ONCE UPON A CURSE

STORIES AND FAIRY TALES FOR ADULT READERS

by

Peter S. Beagle, Nancy Kress,
Patricia C. Wrede, Cindy Lynn Speer,
Lucy A. Snyder, Siobhan Carroll,
Imogen Howson, and Anna Kashina

Dragonwell Publishing

Foreword copyright © 2012 by Anna Kashina
"A Necklace of Rubies" copyright © 2007 by Cindy Lynn Speer
"Come Lady Death" copyright © 1963 by Peter S. Beagle;
copyright renewed 1991 by Peter S. Beagle
"Summer Wind" copyright © 1995 by Nancy Kress
"Stronger than Time" copyright © 1994 by Patricia C. Wrede
"Words Like Pale Stones" copyright © 1994 by Nancy Kress
"Every Word I Speak" copyright © 2007 by Cindy Lynn Speer
"Remains" copyright © 2011 by Siobhan Carroll
"Frayed Tapestry" copyright © 2008 by Imogen Howson
"The Cold Blackness Between" copyright © 2008 by Lucy A. Snyder
"Solstice Maiden" copyright © 2009; 2012 by Anna Kashina
"But Can You Let Him Go" copyright © 2010 by Cindy Lynn Speer

Cover art by Howard David Johnson
Design by Olga Karengina
Editor Anna Kashina

Published by Dragonwell Publishing
(www.dragonwellpublishing.com)

ISBN 978-0-9838320-5-8

CONTENTS

FOREWORD

Stories have everlasting power. Especially legends and fairy tales.

Part of this power lies in their dimensional quality, where every light has a shadow, every hero has an enemy, and every story has a curse to fight and overcome. In the end, light prevails, but it is the darkness, the villains, the curses, that make these stories wedge so firmly in our minds.

In this volume, we bring together a unique collection of stories based on classical fairy tales and legends from different cultures, retold for the modern reader by some of the best writers in this generation, and some upcoming new talents. You will find stories based on Sleeping Beauty (*Stronger than Time* by Patricia C. Wrede and *Summer Wind* by Nancy Kress), Bluebeard (*A Necklace of Rubies* by Cindy Lynn Speer), Rumpelstiltskin (*Words Like Pale Stones* by Nancy Kress), the classical myth of Hades and Persephone (*Frayed Tapestry* by Imogen Howson), a version of Cinderella told from the fairy godmother's point of view (*But Can You Let Him Go* by Cindy Lynn Speer), a dark romance based on Russian myth (*Solstice Maiden* by Anna Kashina), and other tales that feature Death (*Come Lady Death* by Peter S. Beagle), vampires (*Remains* by Siobhan Carroll) and modern-day necromancers (*The Cold Blackness Between* by Lucy A. Snyder). These timeless stories span styles and centuries to blend into a truly compelling collection for adult readers.

1

We named this collection *Once Upon a Curse*, to reflect our focus on the world of shadows, the unforgettable villains that start their existence as the evil opposing the heroes, but end up as irresistible characters in their own right that make fairy tales and myths so compelling through ages and cultures.

Step into the world of myth and magic.

A NECKLACE OF RUBIES

by

Cindy Lynn Speer

He was the handsomest man I'd ever seen.

Tall and slender, he wore his pale-as-snow hair to his collar, a perfect widow's peak accentuating his aesthetic, almost lupine features. His eyes were the color of amber and sparkled strangely in the candlelight. Sometimes it was almost as if his eyes were on fire. I tried not to look him in the eyes too often. I didn't know what he would read in mine.

He was always fashionable. Perfect clothing, tasteful and not ostentatious, perfect manners, perfect style. He followed the rules as if he walked on a knife's edge, knowing just how long it was proper to touch, to stare, careful to never be alone with a woman longer than was proper. Managing to make one feel as if they, too, walked on the knife's edge with him without doing anything that could be remarked upon as unseemly. He was wealthy, and while he did not have the highest of titles, he had all the things that allowed him entrance into the finest circles. Better yet, some would say, he had all these things and he was as yet unmarried.

But the ladies, from the maidens looking for good marriages to the widows desperate for a man's protection, all avoided him. They flirted, yes, but only as far as safety allowed. No one would consent to marry him, it was said, no matter how fine the offer, no matter how beautiful the dowry gifts.

That's not to say he hadn't been married once already. And that was why, thanks to rumor and to superstition, it was said he would never marry again.

"What was she like, this Dona Meriania?" I asked my hostess, Dona Welicide. She was a second cousin who had graciously agreed to take me in after my guardian lost everything we had to gambling debts. He was in debtor's prison in the capital, and there he could remain, really, for all I cared. He had tried to sell me once to avoid imprisonment and I figured better him than me.

Welicide brightened. I knew nothing of the local gossip, stories which, to her circle, were so overtold as to be threadbare. Now she could relate them to a new audience; in fact, I think it was half the reason she invited me, to have someone else to tell her stories to. "She was beautiful. As dark as he is pale, very much the lady of the moment. Everyone wanted her. She had a taste for rubies, I remember."

I found myself smiling. "That's all you can remember of her?"

"Oh, Tessa, I can remember much more than that, but I fear I did not care for the girl. She was my greatest rival, ever since we were little."

"Did you fight over Don Joaquin?"

"Shhh," she breathed. "I was already engaged at the time, so of course not."

Don Joaquin had dipped his fair head to take a sip from the glass he was holding. He was across the room, a room filled with music and laughing people, but still he stopped when I whispered his name, and looked up at me, slowly, first from the corner of his eye, then straight on, meeting my gaze. I smiled slightly, taken aback by his intensity. I could feel the weight of his stare like a touch, over my cheeks and nose and mouth. He returned the smile just as slightly, then turned to address a man who had come off the dance floor.

"Oh, but that man frightens me," my cousin said. I would have been inclined to agree, but the chills running down my spine felt too good to be wrong.

I lost sight of him for a time, until I went outside to get a breath of air. I chose one of the smaller balconies that stood open on the far side of the room. I saw him almost immediately; the light of the moon shone on his hair like a beacon. I paused at the threshold of the doorway, then continued onto the balcony. I leaned against the rail opposite from where he stood, but still, there was only a foot between us.

I imagined I could feel the heat of his presence radiating off of him.

"You are not afraid?" His voice was deep, like the forest at night. He seemed surprised, perhaps even amused.

"I am not afraid." I realized it was true.

"You have not been in our fair country long enough, perhaps."

"Perhaps. Perhaps I do not listen to rumors."

"Or perhaps you simply do not listen."

The coolness of his tone took me aback. What did he know? "I think that you rather like your notoriety, Don Joaquin. Maybe you enjoy being dark and mysterious and dangerous."

He straightened up, cold dark eyes meeting mine. "No," he said. "I do not."

"I'm sorry," I said, but I spoke to the air, for he had already pushed past the doors and back into the ballroom.

That was not the last time I saw him, though perhaps it should have been.

I was lost. Helplessly, and absolutely, regretting that I had agreed to go on the fox hunt in the first place. Welicide was busily trying to introduce me to a wide range of men, any of whom she hoped would sweep me off my feet and give me a home, hearth, and silk dresses. Some of them were nice enough, but I found them all tedious and boring. Sometimes I could feel my brain dying in bits and pieces, as I talked, or rather listened, to them.

Of course, the hunt would have been fine if I hadn't allowed myself to be talked into a race with people much better at riding than I. My run for glory had ended, ignominiously, with my horse running off and me being dumped on my well-skirted rear. I had no idea where the bull-headed animal (who, despite being the meanest horse I'd ever clapped eyes on, nevertheless had a higher IQ than the combined members of the hunting party, myself included) was, and so I was wandering the forest in unsuitable boots and very heavy clothes.

"So, how is the view from the ground?"

"I am not amused," I said, turning. My thoughts disappeared like fog when I saw him, sitting with perfect ease on his white dappled stallion. The black and silver leatherwork of his saddle glistened, and his black suit was cut to emphasize the perfection of the body that sat upon it.

He rode the horse forward with the slightest touch of his knees, stopping next to me. He kicked a foot out of the stirrup and held out a hand. "I doubt I would be, either. Come, it is a long way back to your cousin's manor."

I placed my hand in his. I was surprised at how good it felt. His hand was large, and it enveloped mine. The strength, the warmth, felt wonderful. I put my foot in the free stirrup and with less awkwardness than I feared I was helped up onto the saddle behind him. I sat very straight, trying not to touch him with more than my hands on his shoulders.

"You will fall if you do not relax," he said.

"Again, you mean." And let out a breath I'd been holding and transferred my grip to his waist.

"So, what brings you out here?"

"My horse ran off with me." I don't know if he felt my shrug. "We parted ways."

"I think," he said, pushing aside a low branch, "that you were curious and wanted to explore." I ducked behind his shoulder until he let it go, taking both reins again.

"No. I am the least curious person you will ever meet."

"Really?" He had been polite before, pleasant bordering on cold, but now his voice warmed with real interest.

"Honestly. I like to learn things," I said, not wanting to

sound like a fool, but not wanting to sound too learned, either. "But if it requires anything more than reading a good book, you can count me out. If I am supposed to know it, it will present itself. I shan't go look for it."

He put the reins in one hand and his other came down on my own. Warmth coursed to my toes and back up. My cheeks felt hot. "A wise choice," he muttered, and I felt, somehow, that I had pleased him greatly.

The next day a box was delivered to my cousin's house. My name was written on the label in a quick, graceful script. It held earrings, an ornate confection of silver and brilliant green stones. My cousin was thrilled, until she found who sent them.

"Don't do this," she said.

"Do what?" I was holding one up to my ear, admiring myself in the reflecting glass of the entrance hall. I wiggled the earrings so that I could see how it would flash. They were exquisite. Far more so than I was, I may add.

"He is dangerous. He said his wife fled from him, ran away with another man..."

"How terrible," I said. I was actually thinking about how best to wear my hair to set off the earrings. I wanted to be certain to wear them the very next time he would see me.

"They found her in a ravine, not three miles from his home."

"Perhaps her lover abandoned her. Perhaps she fell."

"I do not know," she said. "But they never recovered her completely."

I looked at her over my shoulder. "Whatever do you mean?"

"She'd been chopped up. They found her head, two of her limbs..."

I shivered and placed the earring next to its mate, and snapped the box closed.

A few days passed, and I forgot my fears again. The weather was bright and hot, so much so that in the gardens of all the noble houses gazebos of bright-colored silk sprung up like flowers, their sides like petals blowing in the wind. None of the manors were very far apart, just a few trees, some knot gardens, some short expanses of perfectly trimmed and watered grass separating us and making us feel as if we lived in our own far off land. The truth was that we were all close enough to walk, easily, from one lawn to another, and that was how the ramble parties began. In the late afternoon the families would all adjourn to the tents outside. Weli favored plums and violet shades this year, and so our family's tent was a pale, lovely lavender, the tied-back sides a combination of lavender with a gauzy plum second curtain that could be pulled shut separately. The pillows were every shade of purple imaginable, from the lightest to the darkest; the rug was patterned in grapes and ivy. My favorite pillow to sit on had pink flowers embroidered on it.

Eventually our turn came at starting the ramble, and we wandered down the road and to our neighbor's home, where a tent the color of buttercups was set out. We drank and ate sparingly, then went on to the next place.

We were halfway through the circle of houses when I finally found myself walking next to my cousin again. She'd just had a slight social scuffle with one of the other members of our party, and they were studiously ignoring each other, so Welicide was alone. She took my arm, and I smiled dreamily at her, thinking of the tiny, rich chocolate square I'd just eaten at the previous house, the only thing I'd eaten all day. I was content, though, turning my thoughts to when we would get to Joaquin's. I was curious to see what he would set out for us to eat, what kind of tea he drank. Just seeing what his house looked like would be interesting. I asked Weli.

"Have you ever seen him on a ramble?"

"No," I admitted.

"He doesn't open his house to it. Besides, he lives too far away to walk to it pleasantly."

I knew from her tone that she wasn't pleased with this topic, so I let the subject slip away, and ignored my disappointment, reminding myself that I wasn't a curious person.

That night there was another party, what they called a gathering of ghouls. It was an excuse to dress in costume and be silly, for all that it was ridiculously structured in an attempt to make certain that no one knew who was behind what mask. People had to disguise their voices and talk in rhyme, yet still attempt to adhere to the strictures of rank and propriety. I had no idea how one was supposed to go about it. How did you pretend you didn't know this person was the Marchioness de Alorna, yet still treat her like one?

I went into the attic to search out a costume, and found a black dress. It was a sheath of black, with a fine gauze overdress of black that was covered with row upon row of tiny beads, almost forming waves. It was loose fitting, so I would not need my corset, and though it covered everything, and the pattered gauze came to a point on the back of my hands, I felt curiously naked in it. I found a plain velvet mask to go with it.

Early in the morning I snuck out and collected peacock feathers, which I used to make myself a suggestion of a tail by carefully sewing the feathers onto the back of the dress. I left my dark brown hair down, tied on the mask, and wondered if anyone would make fun of the odd, musty smell that I couldn't seem to shake out of the dress.

That was the least of my worries. During the party I attracted many more looks that I'd wanted. I ended up embarrassing myself again by fleeing the place, going out the back and into the garden. I was thinking of hiding in the tent, but giggles from that direction stayed me. I walked toward the back of the garden instead, hoping the small stone bench was not taken... or having taking being done upon it. It was in full view of the path and, generally, a fully proper place to sit.

I could see in the bright of the second moon that it was

free, and I sank down on it gratefully.

"I wondered what prey would settle here," Joaquin said from the shadows of the knot work bushes that made the bench seem semi-private. I had not seen him at the party, and in truth he was barely dressed for it...he wore one of his usual suits, only a red-furred fox mask covering his fire-flickered eyes.

"Are you a predator, then, following me?"

He shook his head. "A guardian. You should not be out here alone."

"I intended to hide in the tent."

"Ah." His mouth quirked a little. "Yes, that would not be...advisable."

He sat down beside me, one hand reaching up to untie the mask. He let it drop to his lap.

"It's very realistic." I reached out to touch one jaunty ear.

"It should be," he said. "It once was part of a real fox."

I yanked my hand back. "I thought you disdained the hunt."

"Only unnecessary ones. I am sure that you will agree that some hunts are very necessary."

I folded my hands on my lap and looked at the ground in front of me. I wanted to leave, but I also wanted to stay next to this man, whose pull was so very strong.

"I like your costume," he said. "Though I thought you more of a swan than a peacock."

"Thank you."

"It is missing one thing."

"Oh?"

His fingers traced my collarbone. "You need something right here." He moved closer, and I felt his breath on my neck just a moment before his lips found the soft spot just below my ear. I tilted my head despite myself, enjoying the feel of his warm lips before I reclaimed my senses and pulled firmly away, removing his hand from my clavicle and placing it on his lap. Then I scooted to the very edge of the bench.

"So is this the way you see yourself? A fox?"

10

He picked at the mask. "I am what I am. You can not deny your true nature, correct?"

I stood. It was time to go back to the house. During masques, the rules of propriety were relaxed, but not by much. He blocked me before I could leave, the mask lying forgotten on the ground. We stood a few inches apart, and finally I asked, "And what is your nature, sir?"

He smiled, and tipped my face up to kiss me, instead. Perhaps it was meant to be his answer. His mouth was warm and gentle. He pulled away, and studied me. "I will give you everything you've ever wanted, jewels, clothes, freedom, if you come away with me right now."

I stepped back. "I'm not for sale."

"One night is all I'm asking. And then you will be free from all of this." He looked back at the house. "You'll never have to deal with their games, their foolishness, ever again."

I would lie if I said I did not consider it.

I looked down at my hands. "I should not have allowed that," I said. "Please let me go back to the house now."

He stepped aside, and I left, wondering what he thought of me. The next day brought emeralds. This time, it was a necklace.

Usually we would sit in Weli's purple haven and wait for the ramble to come to us, drinking tea and ignoring the large trays of treats placed on carved white tables set to one side. Eventually a party of nobles would arrive, and we'd lounge together on the pillows, all trying to act very proper despite the fact we were sitting on the ground, and slippery ground at that. Weli's husband cheated by having a small stool brought out for him, which he would usually find himself giving up to an older lady who would find trying to sit on the floor pillows uncomfortable. Eventually the group would be ready to move on, sometimes leaving members, sometimes taking one or even all of us on to the next stop. All day and into the dusk this would continue, wandering back and forth among the houses, eating and drinking and talking about nothing.

On this particular day the party left, and I decided to be the one to stay alone. Weli tried to pull me along, hoping that one of the men might attract me, but as dull and lifeless as they had been to me before I'd met Joaquin, knowing him made it even harder to stand them. Besides, if I was alone, I could actually eat something, not nibble on the same pastry for three hours the way all the other women did. If only there was something left in the carnage that had once been the dessert trays...

I saw him wander out of the woods long before he reached the tent. I kept my eyes down, excited and worried at the same time.

"There is not much left, is there?" he said from behind my shoulder.

"The servants will bring out more soon, I'm sure. May I get you something? Some tea? Or wine, perhaps?"

"No, but thank you."

He was looking at the house. It was all whitewashed stone with black iron shutters on either side of the tall windows. It was a pretty place.

"It's a good home," I said. "It has lovely bones." He blinked, then looked at me. I blushed. "I mean structure. Good structure, underneath it all."

He nodded as if I'd said something of incredible depth, and sat down. He gestured to one of the pillows next to him, but I declined, sitting at an angle from him, stacking a few cushions so I could sit fairly straight.

He remained silent. He looked calm, as if he were enjoying the surroundings. It made me feel uncomfortable, but I learned later that it was supposed to, to make me talk. It was something he did to everyone.

"I would like to thank you again for the earrings and necklace, they're lovely."

"I heard that you favored emeralds. I hope I was not wrong?"

"You heard correct." I realized I was pinching a fold in my

skirt, running my fingernails down it, making a wrinkle. I stopped forcibly, placing my hands on my knees.

"It is an unusual choice, I thought. Most women seem to prefer rubies."

"We don't suit each other," I said, making an implication.

"Everything suits you." If he picked up on it, he was ignoring it. He leaned back, stretching out his long legs. "You should be hearing from your guardian soon."

"I highly doubt that, sir." No one was allowed to write letters from prison.

"Someone has settled his debts."

I met his eyes. They flickered oddly, all shadows. "Why would anyone do that?"

He leaned closer to me. "Perhaps they thought it might please you to have one less worry."

"I was not worried." Actually, I was. If my guardian was released from prison, he could reclaim me. I'd go back to being his slave, keeping his house, avoiding the pawing hands of his fellow card players when they set up an illegal game in the parlor well after the gambling hells had closed.

He thought on this for a moment. "Pity," he said, and made as if to stand.

I caught his arm. "Why do you care?"

He tried to pull away, but I wouldn't allow it. "I could have forced you into marriage. I could have told his, and by proxy your, debtors that I would only settle things when you were my wife. I would not do it."

I stood. "How generous. But if that was all you wanted you might have gotten farther asking first." I felt myself growing very upset. I did not want to go back to the life I had with my guardian, who would rather sell me than protect me. Weli's husband was not precisely pleased to have me, but he wouldn't allow anything bad to happen to me. Don Joaquin had taken away my safety.

I pushed the blowing cloth aside and left the pavilion.

"Marry me, then."

I turned. He was leaning against one of the columns holding the tent up, not relaxed as was his usual wont, but clutching the cloth. His face was in the shade, but I thought he looked... uncertain. Longing. I don't know if it were truth or fancy that made it seem so, but for a moment I felt that I was the most wanted person in the world. My anger evaporated, as did my fear.

"Yes," I said, and walked into the house, never looking back.

He wanted to get married quickly, no ceremony. I agreed, both because I had no one I wanted to invite, and because I was afraid that if I had time to think about it I might change my mind. No one wanted it, you see. Even my cousin's usually disaffected husband, who treated me as a stranger rather than family, stopped me in the halls to tell me on three separate occasions that he was content to shelter me, that I didn't have to rush into marriage.

The servants wept on my wedding day. The children were somber, playing quietly as if afraid to disturb the fragile silence that had gathered around us. Weli, too, wept. "You don't have to do this, you know. You did not ask him to pay your guardian's debts." She was brushing out my hair. Once in awhile she'd stop to rub her face with the back of her hand. "My husband won't allow your guardian to reclaim you, he has high friends... "

"I am doing this because I want to."

"Why? He doesn't... he could have killed her; you do know this."

I was picking at my emerald earrings. The matching necklace lay like lace exactly where he'd kissed me. "It is possible." Admitting it was a weight off of my chest, even as it opened the door to darker imaginings.

She dropped the length of hair she was about to pin up. "Then why?"

"He fascinates me."

"Trust me darling, there are a million fascinating men out

there. Just last night Termind promised that we could all go on a tour." She smiled tremulously. "You have all the time that you want; we could sail the world, visit different places, find you someone extraordinary. . . "

I raised my hand to touch her cheek. Our eyes met in the mirror. "I want him," I said.

Tears stood in her eyes as she began pinning up my hair.

The traditional dress is either pale yellow or pink with exquisite scarlet embroidered flowers in profusion, and arcane symbols indicating the bride's hopes for her future. I dressed in pale green satin, a plain dress with a fitted bodice and a flaring skirt that brushed the top of my feet. I had tacked some gold lace around the hem. It was sleeveless, and I wore white gloves. My only other decorations were the earrings and the necklace, and the emerald-tipped pins that Weli insisted she give me to pin up my hair.

"You should have at least worn a traditional dress. We could have altered mine, for goodness sake."

"That dress is for your daughter, should she want it. Besides, I don't like red."

"Nonsense! Since when?" She was remembering my second best dress, red velvet with black cord decorations. It was now, unbeknownst to her, sitting in the back of her cupboard.

"I don't know." I folded my hands at my waist, and took my place by the door.

We left early, my husband and I.

The wedding itself had been very nice. The groom smiled at me sweetly when I came to stand by him, and I could see he approved of the green of my dress. The vows were simple, and I think they sounded heartfelt on both our parts.

I kept staring at his profile, and once, wondering if this was all truly real and not some wishful dream, I squeezed the hands that held mine so firmly, and ran my thumb lightly over the back of his knuckles. He didn't seem to notice, but at the end, he kissed the back of each of my hands, then my forehead, and everyone sighed, because the ceremony itself was over. Instead of stepping away, as is usual, his mouth slowly lowered to mine. Everyone was silent as death, and when he pulled away, I smiled at him, too dizzy with happiness to care.

It was the happiest moment of the affair, the small party afterward a grim thing of false cheer that seemed more like a wake than a wedding. I didn't understand it. I was outside their circle, why would they care what happened to me? And why, if they were so certain I was going to my doom, did they let me go?

It was uncomfortable, and I couldn't eat, and when Joaquin announced that the ship that was to bear us away on our honeymoon was in early and we had to go, I felt nothing but gratitude. It was, in fact, not true, and we ended up sitting at a portside inn for two hours because of it, but I was very happy. I did not feel as if I was walking down a dangerous path. I was married, and well, my husband solicitous, the food he bought for me at the inn filling and plentiful. I leaned against his arm, and after a moment he drew me closer, holding me while we waited for a ship that would take us beyond the horizon.

I will not bore you with details of our honeymoon. It was lovely. The place he took me was an old ruins, filled with explorers and scientists and wizards trying to discover the meanings of the things the people had left behind. He took me into caverns where the walls had been carefully chiseled flat and covered with mosaics made of tiny stones and tiles that lasted for miles. We traveled to the edge of the desert and visited a gorgeous oasis. After that we traveled north and slept in a palace of ice. It was not an ordinary journey, but one that filled me with wonders and promised me more. He was kind to me, ever watchful, showing very little affection in public, but in private he often touched me, not always for the sake of seduction, though I blush to admit I found myself eagerly fulfilling that part of my duties much more often than was probably proper. I'd find small presents in my pockets, a silver comb, some pretty pebbles, a flower pressed in glass.

I was feeling quite smug with myself, if you must know. And happy. It is hard not to love someone when you are at the center of their most lavish attention.

It faded, though, the closer we got to home. In the carriage, closing in on his estate, it was almost as if we were strangers.

His manor, unlike the other nobles' illusion of space, was situated on a vast stretch of land. The land was covered in a dense forest of pine, and the silence, when we stepped out of the carriage and walked up the pale marble steps to the imposing doors, was complete. The house was so huge, gray marble veined with white, that I could not take it all in with one look. I was relieved when we got near the door, because I would not have to assimilate the absolute vastness of the place.

Over the door, a thick slab of almost black wood with black iron hinges, was carved "Be Bold."

I waited, at his shoulder, for him to do something. The only servant I had seen was the man who drove the carriage and who was, even now, somewhere behind the house putting things away. Perhaps they did not know we were here?

"Tessa," he said. I put my hand on his shoulder, and he placed his own on top of it. It was cold, and I stepped around him to see his face. He looked paler than usual. He was silent for so long that I thought about prompting him, but he spoke again, looking into my eyes. "I give you everything I have. My wealth, my home, my body. Any desire you have, it's yours."

He dug into his pocket and produced a ring of keys. They were all ornate. Some were silver, some were brass. One was black, not as iron would be, but a sort of black whose dullness seemed to suck the life out of everything next to it. It was the smallest key of all. He presented me the ring. The keys clattered together, and I realized my unflappable husband was shaking. I took the keys quickly, hating to see his weakness. He did not let them go, but placed a hand under my chin.

Our eyes met again.

"There is only one thing that you may not do. There is a room by itself, down a dark narrow hall to the back. Its frame is painted red, and it is a small door and takes the smallest key. Under no circumstances are you to ever enter that room." He half whispered, half growled the words, so fierce that his hand on my chin was beginning to hurt.

"I promise" I gasped, and looking surprised, he let go of me.

"Do not place the key to the lock. Do not open the door. Do not enter in. No matter what." He paused, and no longer able to meet my eyes he said, "It would not be good for our marriage."

"I promise never to go anywhere near that room, much less open it."

He nodded, and let go of the keys. He gestured toward the door. "The house is yours, then, my wife. Unlock her and enter in."

I tried to smile, and, knees shaking, I walked past him. I tried the largest key first, because it had a pattern that looked doorlike to me on it. My not so wild guess was right, and the double doors parted to my touch, sliding open on well-oiled hinges. The entryway looked like a church foyer, all wide expanse, with a pair of carefully turned staircases spiraling down the wall on either side. Three smaller replicas of the huge doors we'd entered through interrupted the paleness of it all.

"Where are the..." I began, not knowing how to ask.

"Servants?"

"Yes. I've never entered into a house before without being approached by someone determined to fuss over me."

He smiled, in control again, the shadow of the man I'd honeymooned with returning. "Everything is taken care of. This way, dear. I'll be going away on business tomorrow."

"So soon?"

"And therefore I'll leave the explorations up to you. It will give you something to do while I'm away."

"Can't I come with you?" The last thing I wanted to do was to be left in that... that... mausoleum by myself.

"Next time, perhaps. Don't you want a chance to get yourself situated? I smell food. I am absolutely dying for something to eat, aren't you?" And he kept me distracted like that all evening.

The next morning he was waiting in the dining room. As with the night before, everything was already laid out, not another person in sight.

"Three times a day," he told me, "the servants will lay out a meal. If you require anything else, something between meals, something you would prefer, you merely have to say so in the speaking tube leading to the kitchen." He flicked a finger at a brass tube next to the doorway leading toward the servants' area. It had a cover, so all I had to do was flip the cover up and say what I wanted.

"How will I know that they've heard?" I asked.

"They always hear."

"I've never seen one of them yet. Where are they?"

"Around." He handed me an egg from the basket. It was still warm, and when I cracked open the shell I was pleased to see it was cooked through solid. I listened to the crunch of shells being rolled and cracked on the table, silverware on plates, struck again by how loud all these mundane tasks seemed in contrast to the absolute silence that commanded the residence. It had been too quiet for me, last night, trying to get to sleep. The manor did not creak as it settled for the night. The wind did not whistle through the chimneys. I would have drawn comfort from the breathing of my husband, but once he drifted off his breath became almost imperceptibly shallow. I'd held my hand in front of his face once, to see if he yet lived.

It had not been this way on our travels.

Wherever the servants were, they knew how to cook. The rolls were so sweet and warm they hardly needed the honey that pooled in its etched glass pot. It, like the dinnerware, had a fox motif. In fact, hunting was a major decoration of many of my husband's furnishings. So manly. I wondered if he would mind, now that he was no longer an unwed man, if I replaced a few of his foxes with something more feminine.

I stared down at my plate, at the foxes running along a forested border, outwitting a farmer with an axe, and felt dizzy. Yes. Roses, or perhaps ivy, would be far better for my digestion. Especially since the plates seemed to be telling a story, one that continued around the brim of the salad plate, that blossomed full blown on the side of the teapot. Foxes running, hiding, from foolish-looking men. It would have been cute, even comedic, but for the look on the fox's muzzled face...

"I've lingered longer than I should have," Joaquin said, standing. I made to stand, too, but he stayed me with a kiss. "Sit, finish your dinner. I will see you in a few days, I promise."

"Are you sure?"

He took my chin in his hands and kissed me again. "I always keep my promises." He looked me in the eyes a long moment and I nodded. He stroked my cheek and left, leaving me to sit, wondering what to do next. I ran to the window after a moment, to see him on his white and gray horse, riding down the lane. He had a pair of saddlebags, no more, and I thought that was good. Perhaps he would come home soon. The keys weighed heavily from their chain around my waist, and so I decided to do some of the exploration denied me the night before. I went over to the tube.

"I'm all done. Thank you. It was very nice." I listened for a long second. No banging of pots, no yelling at skivvies, and certainly no acknowledgement of my speech. Odd, I thought as I went off, keys jingling.

Most of the rooms were not locked. Some of them could be, and I had keys for those to prove it. The library, three stories high and filled with books, was one of these; the key marked with an open book fit in the lock and turned easily. It was a perfectly round room, and a set of stairs spiraled around it, up and up to a small platform at the very top, below the stained glass dome. I walked all the way up, admiring the pattern of the large dome. It was intricately done, a forest filled with flowers and life, like a labyrinth that unraveled itself the closer I got to it. On the platform, with its short iron rail, I could see the words around the very bottom, worked into the pattern of the forest floor. "Be bold," it said. "Be bold, be bold... but not too bold." Looking far down to where the bright-colored pattern of the carpet seemed more like a memory than fact, I thought it would take far more than me being bold to ever ascend those steps again.

There were bedrooms done in various colors, and, under lock and key, a nursery, the only place that had any accumulated dust. I pulled the drapes and opened the windows wide, hoping that some of the dust and the underlying stench of decay would fade. I would have to talk to the servants. It smelled as if a rat, or maybe even a cat, had died unattended to. And the dust and webs lay so thick on the furnishings that until I opened the windows I thought they were covered with cloth.

It was the only room in the manor so shamefully taken care of. I took delight in the upper rooms, all of them locked, such as the music room. As I stepped inside it, I was amazed at how airy it seemed, filled with cases displaying all manner of instruments. One corner was taken up with an odd organ that barked nosily at me when I, thinking that I was crossing a different pattern of tile, found myself making music. I did a silly little jig on the wedge-shaped tiles, and every time my foot moved, music came out of the pipes. In front of the windows a many-layered harp sat, speaking softly whenever a whisper of breath from my movements touched it. I opened the windows and stood behind it so that the breeze from outside could play across the strings, and as I stood there I felt as if I was awash in music, bathing in it like something tangible.

Eventually I left. I spent more time than I should admit to in the treasure room, with its small boxes filled with gold coins stamped with symbols from around the world, a chest of nothing but pearls, and a cabinet with various stones of varying hues and sizes. I felt guilty, looking through it, but he had bid me to be free with his home.

And so I was, until I took a wrong turn somewhere, wanting to sneak down into the servants' quarters. I thought I could creep up on one of them, give them a right talking to about the nursery.

The hall was long, dark, but perfectly clean. A window at the very end of it provided the only light, and there was only one door, outlined in red. There was no other way out, forcing me to go back the way I came. Yet I could hear something on the other side, and as I leaned closer I made out whispering. At first I wondered if it was perhaps the housekeeper or the butler's room. I placed my hand on it lightly, pressed my ear to the wood. My other hand held the keys silent.

The smallest key dug into the palm of my hand, and I straightened, looking at it. It was not metal, despite its black, all-absorbing color, but glass. I held it in front of my eyes, studying it. The other keys slid away until I was holding only the small, plain glass key in between my thumb and forefinger. Such a tiny key, for such a tiny room, down such a long, plain hall. It looked so harmless. I had seen all his treasures, surely... his gold and his jewels and his strange, beautiful, wondrous things. What things would this room hold? This out of the way, innocent-looking doorway? Besides, he was my husband, was he not? What right did he have to keep secrets from his wife?

Such a tiny, harmless, innocent key. Such a plain door. Just take a peek, prove them all wrong, no one would ever, ever know...

I lowered the key toward the lock. The doorknob was red glass, smooth and cool to the touch.

It would not go well for our marriage, I heard him say, as clearly as if it were yesterday again. I took my hand away from the knob and put it behind my back. I forced myself to drop the keys so that they hit my thigh. Hand joined hand,

and grasped each other tightly. I backed down the hall, never taking my eyes off the door, wondering, wondering, what was listening to me in the silence; what might come out to get me?

The only sign of my near fall was that my thumb and forefinger were pink, almost as if the key had scalded me. It faded even as I was sitting down to the tea I had requested from the kitchen, telling the silent servants that I was not interested in lunch, thank you; when footsteps, hard, businesslike boot steps, could be heard stomping up the stairs. I thought about cowering in the corner, but realized that the small room, sunny and filled with plants, the only furniture a spindly table and pair of chairs, would afford me no cover. I could throw the teapot at whoever it was, I thought.

"There you are." My husband leaned against the door frame as if trying to capture his breath. There was no warmth in his smile.

"You're home so soon? Was the business that quickly concluded?"

"I hope you're not disappointed. I wanted to rush home to my bride." He crossed to me, and offered his hand. I placed my hand in his and he kissed it with cold lips, turning it over so that he could kiss the palm. His eyes lingered on the tips of my fingers. The pink was merely a blush, almost indiscernible, and he kissed those two. He repeated the process with my other hand, and the more he kissed them, the more he looked, the warmer he became, until he gave me a smile of perfect, unspoiled joy and pulled me close. His lips on mine were warmer than summer, and I felt, oddly, as if I'd passed some test, as if I'd made him incredibly, profoundly happy.

I searched the house from top to bottom, but never found the smallest sign of a servant. My husband always changed the subject even if I asked him outright where they where and why I never saw them.

The nursery door was locked again the next time I went to inspect it, and when I opened the door the curtains were drawn once more. I looked at the floor and noticed that there were only two sets of tracks in the dust, one leading in and one leading out. How did they manage to go in and shut the windows without leaving a sign? I thought it was because they had their own way in. All large houses had a network of tunnels running behind the walls, entrances and exits cleverly concealed by wall seams and wainscoting. I walked around the room, pulling back the curtains and looking for scuffs in the dust beside my own, and came up empty. I stepped into the hallway, pausing for just a moment, wondering if I should prop open the door and go get my husband, when I heard the whisk of the curtains being drawn once more. The door was slammed shut and I heard the lock turn. I fumbled for the keys then stopped, much as I had before another, smaller door, and decided to leave well enough alone.

To quote my husband during a more exasperated moment when I'd been harassing him on the subject, "As long as the food appears on the table on time, the rooms are clean and all of your other needs are seen to, what do you care if you ever see them or not? Most nobles prefer it that way." I admitted he had a point and decided to let it go.

The servants, or lack thereof, were not the worst part.

Every day or so, I would receive visitors. Sometimes my cousin, but more often other noble women from our circle. People, I'd like to point out, who had had very little time for me when I was merely Weli's charity case. And had they behaved as the usual busybodies digging for gossip, I'd have probably dealt better with it, but it was... odd. There were no noisy entrances, no silly useless talk or overly exuberant greetings. The show, in short, was gone.

You know what I mean. Every time a lady visits another, a performance is demanded. Her clothes, her friends, her carriage, everything down to a small, yappy pet is part of a performance. The way she takes your hands, kisses your cheek, looks around your home, are all part of a larger thing. They did not do this with me.

They were quiet when they came, and their clothes, while

24

respectable, were darker in tone. They took turns coming, and always came early in the day, well before sunset. The most daunting realization was that, from the closest friend to the most distant near enemy, without fail, they always looked so worried until they saw me, until they took my hand. They would search my face, talk to me, until little by little the worry would fade into an almost palatable relief. I thought as time went on they would stop coming, but they never did. Every other day, early afternoon. I could predict with near perfect precision when and who.

But that wasn't the worst part, either.

That would be the whispering. Every night on the edge of my dreams. It was a murmur if my husband was there, but it only grew louder when he wasn't. Sometimes I would wake up in the middle of the darkness to an empty bed, chitterings and whisperings and moanings echoing between my ears so loudly that sleep was impossible and I could only lie there and wait for my husband's return. He would come in, naked, cold, damp, and throw himself under the covers. He'd slide his hand into mine, and we'd never speak, just wait until his shivering stopped and the screeching in my head died down to faint whispers once more.

It amazes me still, that I could be obsessed with making him confess the secret of the servants, but never once ask him about the sounds in my head. Perhaps I was afraid that my listening at the door had contaminated me somehow, that it would be a confession of how I'd almost slipped the key in and opened it.

"Be bold," I said.

He jumped a little, and looked up from his reading. "What did you say?"

We were in his study, and I was standing next to the fireplace. The painting above it disturbed me, continuing as it did the fox motif. I'd never gotten quite comfortable with it, but the picture of it, with a group of farmers hunkered down around a fire, the fox spitted over the flames, was horrifying. I felt bad for the fox, which chased my food around the dishes and followed me in the woodwork of the house. I'd read the brass plaque underneath it.

"That's what the painting's called, I suppose," I said, pointing at it. "'Be Bold'."

"No," he said. "That's the motto of our house."

"Be bold? Is that all?"

He nodded and returned to his reading. "It's enough."

I looked outside. There were another couple of hours of light. "I'm going riding." I looked to see if he would jump up and congratulate me on my wonderful idea, but all he did was nod and turn the page. I left the study, feeling nervous. I'd never ridden anywhere by myself, at least not since the last time. His voice echoed down the hall after me, comfortingly, as if he knew my worries.

"I'll come after you in an hour," he said, "should I not see you sooner." And suddenly I felt much braver.

The forest around our home was dense, as if no one had been permitted to thin it, even for a stick of wood to feed the fire. The only thing that made it passable was the trails beat down by horses like mine, and the patches of land where the needles had landed too deep for anything to grow. I had set off meaning to go in a straight direction, stopping when we reached the edge of the land, which I hoped would be marked by some sign, such as a line of low stone fence. This idea was soon discarded. I'd be fine for a long time, until a thicket of brambles and brush forced me to turn right or left. Sometimes I would see burrows dug out of the floor, and as I carefully steered my gentle mare around them, I wondered what lived inside them, and hoped for a glimpse of animal. I saw birds occasionally, but did not hear them sing or even chirp. I startled something large as I came around a corner, and though I heard its panicked flight, I saw nothing. Otherwise, all was silence as steady and as unsettling as inside the house.

I got off the mare, meaning to lead her to the stream I thought I saw through a wall of weed and brush. I knew if there was water, there were animals, thus there would be a way down. And there was. Narrow, muddy, I took the reins and walked down slowly. In her eagerness for a fresh drink she pushed me, and my boots, pretty and pretty useless, skidded in the soft soil. I let go of the reins and fell backwards, skidding until my feet and one hand splashed into the water, managing to keep most of myself out of it. I grabbed a few pale twigs sticking out from the mud to pull me up, but they pulled free, and I fell back.

The sticks felt strange and I opened my fist to inspect its contents. Barely held together by mud and something else, finger bones lay in my hand, surprisingly heavy. In the dying rays of the sun, a ruby winked through the sludge and I realized the rough, filthy lump encircling one bone was a ring.

I went into shock, I think, because I didn't scream. I didn't throw the fingers as far from me as possible. I was filled with dread, but not worried. After all, I knew that his wife had been found, and how. The searchers simply missed something. Instead, I sat, got colder, shivered, while I wondered.

Now what does one do? I have been poor, as you might have gathered from my story so far; hungry, putting my coppers and silvers together to buy enough trim to pretty up a dress to keep up appearances when I'd rather be buying bread; watching money I would rather have spent on supper being sent off to pay the previous night's losses. Knowing this, perhaps, you won't be surprised that one of my first thoughts was whether or not to keep the ring.

Eventually, I worked my way back up the bank. I saw a curve of bone that I'd earlier confused with a rock. I pulled at it, bringing a skull out of the muck.

And that was when I began to worry; for you see, I knew that they'd found her head. That's how they would have identified her, his wife, the one who loved rubies. In the hole made by removing the skull, I found something that glittered, despite the mud, and I took it out and walked it down to the water, and rinsed it until the mud was gone. It was a sapphire earring, some of the stones missing, but nevertheless, it was not something a woman who favored rubies would mistakenly wear.

My horse raised her head and nickered, and I shoved the skull and the fingers back into the bank. I pocketed the ring and the earring and walked over to the edge of the path.

I held my hands out from my body, lifting a drenched skirt. Joaquin, from on top of his stallion, winced. "What must you think of me," I said, walking up to him. His eyes flickered over my shoulder, along the bank, and back to me. I kept my smile on straight, just as I had when creditors came and assessed my family's possessions. *He knows*, a voice in the back of my head whispered. *He knows that they're there. You had best pray that he doesn't think you do.*

He got down from his horse. I could see that he intended to come down to the river, perhaps disguising his need to look at the grave by fetching my horse.

"Rachel, come now," I called, and thank God, she actually listened, blocking the path down by coming up it. He grabbed the reins, and in the moment it took him to pull her around, I made a decision. As he made to hand them back to me, I wrapped my arms around him and pressed close, not worrying that I was getting mud and water all over his nice clothes. "I'm cold. Let's go home. Perhaps you can help me get warm again?" I pulled his face to mine and kissed him, making the meaning behind my words clear. He pulled away, looking down at me with thinly disguised suspicion, but then the hard set of his shoulders loosened, and he kissed me back.

It was late, when we finally sat down to dinner, but the food was still warm.

He awoke me with a kiss.

I unwillingly opened my eyes. It was still quite dark out; a peek out the window showed the last stars of night and a gray line of sky. I flopped back down with a sigh, and snuggled closer to him. He laughed and said, "I have to go."

"Already?" I wrapped my arms tighter and squeezed my eyes shut. He carefully pulled my arm from around his waist.

"While you were out yesterday I received an urgent letter from one of my business associates. I have matters to attend to. I'll be back."

"You didn't say anything about this last night." I managed to pry one eye open. This was my favorite time of day, to be honest. He was always softer when we first woke up. He looked younger, gentler. It was easier to delight him.

He grinned wickedly. "You kept me quite busy last night."

"How long will you be?"

"Only a couple of days. I'll hurry back to you, I promise."

"Very well." I closed my eyes and turned over again.

"Shall I bring you something?" I felt the bed move as he sat up.

"Sapphires," I whispered, half back into dreams. I'd been floating in the ocean, and the water had been so warm.

His motions, reaching for things, getting dressed, stilled. My eyes opened, and I cursed myself. I forced them closed again, and said sleepily. "You know, something purple."

He put a hand on my waist. "You mean amethysts, sweetheart?"

I sighed. "Yes. To go with the new lavender dress you bought me."

"I thought you bought the lavender dress to go with your emeralds?" His teasing tone was there. I wondered if I detected the edge of hardness, or if I imagined it out of some weird guilt.

"I did, but Weli said that was gauche. I'm not sure what gauche means, but it sounds horrible, doesn't it?"

"I've never known a woman who liked amethysts," he said, then laughed and kissed my temple.

I am told that people keep huge hunting cats, cared for from birth, as pets. They walk them around on leashes; they feed them raw meat from their fingers.

Living with him was like that. He'd love me up, eat morsels from my fingers, be the perfect husband. But I always knew, someday, he might just turn on me. And worse, I'd never be sure why.

The ring and earring burned in my pocket. Not literally, but I knew constantly where they were and couldn't help but think on them.

Finally, I walked into the treasury room. I poked through boxes, looking for jewelry. Surely, if his first wife was so enamored of rubies, there would be more left of her collection than a ring. In my own jewelry box, since I had told him that I loved emeralds, I had four rings of various kinds for each hand, a half dozen bracelets, some gold or silver, but most studded with emerald chips in different patterns. I also had five necklaces, three sets of earrings, and one tiara. Surely she would have just as much, maybe even more, since rumor had it he'd courted her for years.

The room was made up of shelves. The shelves were mostly covered in boxes that you pulled out and opened. He had a work table, the tools of his trade—for that was what he did, he traded in valuables—lay neatly along one side. Most of the boxes were filled with metals, gold, silver, copper. There was even some brass and mithril. There were also a few stones, and I could tell how valuable they were by how they were stored. Some were loose in their perfectly organized box, some were sheathed in fine cloth pouches. I was very careful because everything was very neat. My favorite object was a chunk of purple stone the size of my fist, perfect for a paperweight, and I wondered if I could ask for it. It had an inclusion shaped like a butterfly.

I went over to the work bench and inspected the tools—a tiny smelter, weighing scales, a mortar and pestle, and tweezers were the things I knew right off. I opened a drawer, and saw boxes of various sizes and small velvet bags. They contained resins and herbals, as far as I could tell, some so pungent that when I opened them they brought tears to my eyes. I started to close the drawer when I saw a flash of gold filigree. I pulled the drawer out a little further and saw a thick black leather-bound box, decorated in a pattern of gold vines and flowers. Inside was a jackdaw's treasure chest—ruby necklaces lay entwined with beads of amber, onyx and jet, diamond and sapphire, topazes and opals all lay in a knotted mess. I pulled out half-mashed links of what had once been a diamond collar, halves of a sapphire-studded bangle that had been sliced in two. I pulled the earring out of my pocket and began matching it with the pieces I saw, looking for a mate, or a necklace that would have been part of its set.

I found the mate in a nest of fine silver links with beads of jet strung on it, spaced so many inches a part. I held them together. Some of the chips were missing from the edge of it, but I knew they had been made to be together. The teardrop-shaped sapphire that hung in the center was exactly the same shade of blue. I heard something clatter down the hall, and I shoved everything back into the box, put the box back into the drawer, and put the purple stone on the shelf by the door to give me an alibi. I closed the door and ran down the hall, looking for Joaquin.

The hall by the red-framed door faced the stable yard, and so I ran down the corridor to look out the window. No sign of his horse, though I could see Rachel contentedly grazing in the paddock.

A flare of cold light behind me reflected off the panes, and I turned.

Around the red frame of the forbidden door, words had been burned, black against the blood red.

"Be bold," they read, "Be bold..."

"But not too bold," Joaquin said. I looked around. He wasn't in the hall. I stepped closer to the door. I'd heard him, plain as day.

"Yes," I heard him say. "'Tis I."

I pressed my ear to the door. "Joaquin?"

"I've locked myself in, wife." There was a mocking quality to his words, and while one would assume he was making fun of himself—after all, he'd locked himself in—I felt that the humor was directed at me. And it wasn't quiet, delighted humor, as if he found me constantly endearing, but something much crueler.

"How... how did you do that?"

"I came back to fetch something and now the door won't open. It must be locked from the outside. Perhaps you...?"

"I didn't hear your return. And I didn't see your horse..."

"The servant must have taken him inside to groom him. And perhaps you were yet asleep. I've been stuck in here for such a long time."

I fumbled at my chatelaine belt. The little black key slipped into my hands.

"I'm so thirsty," he whispered. I lay one hand flat on the door while the other hand slowly brought the key to the lock. My hand shook so badly that it knocked against the metal. I thought again of the first day here.

"Do not place the key to the lock," he had said. "Do not open the door. Do not enter in."

I dropped the keys and stepped away.

"No matter what," I whispered.

"Wife, what is going on?"

"I do love you," I said, backing away. I felt dazed. I tripped over my own feet and had to put a hand out on the wall to support myself.

"You can't leave me like this! Wife!"

"I'm so sorry," I said, as something began to howl and throw itself against the door.

I fainted at the mouth of the hallway, and when I came to, it was night again.

He found me lying on the sofa, as uncomfortable as it was, staring wide-eyed at the fire. I was not going upstairs by myself for any reason. It did not occur to me to ask how he got out of the room. I knew that, whomever I had spoken with, it wasn't with him.

You might be thinking that this would be the right time to introduce my peculiar thoughts into the conversation. "Hello, husband. While you were out I went to the door. Don't worry, I didn't open it, but I did have a conversation with some fell creature that spoke with your voice." Or, "By the way, when I was riding the other day, I found some body parts—would you happen to know why you have an earring belonging to a dead body lying in your drawer?"

It doesn't much matter, you see. It's what I was saying about the hunting cats. He may be a murderer, and I may be the next victim. But when he scolds me gently for sleeping on the sofa ("It's freezing in this room. You'll be sick.") and when he picks me up and carries me upstairs promising a present for me; he's so soft and so loving, I cannot feature it.

He's often a cold, hard man, but he softens for me. He cherishes me. It makes me feel special, as if I've done something no other woman could.

At the top of the stairs he put me down, and took a sack off his back. "Let's put this away," he said, and headed over to the treasure room. I unlocked the door for him, and he stepped inside, lighting torches with a flicker of his hand. He opened the sack and beckoned me over, pulling out a length of pale purple pearls, each as large around as a fingernail, and long enough for him to loop it around my neck and drape it over my hair. They felt like warm satin.

"They're beautiful," I said as he stepped back to admire the effect. Something crunched under his foot, and he moved his boot slowly. His nostrils flared, and I could tell that he recognized the mangled bit of blue and silver.

"I'm so sorry," I managed, thrusting my hand into my pocket, where I had been certain I'd shoved the earring in my rush. It wasn't there, of course, and neither was the ruby ring. There was a hole, one that should not and had not been there before.

Where was the ruby ring? I looked around, trying not to be transparent. "What were you doing in here?" he asked casually as he opened the drawer.

"Being careless with valuable things, obviously." I could not conceal the nervousness in my voice as he opened the box. Of course, the mate was sitting right on top of the scramble. It even sparkled in the light.

"I found it outside," I said before he could ask. "In the garden. I don't like sapphires, and was looking for a place in here to store it."

He nodded and knelt to scoop up the earring pieces, then threw them in the box. He slammed it shut, then closed the drawer with much more force than was needed.

"The rest can wait until tomorrow," he said, taking my arm. The torches went out, and in the darkness, he placed his lips to my ear. "I believe you because I choose to; not because I do."

I lay, almost asleep, pillowed against his shoulder. I had coaxed and charmed him until his anger eased, and now I listened to him breathing in sleep, my cheek warm against his bare skin. His breathing was becoming increasingly softer and soon it would fade into silence, so I was enjoying it while I could.

I tried to let myself doze off, determined to continue not thinking. Not thinking about the fact that breakfast that morning had consisted of chocolate-covered cherries and green beer. Of the fact that sometimes I found a scuff mark here, a bit of dust there. It was as if the house spirit, for I had given up on believing in servants I'd never seen or heard, was getting tired.

Or perhaps was stretched thin, somehow. Did I make much more work for it? Or were its resources stretched by something else?

I had managed to sweep my mind clean and could feel myself just on the edge of sleep-induced placidity, when my husband sat up in bed.

"No!" he yelled, and I fancied I saw a shadow move across the window. "You will not have her." His words came out as an agonized groan. The lights came on in the room, too bright. I blinked until I could see.

"Joaquin?" I whispered, hugging myself.

He looked at me, his eyes narrowed. "You." He crawled across the bed until his face was an inch from mine. "You touched the door. I saw it."

"W-when?"

He pulled away slightly. "Did you touch. the door?"

"Yes." My half-breathed word was covered by his growl of frustration. He grabbed my arm and pulled me out of bed, half dragging me behind him. The doors slammed opened before we reached them as we raced down the hall. The etched glass doors of the library shattered as they hit the walls. A wind gathered around us as we walked, cold and clammy. Even naked, he did not seem to feel the cold, but I wore my thinnest shift, and felt it like a blade across my skin. He was muttering something furiously under his breath, words I could not catch. The kitchen door opened, and he pulled me closer to him.

"Women, women you're all the same," he spat out.

"I did not open the door," I said calmly. "I did not put the key to the lock. Because I love you and respect your wishes."

The kitchen torches lit, and I saw that there were tears on his face. "He's in your head now. It's only a matter of time." He threw me into the kitchen and I caught myself on the table just as he slammed the door shut.

He did not come back.

Here is how I lived for two days in the kitchen. During the first night, in the dark, I huddled in a corner under a table, scared witless because I could finally see the servants. They were shadow against shadow, movement that flickered in and out of the corner of my eye. A flash of phantom knife here, a flicker of peeling falling there, things didn't float or look as if they were being moved about by invisible hands so much as appear when I wasn't looking.

The first morning I had, by some miracle, managed to fall asleep, and when I awoke I saw a bowl of oatmeal and a cup of tea placed on the floor beside me. The kitchen itself, a place of perfect order the one time I'd bothered to look at it, was now completely dilapidated. There was dust and one of the widow panes was cracked, a small square of glass broken out. The dry sink was rimed with filth, the pump disused-looking. Neither the oatmeal nor the tea had any taste. True, it's hard for oatmeal to have any real taste, and when one is upset food tastes like wet parchment anyway, but still, the complete absence of flavor, the nothing that sat on my tongue, was disturbing.

There was a blanket, half mangled but clean, draped on one chair. It had not been there the night before. "Thank you," I said out loud, before wrapping myself in it. I stuck my head through the largest of the holes, then ran my fingers up and down the horribly scarred table. It was filthy. I looked for a bucket, and worked the water pump. Nothing.

"If you get this pump to work, I'll clean the kitchen. Fair trade?" There was silence, but a few moments later, when I tried the pump, it gurgled deep inside itself. I worked it until water, rusted but usable, finally came out. A few more pumps and the water ran clean.

When he comes for me, at least he'll find me useful, I thought. Once in a while I checked the door carefully, just in case he'd unlocked it and left, but it was stuck fast. So, I attacked the kitchen, starting with the table.

In some ways I wish I hadn't.

The kitchen tells a story. I cannot tell you what it is, but I have an idea.

The filth-covered axe shoved under the sink. The table, covered in dark brown blotches that look like rust in the scores the axe made, where a liquid puddled and stained the fresher wood. The corner of the table was sheared off by the axe. I found the piece lying underneath.

Blotches everywhere, layer upon layer. The stone of the floor, the countertop, the bowl of the dry sink, all stained. Some of it comes up dark flaky brown on my clothes, now clotted with filth.

The big, heavy fireplace is perfectly clean except for a light layer of dust, and the lack of ash just makes me feel sicker.

"Why did you put me here, Joaquin?" I opened the pantry, fearing what I'd find. Save for one smeared blotch in the middle of the floor, the place was clean. Jars of preserved fruits, vegetables, smoked meats, hung in perfect order. He put me where the food was, I realized, but why? So that I would not go hungry, of course, but did he mean me to stay here until he came for me? Did he think something would happen to the house spirit, and I would have to fend for myself?

No lunch came, nor did dinner. The sunlight faded and was not replaced. I fended for myself with cheese and meat I cut with a small sharp knife. I drank water and wondered what the new day would bring, praying that the night would bring nothing. My prayers were answered, mostly, though in the distance I could hear anguished howling, punctuated sometimes by something shattering.

I slept on the counter in the pantry that night, wrapped in my ragged blanket. The knife stayed in my hand.

The next day breakfast was laid out on the table, thin slices of white and yellow cheese alternated in a many-petaled flower pattern with slices of pale green fruit. A pitcher of pale peach juice sat in the center. "How very pretty!" I said, yet when I reached out to pluck a piece of cheese from the display it crumbled to dust in my hand.

Breakfast: dried fruit, a little smoked ham, water.

I cleaned up, then scrubbed the walls, ignoring the spots of irregular brown that splattered them.

The night was silent.

Still, Joaquin did not come.

The next morning a pitcher of boiling water was set out for me. It remained hot as I prepared a little tea. I ate from a jar of tiny, stale biscuits and stared at the door. My keys were upstairs on my dresser, yet even so it didn't look as if I could lock or unlock the door from this side. In fact, there was a sort of bar set across the door, that pulled back when the latch on the other side was turned.

The axe was in the corner, cleaned of the worst of the mess, its cream-colored handle spotted with many finger-shaped prints. I hefted it, a sense of dizziness coming over me. I went to the door, and as I lifted it over my shoulder, the kitchen came into sharp focus. I turned and looked behind me.

There were four of them, dressed in the same colors, serviceable gray for servants, a bright blue for the family's crest. A man, his haggard looks belying the strength in his scarred hands, the hostler, I thought, and a glance at the heavy boots proved that he was the one who took care of the stables. A young boy with dark hair, his ears sticking out like saucers. A flat-chested scarecrow of a girl, her dull straw hair almost all hidden underneath her tightly drawn scarf. An older woman, her face like leather, her hair like wool. They all stood perfectly still, hands folded in front of them, as if lined up for inspection.

The hostler's eyes lit up like flame. "Be bold," he said, and it was almost fatherly, the way he looked at me. The flames dulled, and he disappeared, the fire passing on to the boy.

"Be bold," he said earnestly. The fire passed on. He, too, was gone. "Be bold," the girl said, a flicker of flirtation in it.

Now only the housekeeper was left. She stared at me for a long time. I recognized pity in her eyes, along with the flicker of flame. "Be bold," she said. She started to say something else, but she, like the others, faded.

I took the axe to the door bar.

When I walked out I half expected to see Joaquin, drawn by the noise. No one sat at the table, though a book and some dishes lay scattered upon it. The food looked like offerings left for mice, so old and desiccated it was. I looked down at the axe in my hand, then turned around and put it back in the kitchen. I did not wish to approach my husband so obviously armed. I settled, instead, for a small knife that fit in my pocket.

I wrapped the blanket around myself like a stole, and with my back straight, I marched out of the dining room.

She was beautiful, the woman who stood near the bottom of the stairs, her hand on the rail. She wore a white dress, beaded and embroidered lavishly in red, and a velvet coat that pooled onto the pale marble below. She wore her rich black hair pulled slightly up to one side, graced by a ruby tiara. She had on a choker of rubies, and rubies dripped from her wrists and from her elbows. As I got closer one ruby drop fell to the steps and splashed, and as I took another step I realized that the line around her neck, her elbows, fingers and wrists were all made of blood. The embroidery became splashes of blood, and she dripped, calmly staring at me, on the marble of the white stairs. The only rubies she truly wore were on her ears and in her crown.

I stood only a foot from her. "Hello," I said.

Her mouth almost lifted. Her expression almost mocking and amused, but only slightly, as if she had not the energy to gather anymore.

I walked up the steps, scraping the wall to put as much space between me and wife number one as possible. Only her eyes moved.

"But not too bold," she said. I looked at her, and realized that her hair was not half pulled up, but shorn on one side, as if it had been between the blade and the flesh. I kept going, and her head turned. "Lest your heart's blood grow cold." And then she laughed. "God knows mine did." She fell to pieces then, whatever had been holding her together vanished, and she lay in a pile, her head rolling down the few steps and coming to a stop near the door.

I managed to make it to my bedroom without further incident, where I began to pull my warmest dress out of the cupboard, then stopped. Instead I pulled out the dress I'd married Joaquin in, and slowly, bit by bit, dressed myself in my finest things. My most beautiful jewelry, the intricately embroidered shawl. I decorated my hair as finely as I could, and carefully applied a subtly enhancing layer of cosmetics. My fingers twitched to put on my heavy walking boots in case I decided to run for it, but, knowing they'd look amiss, I slipped on soft slippers instead.

When I was done I looked just like the woman he'd married.

The library was a mess. The dome was shattered, books scattered everywhere. I crunched and slid through the room until I got to the study. The painting had been ripped from the mantel and thrown aside. In the direct light from the sun I realized that the hunters had the faces and hands of foxes, and that the creature on the spit was a man. "We'll have to burn that," I muttered, and made my way back and up the stairs.

He was sitting in the middle of the music room, the wind blowing in and twanging across half broken strings. He looked up at me slowly. "There you are," he said, offhandedly, as if I'd wandered off somewhere.

"You look like you smashed your face into a glass cabinet." I said, and he did. Crisscrossed scratches covered his face and hands. Three lines that looked like claw marks stuck out against the brutal purple collar of flesh that decorated his throat. Dried blood pooled in the shell of one ear.

His eyes looked out into the distance. He didn't seem to even see me. "I think," he said, after awhile, "that you should go and visit your cousin. It will do you good, to be away for awhile."

"I don't want to."

His eyes focused, and he looked at me with that searing expression he used to grant me when he was not to be coaxed. "I was not making a suggestion."

I stepped forward, wanting to keep his attention, wanting to keep him. "We should both go. Together. It doesn't matter where. You can run your business anywhere."

His eyes unfocused again, and he drifted away from me. "I can't leave. Not for long."

"Why not?"

"I am the house," he said, and then buried his face in his hands and laughed, a soft, angry chuckle that was half sob, half acceptance. The house had to get its power from somewhere, I realized, and though he was trying, he couldn't fight against himself.

I placed my hand on his head. "I really do love you," I said, then sighed. "Right, then. It's up to me."

"What are you going to do?" he asked me as I left.

"You'll see," I said. "Lock, door." And it did as I bid it.

The axe was where I left it, and so was wife number one. I shuddered both times I passed her, and hoped she'd be gone when I got back.

I finally stood before the red framed door. The wood was scratched and splintered, and someone had written nasty-looking curses and spells around the frame with a nail or a knife. The voices were loud inside my head, the whispers beating in time with the drum of my heart, but they did not need to urge me to take the key to the lock. It turned easily, the glass almost too hot to hold. The door opened slowly.

The odor was nearly overwhelming, death and animal mixed together. Things lay scattered everywhere. Balled-up and stained dresses of bright cloth in piles, sapphire and ruby, one of them a wedding dress. Gnawed bones mixed with shattered plates. Next to the room's only window, Joaquin stood, dressed in perfect black mourning, polished boots and starched white cuffs. He turned to me, shutting the book he held in his hands with a snap. A fine mist of fur covered the back of his hands, and climbed up his neck, surrounding his face in a soft fuzz. His fingernails were quite longer than he was in the habit of keeping them, and his teeth were very sharp when he smiled.

"Well, then," I said. "I am pleased to finally meet the rest of the family."

He smirked at me. "I knew you would come." He threw

the book aside. "They always do." He walked closer, and my hand tightened on the axe. He rested his paws on the back of a chair. "Tell me, what did you expect to find? More fine jewels, more fair wonders? What did you expect to find in this room that made all of the other treasures seem so inadequate?"

"I found what I expected," I said. "A monster who preys on the innocent, who enjoys chopping up the servants just because he can. I revile you, and I want you out of my house and away from my husband."

"But I am the house," he said, feigning shock.

"It is time, then, for some remodeling." I hefted the axe and struck the wall. I was rewarded by a pained scream that barely muffled my own as a shock of pain ran down my elbow. The scream came from Joaquin, not from the monster I shared the room with.

He smiled, all his sharp teeth glittering. "He came out first," he said, "and he'll die before me."

I pulled the axe from the wall.

"I would thank you to be kinder to the walls," Joaquin, the real Joaquin, was leaning on the door frame, one hand holding his shoulder.

"What are you? What is he?"

He straightened slowly, and came toward me. "My father was a man," he said, reaching for the axe. I resisted his tug on the handle before letting it slide from my fingers. "My mother was a fox."

"They lured women here," his twin continued, "to feed the family." He ran his eyes down my form, and I could feel his gaze is if it were his tongue, tasting and testing, deciding where he'd like to begin eating.

"Is this true?"

Joaquin was looking at the balled-up wedding dress. "Yes," he said.

"But you don't look like him," I said. "I mean, you do, but..."

"He shaves," his brother sneered. "And he leaves you to hunt game in the deep woods. What do you hunt now?

Chickens? A stray goat? While I stayed locked up in this room, forgotten like yesterday's meal."

"If that's so, how have you survived?"

"It's the house. We are the house, the house takes care of us." Joaquin's hand flexed on the axe. "There must always be two."

I tucked my hand in my pocket. The small kitchen knife was there. "I am your flesh," I said to him. "We swore before God." He looked at me, and I tried to read his eyes ."You've lived too long with this. You must choose."

"He can't choose!" his brother snarled. "His choices were taken from him long ago. Without the house, he dies. Without me, he dies."

"Because you are the house?"

"That's right," he snarled, his fingers ripping open his coat.

"I have a message for you, from the house," I said, pulling the knife out. "It doesn't want you anymore."

Joaquin brushed past me. "I'll go first," he said.

Of course, I must have lived, or I would not be telling you this.

The house showed itself to me when I picked up the axe and proved that I was willing to take things into my own hands. It showed me the servants, murdered so long ago by my in-laws, and when I struck it, it hurt my shoulder as it hurt Joaquin's and so I knew, or hoped.

Sometimes I walk past that room. It is empty, the occupant buried, but I do not open the door. I do not want to see his ghost, taunting me with my husband's face.

I would like to leave the house sometimes but I no longer can for more than a few weeks else I begin to pine. I feel weak and hungry and no amount of food fills me.

I always see the ghosts now, the servants at their work, bound to me and the house; unwilling to go even if I could free them. Sometimes I see wife number one and a woman I call sapphire earrings, and both of them shoot daggers at

Joaquin, who seems never to notice. Once I saw a woman with wild red curls, beads of amber twined about her throat. She stood behind Joaquin's chair cheerfully petting the air above his head. When she looked up at me I saw that they shared the same eyes, and she smiled at me, her teeth sharp. Her ears twitched and she bounded off, a bush of tail ruining the line of her loose, colorful skirts.

"Don't you see them?" I asked.

"God forbid that it should ever be so." He shuddered, and I decided not to discuss it again. Even when a man with hair so black that it was blue, the stubble from the late day beginnings of a beard making his skin cobalt, was awaiting for me at the front landing, cleaning his nails with a small, sharp knife not unlike the one I always carried. He gave me a look filled with lust and menace, and took a step forward.

"If you don't behave yourself, I can have you kicked out and then you'll be even less than you are now." I did not look back to see what he made of it, but in the kitchen the housekeeper gave me a pleased wink.

I am heavy with child now and Joaquin thinks it will be twins. He does not look pleased, and sometimes, when he seems to be happy, his hand on my swelling belly, talking nonsense to me and our children, waiting for one to kick, a shadow will cross his face, and I realize that he is afraid.

I'm not. The house and I have an agreement and I will do what I have to.

It is what mothers always do, in the woods.

COME LADY DEATH

by
Peter S. Beagle

This all happened in England a long time ago, when that George who spoke English with a heavy German accent and hated his sons was King. At that time there lived in London a lady who had nothing to do but give parties. Her name was Flora, Lady Neville, and she was a widow and very old. She lived in a great house not far from Buckingham Palace, and she had so many servants that she could not possibly remember all their names; indeed, there were some she had never even seen. She had more food than she could eat, more gowns than she could ever wear; she had wine in her cellars that no one would drink in her lifetime, and her private vaults were filled with great works of art that she did not know she owned. She spent the last years of her life giving parties and balls to which the greatest lords of England—and sometimes the King himself—came, and she was known as the wisest and wittiest woman in all London.

But in time her own parties began to bore her, and though she invited the most famous people in the land and hired the greatest jugglers and acrobats and dancers and magicians to entertain them, still she found her parties duller and duller. Listening to court gossip, which she had always loved, made her yawn. The most marvelous music, the most exciting feats of magic put her to sleep. Watching a beautiful young couple

45

dance by her made her feel sad, and she hated to feel sad.

And so, one summer afternoon she called her closest friends around her and said to them, "More and more I find that my parties entertain everyone but me. The secret of my long life is that nothing has ever been dull for me. For all my life, I have been interested in everything I saw and been anxious to see more. But I cannot stand to be bored, and I will not go to parties at which I expect to be bored, especially if they are my own. Therefore, to my next ball I shall invite the one guest I am sure no one, not even myself, could possibly find boring. My friends, the guest of honor at my next party shall be Death himself!"

A young poet thought that this was a wonderful idea, but the rest of her friends were terrified and drew back from her. They did not want to die, they pleaded with her. Death would come for them when he was ready; why should she invite him before the appointed hour, which would arrive soon enough? But Lady Neville said, "Precisely. If Death has planned to take any of us on the night of my party, he will come whether he is invited or not. But if none of us are to die, then I think it would be charming to have Death among us—perhaps even to perform some little trick if he is in a good humor. And think of being able to say that we had been to a party with Death! All of London will envy us, all of England!"

The idea began to please her friends, but a young lord, very new to London, suggested timidly, "Death is so busy. Suppose he has work to do and cannot accept your invitation?"

"No one has ever refused an invitation of mine," said Lady Neville, "not even the King." And the young lord was not invited to her party.

She sat down then and there and wrote out the invitation. There was some dispute among her friends as to how they should address Death. "His Lordship Death" seemed to place him only on the level of a viscount or a baron. "His Grace Death" met with more acceptance, but Lady Neville said it sounded hypocritical. And to refer to Death as "His Majesty" was to make him the equal of the King of England, which even

Lady Neville would not dare to do. It was finally decided that all should speak of him as "His Eminence Death," which pleased nearly everyone.

Captain Compson, known both as England's most dashing cavalry officer and most elegant rake, remarked next, "That's all very well, but how is the invitation to reach Death? Does anyone here know where he lives?"

"Death undoubtedly lives in London," said Lady Neville, "like everyone else of any importance, though he probably goes to Deauville for the summer. Actually, Death must live fairly near my own house. This is much the best section of London, and you could hardly expect a person of Death's importance to live anywhere else. When I stop to think of it, it's really rather strange that we haven't met before now, on the street."

Most of her friends agreed with her, but the poet, whose name was David Lorimond, cried out, "No, my lady, you are wrong! Death lives among the poor. Death lives in the foulest, darkest alleys of this city, in some vile, rat-ridden hovel that smells of—" He stopped here, partly because Lady Neville had indicated her displeasure, and partly because he had never been inside such a hut or thought of wondering what it smelled like. "Death lives among the poor," he went on, "and comes to visit them every day, for he is their only friend."

Lady Neville answered him as coldly as she had spoken to the young lord. "He may be forced to deal with them, David, but I hardly think that he seeks them out as companions. I am certain that it is as difficult for him to think of the poor as individuals as it is for me. Death is, after all, a nobleman."

There was no real argument among the lords and ladies that Death lived in a neighborhood at least as good as their own, but none of them seemed to know the name of Death's street, and no one had ever seen Death's house.

"If there were a war," Captain Compson said, "Death would be easy to find. I have seen him, you know, even spoken to him, but he has never answered me."

"Quite proper," said Lady Neville. "Death must always speak first. You are not a very correct person, Captain," but she smiled at him, as all women did.

Then an idea came to her. "My hairdresser has a sick child, I understand," she said. "He was telling me about it yesterday, sounding most dull and hopeless. I will send for him and give him the invitation, and he in his turn can give it to Death when he comes to take the brat. A bit unconventional, I admit, but I see no other way."

"If he refuses?" asked a lord who had just been married.

"Why should he?" asked Lady Neville.

Again it was the poet who exclaimed amidst the general approval that it was a cruel and wicked thing to do. But he fell silent when Lady Neville innocently asked him, "Why, David?"

So the hairdresser was sent for, and when he stood before them, smiling nervously and twisting his hands to be in the same room with so many great lords, Lady Neville told him the errand that was required of him. And she was right, as she usually was, for he made no refusal. He merely took the invitation in his hand and asked to be excused.

He did not return for two days, but when he did he presented himself to Lady Neville without being sent for and handed her a small white envelope. Saying, "How very nice of you, thank you very much," she opened it and found therein a plain calling card with nothing on it except these words:

Death will be pleased to attend Lady Neville's ball.

"Death gave you this?" she asked the hairdresser eagerly. "What was he like?" But the hairdresser stood still, looking past her, and said nothing, and she, not really waiting for an answer, called a dozen servants to her and told them to run and summon her friends. As she paced up and down the room waiting for them, she asked again, "What is Death like?" The hairdresser did not reply.

When her friends came they passed the little card excitedly from hand to hand, until it had gotten quite smudged and bent from their fingers. But they all admitted that, beyond its message, there was nothing particularly unusual about it. It was neither hot nor cold to the touch, and what little odor clung to it was rather pleasant. Everyone said that it was a very familiar smell, but no one could give it a name. The poet said that it reminded him of lilacs but not exactly.

It was Captain Compson, however, who pointed out the one thing that no one else had noticed. "Look at the handwriting itself," he said. "Have you ever seen anything more graceful? The letters seem as light as birds. I think we have wasted our time speaking of Death as His This and His That. A woman wrote his note."

Then there was an uproar and a great babble, and the card had to be handed around again so that everyone could exclaim, "Yes, by God!" over it. The voice of the poet rose out the hubbub saying, "It is very natural, when you come to think of it. After all, the French say *la mort*. Lady Death. I should much prefer Death to be a woman."

"Death rides a great black horse," said Captain Compson firmly, "and wears armor of the same color. Death is very tall, taller than anyone. It was no woman I saw on the battlefield, striking right and left like any soldier. Perhaps the hairdresser wrote it himself, or the hairdresser's wife."

But the hairdresser refused to speak, though they gathered around him and begged him to say who had given him the note. At first they promised him all sorts of rewards, and later they threatened to do terrible things to him. "Did you write this card?" he was asked, and "Who wrote it, then? Was it a living woman? Was it really Death? Did Death say anything to you? How did you know it was Death? Is Death a woman? Are you trying to make fools of us all?"

Not a word from the hairdresser, not one word, and finally Lady Neville called her servants to have him whipped and thrown into the street. He did not look at her as they took him away, or utter a sound.

Silencing her friends with a wave of her hand, Lady Neville said, "The ball will take place two weeks from tonight. Let Death come as Death pleases, whether as a man or woman or strange, sexless creature." She smiled calmly. "Death may well be a woman," she said. "I am less certain of Death's form than I was, but I am also less frightened of Death. I am too old to be afraid of anything that can use a quill pen to write me a letter. Go home now, and as you make your preparations for the ball see that you speak of it to your servants, that they may spread the news all over London. Let it be known that on this one night no one in the world will die, for Death will be dancing at Lady Neville's ball."

For the next two weeks Lady Neville's great house shook and groaned and creaked like an old tree in a gale as the servants hammered and scrubbed, polished and painted, making ready for the ball. Lady Neville had always been very proud of her house, but as the ball drew near she began to be afraid that it would not be nearly grand enough for Death, who was surely accustomed to visiting in the homes of richer, mightier people than herself. Fearing the scorn of Death, she worked night and day supervising her servants' preparations. Curtains and carpets had to be cleaned, goldwork and silverware polished until they gleamed by themselves in the dark. The grand staircase that rushed down into the ballroom like a waterfall was washed and rubbed so often that it was almost impossible to walk on it without slipping. As for the ballroom itself, it took thirty-two servants working at once to clean it properly, not counting those who were polishing the glass chandelier that was taller than a man and the fourteen smaller lamps. And when they were done she made them do it all over, not because she saw any dust or dirt anywhere, but because she was sure that Death would.

As for herself, she chose her finest gown and saw to the laundering personally. She called in another hairdresser and had him put up her hair in the style of an earlier time, wanting to show Death that she was a woman who enjoyed her age and did not find it necessary to ape the young and beautiful. All the day of the ball she sat before her mirror, not making herself up much beyond the normal touches of rouge and eye shadow and fine rice powder, but staring at the lean old face she had been born with, wondering how it would appear to Death. Her steward asked her to approve his wine selection, but she sent him away and stayed at her mirror until it was time to dress and go downstairs to meet her guests.

Everyone arrived early. When she looked out of a window, Lady Neville saw that the driveway of her home was choked with carriages and fine horses. "It all looks like a funeral procession," she said. The footman cried the names of her guests to the echoing ballroom. "Captain Henry Compson, His Majesty's Household Cavalry! Mr. David Lorimond! Lord and Lady Torrance!!" (They were the youngest couple there, having been married only three months before.) "Sir Roger Harbison! The Contessa della Candini!" Lady Neville permitted them all to kiss her hand and made them welcome.

She had engaged the finest musicians she could find to play for the dancing, but though they began to play at her signal, not one couple stepped out on the floor, nor did one young lord approach her to request the honor of the first dance, as was proper. They milled together, shining and murmuring, their eyes fixed on the ballroom door. Every time they heard a carriage clatter up the driveway they seemed to flinch a little and draw closer together; every time the footman announced the arrival of another guest, they all sighed softly and swayed a little on their feet with relief.

"Why did they come to my party if they were afraid?" Lady Neville muttered scornfully to herself. "I am not afraid of meeting Death. I ask only that Death may be impressed by the magnificence of my house and the flavor of my wines. I will die sooner than anyone here, but I am not afraid."

Certain that Death would not arrive until midnight, she moved among her guests, attempting to calm them, not with her words, which she knew they would not hear, but with the tone of her voice as if they were so many frightened horses. But little by little, she herself was infected by their nervousness: whenever she sat down she stood up again immediately, she tasted a dozen glasses of wine without finishing any of them, and she glanced constantly at her jeweled watch, at first wanting to hurry the midnight along and end the waiting, later scratching at the watch face with her forefinger, as if she would push away the night and drag the sun backward into the sky. When midnight came, she was standing with the rest of them, breathing through her mouth, shifting from foot to foot, listening for the sound of carriage wheels turning in gravel.

When the clock began to strike midnight, everyone, even Lady Neville and the brave Captain Compson, gave one startled little cry and then was silent again, listening to the tolling of the clock. The smaller clocks upstairs began to chime. Lady Neville's ears hurt. She caught sight of herself in the ballroom mirror, one gray face turned up toward the ceiling as if she were gasping for air, and she thought, "Death will be a woman, a hideous, filthy old crone as tall and strong as a man. And the most terrible thing of all will be that she will have my face." All the clocks stopped striking, and Lady Neville closed her eyes.

She opened them again only when she heard the whispering around her take on a different tone, one in which fear was fused with relief and a certain chagrin. For no new carriage stood in the driveway. Death had not come.

The noise grew slowly louder; here and there people were beginning to laugh. Near her, Lady Neville heard young Lord Torrance say to his wife, "There, my darling, I told you there was nothing to be afraid of. It was all a joke."

"I am ruined," Lady Neville thought. The laughter was increasing; it pounded against her ears in strokes, like the chiming of the clocks. "I wanted to give a ball so grand that those who were not invited would be shamed in front of the whole city, and this is my reward. I am ruined, and I deserve it."

Turning to the poet Lorimond, she said, "Dance with me, David." She signaled to the musicians, who at once began to play. When Lorimond hesitated, she said, "Dance with me now. You will not have another chance. I shall never give a party again."

Lorimond bowed and led her onto the dance floor. The guests parted for them, and the laughter died down for a moment, but Lady Neville knew that it would soon begin again. "Well, let them laugh," she thought. "I did not fear Death when they were all trembling. Why should I fear their laughter?" but she could feel a stinging at the thin lids of her eyes, and she closed them once more as she began to dance with Lorimond.

And then, quite suddenly, all the carriage horses outside the house whinnied loudly, just once, as the guests had cried out at midnight. There were a great many horses, and their one salute was so loud that everyone in the room became instantly silent. They heard the heavy steps of the footman as he went to open the door, and they shivered as if they felt the cool breeze that drifted into the house. Then they heard a light voice saying, "Am I late? Oh, I am so sorry. The horses were tired," and before the footman could re-enter to announce her, a lovely young girl in a white dress stepped gracefully into the ballroom doorway and stood there smiling.

She could not have been more than nineteen. Her hair was yellow, and she wore it long. It fell thickly upon her bare shoulders that gleamed warmly through it, two limestone islands rising out of a dark golden sea. Her face was wide at the forehead and cheekbones, and narrow at the chin, and her skin was so clear that many of the ladies there—Lady Neville among them—touched their own faces wonderingly, and instantly drew their hands away as though their own skin had rasped their fingers. Her mouth was pale, where the mouths of other women were red and orange and even purple. Her eyebrows, thicker and straighter than was fashionable, met over dark, calm eyes that were set so deep in her young face and were so black, so uncompromisingly black, that the middle-aged wife of a middle-aged lord murmured, "Touch of a gypsy there, I think."

"Or something worse," suggested her husband's mistress.

"Be silent!" Lady Neville spoke louder than she had intended, and the girl turned to look at her. She smiled, and

Lady Neville tried to smile back, but her mouth seemed very stiff. "Welcome," she said. "Welcome, my lady Death."

A sigh rustled among the lords and ladies as the girl took the old woman's hand and curtsied to her, sinking and rising in one motion, like a wave. "You are Lady Neville," she said. "Thank you so much for inviting me." Her accent was as faint and almost familiar as her perfume.

"Please excuse me for being late," she said earnestly. "I had to come from a long way off, and my horses are so tired."

"The groom will rub them down," Lady Neville said, "and feed them if you wish."

"Oh, no," the girl answered quickly. "Tell him not to go near the horses, please. They are not really horses, and they are very fierce."

She accepted a glass of wine from a servant and drank it slowly, sighing softly and contentedly. "What good wine," she said. "And what a beautiful house you have."

"Thank you," said Lady Neville. Without turning, she could feel every woman in the room envying her, sensing it as she could always sense the approach of rain.

"I wish I lived here," Death said in her low, sweet voice. "I will, one day."

Then, seeing Lady Neville become as still as if she had turned to ice, she put her hand on the old woman's arm and said, "Oh, I'm sorry, I'm so sorry. I am so cruel, but I never mean to be. Please forgive me, Lady Neville. I am not used to company, and I do such stupid things. Please forgive me."

Her hand felt as light and warm on Lady Neville's arm as the hand of any other young girl, and her eyes were so appealing that Lady Neville replied, "You have said nothing wrong. While you are my guest, my house is yours."

"Thank you," said Death, and she smiled so radiantly that the musicians began to play quite by themselves, and with no sign from Lady Neville. She would have stopped them, but Death said, "Oh, what lovely music! Let them play, please."

So the musicians played a gavotte, and Death, unabashed by eyes that stared at her in greedy terror, sang softly to herself without words, lifted her white gown slightly with both hands, and made hesitant little patting steps with her small feet. "I have not danced in so long," she said wistfully. "I'm quite sure I've forgotten how."

She was shy; she would not look up to embarrass the young lords, not one of whom stepped forward to dance with her. Lady Neville felt a flood of shame and sympathy, emotions she thought had withered in her years ago. "Is she to be humiliated at my own ball?" she thought angrily. "It is because she is Death; if she were the ugliest, foulest hag in all the world they would clamor to dance with her, because they are gentlemen and they know what is expected of them. But no gentleman will dance with Death, no matter how beautiful she is." She glance sideways at David Lorimond. His face was flushed, and his hands were clasped so tightly as he stared at Death that his fingers were like glass, but when Lady Neville touched his arm he did not turn, and when she hissed, "David!" he pretended not to hear her.

Then Captain Compson, gray-haired and handsome in his uniform, stepped out of the crowd and bowed gracefully before Death. "If I may have the honor," he said.

"Captain Compson," said Death, smiling. She put her arm in his. "I was hoping you would ask me."

This brought a frown from the older women, who did not consider it a proper thing to say, but for that Death cared not a rap. Captain Compson led her to the center of the floor, and there they danced. Death was curiously graceless at first— she was too anxious to please her partner, and she seemed to have no notion of rhythm. The Captain himself moved with the mixture of dignity and humor that Lady Neville had never seen in another man, but when he looked at her over Death's shoulder, she saw something that no one else appeared to notice: that his face and eyes were immobile with fear, and that, though he offered Death his hand with easy gallantry, he flinched slightly when she took it. And yet he danced as well as Lady Neville had ever seen him.

"Ah, that's what comes of having a reputation to maintain,"

she thought. "Captain Compson too must do what is expected of him. I hope someone else will dance with her soon."

But no one did. Little by little, other couples overcame their fear and slipped hurriedly out on the floor when Death was looking the other way, but nobody sought to relieve Captain Compson of his beautiful partner. They danced every dance together. In time, some of the men present began to look at her with more appreciation than terror, but when she returned their glances and smiled at them, they clung to their partners as if a cold wind were threatening to blow them away.

One of the few who stared at her frankly and with pleasure was young Lord Torrance, who usually danced only with his wife. Another was the poet Lorimond. Dancing with Lady Neville, he remarked to her, "If she is Death, what do these frightened fools think they are? If she is ugliness, what must they be? I hate their fear. It is obscene."

Death and the Captain danced past them at that moment, and they heard him say to her, "But if that was truly you that I saw in the battle, how can you have changed so? How can you have become so lovely?"

Death's laughter was gay and soft. "I thought that among so many beautiful people it might be better to be beautiful. I was afraid of frightening everyone and spoiling the party."

"They all thought she would be ugly," said Lorimond to Lady Neville. "I—I knew she would be beautiful."

"Then why have you not danced with her?" Lady Neville asked him. "Are you also afraid?"

"No, oh, no," the poet answered quickly and passionately. "I will ask her to dance very soon. I only want to look at her a little longer."

The musicians played on and on. The dancing wore away the night as slowly as falling water wears down a cliff. It seemed to Lady Neville that no night had ever endured longer, and yet she was neither tired nor bored. She danced with every man there, except with Lord Torrance, who was dancing with his wife as if they had just met that night, and, of course, with Captain Compson. Once he lifted his hand and touched Death's golden hair very lightly. He was a striking man still, a fit partner for so beautiful a girl, but Lady Neville looked at his face each time she passed him and realized that he was older than anyone knew.

Death herself seemed younger than the youngest there. No woman at the ball danced better than she now, though it was hard for Lady Neville to remember at what point her awkwardness had given way to the liquid sweetness of her movements. She smiled and called to everyone who caught her eye—and she knew them all by name; she sang constantly, making up words to the dance tunes, nonsense words, sounds without meaning, and yet everyone strained to hear her soft voice without knowing why. And when, during a waltz, she caught up the trailing end of her gown to give her more freedom as she danced, she seemed to Lady Neville to move like a little sailing boat over a still evening sea.

Lady Neville heard Lady Torrance arguing angrily with the Contessa della Candini. "I don't care if she is Death, she's no older than I am, she can't be!"

"Nonsense," said the Contessa, who could not afford to be generous to any other woman. "She is twenty-eight, thirty, if she is an hour. And that dress, that bridal gown she wears—really!"

"Vile," said the woman who had come to the ball as Captain Compson's freely acknowledged mistress. "Tasteless. But one should know better than to expect taste from Death, I suppose." Lady Torrance looked as if she were going to cry.

"They are jealous of Death," Lady Neville said to herself. "How strange. I am not jealous of her, not in the least. And I do not fear her at all." She was very proud of herself.

Then, as unbiddenly as they had begun to play, the musicians stopped. They began to put away their instruments. In the sudden shrill silence, Death pulled away from Captain Compson and ran to look out of one of the tall windows, pushing the curtains apart with both hands. "Look!" she said, with her back turned to them. "Come and look. The night is almost gone."

The summer sky was still dark, and the eastern horizon was only a shade lighter than the rest of the sky, but the stars had vanished and the trees near the house were gradually becoming distinct. Death pressed her face against the window and said, so softly that the other guests could barely hear her, "I must go now."

"No," Lady Neville said, and was not immediately aware that she had spoken. "You must stay a while longer. The ball was in your honor. Please stay."

Death held out both hands to her, and Lady Neville came and took them in her own. "I've had a wonderful time," she said gently. "You cannot possibly imagine how it feels to be actually invited to such a ball as this, because you have given them and gone to them all your life. One is like another to you, but for me it is different. Do you understand me?" Lady Neville nodded silently. "I will remember this night forever," Death said.

"Stay," Captain Compson said. "Stay just a little longer." He put his hand on Death's shoulder, and she smiled and leaned her cheek against it. "Dear Captain Compson," she said. "My first real gallant. Aren't you tired of me yet?"

"Never," he said. "Please stay."

"Stay," said Lorimond, and he too seemed about to touch her. "Stay. I want to talk to you. I want to look at you. I will dance with you if you stay."

"How many followers I have," Death said in wonder. She stretched her hand toward Lorimond, but he drew back from her and then flushed in shame. "A soldier and a poet. How wonderful it is to be a woman. But why did you not speak to me earlier, both of you? Now it is too late. I must go."

"Please, stay," Lady Torrance whispered. She held on to her husband's hand for courage. "We think you are so beautiful, both of us do."

"Gracious Lady Torrance," the girl said kindly. She turned back to the window, touched it lightly, and it flew open. The cool dawn air rushed into the ballroom, fresh with rain but already smelling faintly of the London streets over which it had passed. They heard birdsong and the strange, harsh nickering of Death's horses.

"Do you want me to stay?" she asked. The question was put, not to Lady Neville, nor to Captain Compson, nor to any of her admirers, but to the Contessa della Candini, who stood well back from them all, hugging her flowers to herself and humming a little song of irritation. She did not in the least want Death to stay, but she was afraid that all the other women would think her envious of Death's beauty, and so she said, "Yes. Of course I do."

"Ah," said Death. She was almost whispering. "And you," she said to another woman, "do you want me to stay? Do you want me to be one of your friends?"

"Yes," said the woman, "because you are beautiful and a true lady."

"And you," said Death to a man, "and you," to a woman, "and you," to another man, "do you want me to stay?" And they all answered, "Yes, Lady Death, we do."

"Do you want me, then?" she cried at last to all them. "Do you want me to live among you and to be one of you, and not to be Death anymore? Do you want me to visit your houses and come to all your parties? Do you want me to ride horses like yours instead of mine, do you want me to wear the kind of dresses you wear, and say the things you would say? Would one of you marry me, and would the rest of you dance at my wedding and bring gifts to my children? Is that what you want?"

"Yes," said Lady Neville. "Stay here, stay with me, stay with us."

Death's voice, without becoming louder, had become clearer and older; too old a voice, thought Lady Neville, for such a young girl. "Be sure," said Death. "Be sure of what you want, be very sure. Do all of you want me to stay? For if one of you says to me, no, go away, then I must leave at once and never return. Be sure. Do you all want me?"

And everyone there cried with one voice, "Yes! Yes, you must stay with us. You are so beautiful that we cannot let you go."

"We are tired," said Captain Compson.

"We are blind," said Lorimond, adding, "especially to poetry."

"We are afraid," said Lord Torrance quietly, and his wife took his arm and said, "Both of us."

"We are dull and stupid," said Lady Neville, "and growing old uselessly. Stay with us, Lady Death."

And then Death smiled sweetly and radiantly and took a step forward, and it was as though she had come down among them from a very great height. "Very well," she said. "I will stay with you. I will be Death no more. I will be a woman."

The room was full of a deep sigh, although no one was seen to open his mouth. No one moved, for the goldenhaired girl was Death still, and her horses still whinnied for her outside. No one could look at her for long, although she was the most beautiful girl anyone there had ever seen.

"There is a price to pay," she said. "There is always a price. Some one of you must become Death in my place, for there must forever be Death in the world. Will anyone choose? Will anyone here become Death of his own free will? For only thus can I become a human girl."

No one spoke, no one spoke at all. But they backed slowly away from her, like waves slipping back down a beach to the sea when you try to catch them. The Contessa della Candini and her friends would have crept quietly out of the door, but Death smiled at them and they stood where they were. Captain Compson opened his mouth as though he were going to declare himself, but he said nothing. Lady Neville did not move.

"No one," said Death. She touched a flower with her finger, and it seemed to crouch and flex itself like a pleased cat. "No one at all," she said. "Then I must choose, and that is just, for that is the way I became Death. I never wanted to be Death, and it makes me so happy that you want me to become one of yourselves. I have searched a long time for people who would want me. Now I have only to choose someone to replace me and it is done. I will choose very carefully."

"Oh, we were so foolish," Lady Neville said to herself. "We were so foolish." But she said nothing aloud; she merely clasped her hands and stared at the young girl, thinking vaguely that if she had had a daughter she would have been greatly pleased if she resembled the lady Death.

"The Contessa della Candini," said Death thoughtfully, and that woman gave a little squeak of terror because she could not draw her breath for a scream. But Death laughed and said, "No, that would be silly." She said nothing more, but for a long time after that the Contessa burned with humiliation at not having been chosen to be Death.

"Not Captain Compson," murmured Death, "because he is too kind to become Death, and because it would be too cruel to him. He wants to die so badly." The expression on the Captain's face did not change, but his hands began to tremble.

"Not Lorimond," the girl continued, "because he knows so little about life, and because I like him." The poet flushed, and turned white, and then turned pink again. He made as if to kneel clumsily on one knee, but instead he pulled himself erect and stood as much like Captain Compson as he could.

"Not the Torrances," said Death, "never Lord and Lady Torrance, for both of them care too much about another person to take any pride in being Death." But she hesitated over Lady Torrance for a while, staring at her out of her dark and curious eyes. "I was your age when I became Death," she said at last. "I wonder what it will be like to be your age again. I have been Death for so long." Lady Torrance shivered and did not speak.

And at last Death said quietly, "Lady Neville."

"I am here," Lady Neville answered.

"I think you are the only one," said Death. "I choose you, Lady Neville."

Again Lady Neville heard every guest sigh softly, and although her back was to them all she knew that they were sighing in relief that neither themselves nor anyone dear to themselves had been chosen. Lady Torrance gave a little cry of protest, but Lady Neville knew that she would have cried out at whatever choice Death made. She heard herself say calmly, "I am honored. But was there no one more worthy than I?"

"Not one," said Death. "There is no one quite so weary of being human, no one who knows better how meaningless it is to be alive. And there is no one else here with the power to treat life"—and she smiled sweetly and cruelly—"the life of your hairdresser's child, for instance, as the meaningless thing it is. Death has a heart, but it is forever an empty heart, and I think, Lady Neville, that your heart is like a dry riverbed, like a seashell. You will be very content as Death, more so than I, for I was very young when I became Death."

She came toward Lady Neville, light and swaying, her deep eyes wide and full of the light of the red morning sun that was beginning to rise. The guests at the ball moved back from her, although she did not look at them, but Lady Neville clenched her hands tightly and watched Death come toward her with little dancing steps. "We must kiss each other," Death said. "That is the way I became Death." She shook her head delightedly, so that her soft hair swirled about her shoulders. "Quickly, quickly," she said. "Oh, I cannot wait to be human again."

"You may not like it," Lady Neville said. She felt very calm, though she could hear her old heart pounding in her chest and feel it in the tips of her fingers. "You may not like it after a while," she said.

"Perhaps not." Death's smile was very close to her now. "I will not be as beautiful as I am, and perhaps people will not love me as much as they do now. But I will be human for a while, and at last I will die. I have done my penance."

"What penance?" the old woman asked the beautiful girl. "What was it you did? Why did you become Death?"

"I don't remember," said the lady Death. "And you too will

forget in time." She was smaller than Lady Neville, and so much younger. In her white dress she might have been the daughter that Lady Neville had never had, who would have been with her always and held her mother's head lightly in the crook of her arm when she felt old and sad. Now she lifted her head to kiss Lady Neville's cheek, and as she did so she whispered in her hear, "You will still be beautiful when I am ugly. Be kind to me then."

Behind Lady Neville the handsome gentlemen and ladies murmured and sighed, fluttering like moths in their evening dress, in their elegant gowns. "I promise," she said, and then she pursed her dry lips to kiss the soft, sweet-smelling cheek of the young Lady Death.

SUMMER WIND

by
Nancy Kress

Sometimes she talked to them. Which of course was stupid, since they could neither hear nor answer. She talked anyway. It made the illusion of company.

Her favorite to talk to was the stableboy, frozen in the stableyard beside the king's big roan, the grooming brush still in his upraised hand. The roan was frozen too, of course, brown eyes closed, white forelock blowing gently in the summer wind. She used to be a little frightened of the roan, so big it was, but not of the stableboy, who had had merry red lips and wide shoulders and dark curling hair.

He had them still.

Every so often she washed off a few of them: the stableboy, or the cook beside his pots, or the lady-in-waiting sewing in the solarium, or even the man and woman in the north bedchamber, locked in naked embrace on the wide bed. None of them ever sweated or stank, but still, there was the dust— dust didn't sleep—and after years and years the people became coated in fine, gray powder. At first she tried to whisk them clean with a serving maid's feather duster, but it was very hard to dust eyelashes and earlobes. In the end she just threw a pot of water over them. They didn't stir, and their clothes dried eventually, the velvets and silks a little stiff and water-marked, the coarse-weaved breeches and skirts of the servants none the worse off. Better, maybe. And it wasn't as if any of them would catch cold.

"There you are," she said to the stableboy. "Now, doesn't that feel better? To be clean?"

Water glistened in his black curls.

"I'm sure it must feel better."

A droplet fell onto his forehead, slid over his smooth brown cheek, came to rest in the corner of his mouth.

"It was not supposed to happen this way, Corwin."

He didn't answer, of course. She reached out one finger and patted the droplet from his sleeping lips. She put the finger in her own mouth and sucked it.

"How many years was I asleep? How many?"

His chest rose and fell gently, regularly.

She wished she could remember the color of his eyes.

A few years later, the first prince came. Or maybe it wasn't even the first. Briar Rose was climbing the steps from the cool, dark chambers under the castle, her spread skirt full of wheat and apples and cheese as fresh as the day they were stored. She passed the open windows of the Long Gallery and heard a tremendous commotion.

Finally! At last!

She dropped her skirts; wheat and apples rolled everywhere. Rose rushed through the gallery and up the steps to her bedchamber in the highest tower. From her stone window she could just glimpse him beyond the castle wall, the moat, the circle of grass between moat and Hedge. He sat astride a white stallion on the far side of the Hedge, hacking with a long silver sword. Sunlight glinted on his blond hair.

She put her hand to her mouth. The slim white fingers trembled.

The prince was shouting, but wind carried his words away from her. Did that mean the wind would carry hers toward him? She waved her arms and shouted.

"Here! Oh, brave prince, here I am! Briar Rose, princess of

all the realm! Fight on, oh good prince!"

He didn't look up. With a tremendous blow, he hacked a limb from the black Hedge, so thick and interwoven it looked like metal, not plant. The branch shuddered and fell. On the backswing, the sword struck smaller branches to the prince's right. They whipped aside and then snapped back, and a thorn-studded twig slapped the prince across the eyes and blinded him. He screamed and dropped his sword. The sharp blade caught the stallion in the right leg. It shied in pain. The blinded prince fell off, directly into the Hedge, and was impaled on thorns as long as a man's hand and hard as iron.

Rose screamed. She rushed down the tower steps, not seeing them, not seeing anything. Over the drawbridge, across the grass. At the Hedge she was forced to stop by the terrible thorns, as thick and sharp on this side as on the other. She couldn't see the prince, but she could hear him. He went on screaming for what seemed an eternity, although of course it wasn't.

Then he stopped.

She sank onto the green grass, sweet with unchanging summer, and buried her face in her apple-smelling skirts. Somewhere, faintly on the wind, she heard a sound like old women weeping.

After that, she avoided all the east-facing windows. It was years before she convinced herself that the prince's body was, must be, gone from the far side of the Hedge. Even though the carrion birds did not stay for nearly that long.

Somewhere around the thirteenth year of unchanging summer, the second prince came. Rose almost didn't hear him. For months, she had rarely left her tower chamber. Blankets draped the two stone windows, darkening the room almost to blackness. She descended the stone steps only to visit the storage rooms. The rest of the long hours, she lay on her bed and drank the wine stored deep in the cool cellars under the castle. Days and nights came and went, and she lifted the gold goblet to her lips and let the red foregetfulness slide down her throat and tried not to remember. Anything.

After the first unmemoried months of this, she caught sight of herself in her mirror. She found another blanket to drape over the treacherous glass.

But still the chamberpot must be emptied occasionally, although not very often. Rose shoved aside the blanket over the south window and leaned far out to dump the reeking pot into the moat far below. Her bleary eyes caught the flash of a sword.

He was red-headed this time, hair the color of warm flame. His horse was black, his sword set with green stones. Emeralds, perhaps. Or jade. Rose watched him, and not a muscle of her face moved.

The prince slashed at the Hedge, rising in his stirrups, swinging his mighty sword with both hands. The air rang with his blows. His bright hair swirled and leaped around his strong shoulders. Then his left leg caught on a thorn and the Hedge dragged him forward. The screaming started.

Rose let the edge of the blanket drop and stood behind it, the unemptied chamber pot splashing over her trembling hands. She thought she heard sobs, the dry juiceless sobs of the very old, but of course the chamber was empty.

She lost a year. Or maybe more than a year; she couldn't be sure. There was only the accumulation of dust to go by, thick on the Gallery floor, thick on the sleeping bodies. A year's worth of drifting dust.

When she came again to herself, she lay outside, on the endlessly green summer grass. Her naked body was covered with scars. She walked, dazed, through the castle. Clothes on the sleepers had been slashed to ribbons. Mutilated doublets, breeches, sleeves, redingotes, kirtles. Blood had oozed from exposed shoulders and thighs where the knife had cut too deep, blood now dried on the sleeping flesh. In the north bedchamber, the long tumbled hair of the woman had been hacked off, her exposed scalp clotted with blood, her lips still smiling as she slept in her lover's arms.

Rose stumbled, hand to her mouth, to the stableyard. Corwin sat beside the big roan, black curls unshorn, tunic unslashed. Beside him, ripped and bloody, lay Rose's own dress, the blue dress with pink forget-me-nots she had worn for the ball on her sixteenth birthday.

She buried it, along with all the other ruined clothing and the bloody rags from washing the clotted wounds, in a deep hole beside the Hedge.

On the wind, old women keened.

Although the spinning wheel was heavy, she dragged it down the tower stairs to the Long Gallery. For a moment she looked curiously at the sharp needle, but for only a moment. The storage rooms held wool and flax, bales of it, quintals of it. There were needles and thread and colored ribbon. There were wooden buttons, and jeweled buttons, and carved buttons of a translucent white said to be the teeth of far-away animals large enough to lay siege to a magic Hedge. Briar Rose knew better, but she took the white buttons and smoothed them between her fingers.

She weaved and sewed and embroidered new clothes for every sleeper in the castle, hundreds of people. Pages and scullery maids and mummers and knights and ladies and the chapel priest and the king's fool, for whom she made a particolored doublet embroidered with small sharp thorns. She weaved clothes for the chancellor and the pastry chef and the seneschal and the falconer and the captain of the guards and the king and queen, asleep on their thrones. For herself Rose weaved a simple black dress and wore it every day. Sometimes, tugging a chemise or kirtle or leggings over an unresisting sleeping body, she almost heard voices on the summer breeze. Voices, but no words.

She spun and weaved and embroidered sixteen hours a day, for years. She frowned as she worked, and a line stitched itself across her forehead, perpendicular to the lines in her neck. Her golden hair fell forward and interferred with the spinning and so she bound it into a plait, and saw the gray among the gold, and shoved the plait behind her back.

She had finished an embroidered doublet for a sous-cook and was about to carry it to the kitchen when she heard a great noise without the walls.

Slowly, with great care, Rose laid the sous-cook's doublet neatly on the polished Gallery floor. Slowly, leaning against the stone wall to ease her arthritic left knee, she climbed the circular stairwell to her bedchamber in the tower.

He attacked the Hedge from the northwest, and he had brought a great retinue. At least two dozen young men hacked and slashed, while squires and pages waited behind. Flags snapped in the wind; horses pawed the ground; a trumpet blared. Rose had no trouble distinguishing the prince. He wore a gold circlet in his glossy dark hair, and the bridle of his golden horse was set with black diamonds. His sword hacked and slashed faster than the others', and even from the high tower, Rose could see that he smiled.

She unfurled the banner she had embroidered, fierce yellow on black, with the two curt words: BE GONE! None of the young men looked up. Rose flapped the banner, and a picture flashed through her mind, quick as the prince's sword: her old nurse, shaking a rug above the moat, freeing it of dust.

The prince and his men continued to hack at the Hedge. Rose called out—after all, she could hear them, should they not be able to hear her? Her voice sounded thin, pale. She hadn't spoken in years. The ghostly words disappeared in the other voices, the wordless ones on the summer wind. No one noticed her.

The prince fell into the Hedge, and the screaming began, and Rose bowed her head and prayed for them, the lost souls, the ones for whom she would never spin doublets or breeches or whispered smiles like the one on the woman with hacked-off hair asleep in her shared bed in the north chamber.

Her other dead.

After years, decades, everyone in the castle was clothed, and dusted, and pillowed on embroidered cushions rich with intricate designs in jewelled-colored thread. The pewter in the kitchen gleamed. The wooden floor of the Long Gallery shone. Tapestries hung bright and clean on the walls.

Rose no longer sat at the spinning wheel. Her fingers were knotted and twisted, the flesh between them thin and tough as snakeskin. Her hair, too, had thinned but not toughened, its lustrous silver fine as spun flax. When she brushed it at night, it fell around her sagging breasts like a shower of light.

Something was happening to the voices on the wind. They spun their wordless threads more strongly, more distinctly, especially outside the castle. Rose slept little now, and often she sat in the stableyard through the long unchanging summer afternoon, listening. Corwin slept beside her, his long lashes throwing shadows on his downy cheeks. She watched him, and listened to the spinning wind, and sometimes her lined face turned slowly in a day-long arc, as if following a different sun than the one that never moved.

"Corwin," she said in her quavery voice, "did you hear that?"

The wind hummed over the cobblestones, stirred the forelock of the sleeping roan.

"There are almost words, Corwin. No, better than words."

His chest rose and fell.

"I am old, Corwin. Too old. Princes are much younger men."

Sunlight tangled in his fresh black curls.

"They aren't really supposed to be words. Are they."

Rose creaked to her feet. She walked to the stableyard well. The oak bucket swung suspended from its windlass, empty. Rose put a hand on the winch, which had become very hard for her twisted hands to turn, and closed her eyes. The wind spun past her, then through her. Her ears roared. The bucket descended of itself, filled with water. Cranked back up. Rose opened her eyes.

"Ah," she said quietly. And then, "So."

The wind blew.

She hobbled through the stableyard gate to the Hedge. One hand she laid on it, and closed her eyes. The wind hummed in her head, barely rustling the summer grass.

When she opened her eyes, nothing about the Hedge had changed.

"So," Rose said, and went back into the bailey, to dust the royal guard.

But each day she sat in the wordless wind, or the wind whose words were not what mattered, or in her own mind. And listened.

No prince had arrived for decades. A generation, Rose decided; a generation who knew the members of the retinue led by the young royal on the black horse. But that generation must grow older, and marry, and give birth to children, and one day a trumpet sounded and men shouted and banners snapped in the wind.

It took Rose a long time to climb the tower staircase. Often she paused to rest, leaning against the cool stone, hand pressed to her heart. At the top she paused again, to look curiously around her old room, the one place she never cleaned. The bedclothes lay dirty and sodden on the stained floor. Rose picked them up, folded them across the bed, and hobbled to a stone window.

The prince had just begun to hack at the Hedge. He was the handsomest one yet: hair and beard of deep burnished bronze, dark blue doublet strained across strong shoulders, silver fittings on epaulets and sash. Rose's vision had actually improved with age; she could see his eyes. They were the green of stained-glass windows in bright sun.

She knew better, now, than to call to him. She stared at his hacking and slashing, at the deadly Hedge, and then closed her eyes. She let the wind roar in her ears, and through her head, and into the places that had not existed when she was young. Not even when she heard him scream did she open her eyes.

But finally, when the screams stopped as quickly as they had come, she leaned through the tower window and scanned the ground far below. The prince lay on the trampled grass, circled by kneeling, shouting men. Rose watched him wave them away, rise unsteadily, and remount his horse. She saw the horrified gaze he bent upon the Hedge.

Later, after they had all ridden away, she made her way back down the steps, over the drawbridge, across the grass to the Hedge. It loomed as dark, as thick, as impenetrable as ever. The black thorns pointed in all directions, in and out, and nothing she could do with the wind could change them at all.

But then, one day, the Hedge melted.

Rose was very old. Her silver plait had become a bother and she'd cut it, trimming her hair into a neat white cap. There were ten hairs on her chin, which sometimes she remembered to pull out and sometimes she didn't. Her body had gone skinny as a bird's, with thin bird bones, except for a soft rounded belly that fluttered when she snored. The arthritis in her hands had eased and they, too, were skinny, long darting hands, worn and capable as a spinning shuttle. Her sunken blue eyes spun power.

She was sitting on the unchanging grass when she heard the tumult behind the Hedge. Creakily she rose to start for the tower. But there was no need. Before her eyes the black thorns melted, running into the ground like so much dirty water from washing the kitchen floor. And then the rest of the Hedge melted. Beside her a sleeping groom stirred, and beside the drawbridge, another.

The prince rode through the dissolving Hedge as if it had never been. He had brown hair, gold sash, a chestnut horse. As he dismounted, the solid mass of muscle in his thighs shifted above his high polished boots.

"The bedchamber of the princess—where is it?"

Rose pointed at the highest tower.

He strode past her, trailed by his retinue. When the last squire had crossed the drawbridge, Rose followed.

All was commotion. Guards sprang forward, found themselves dressed in embroidered velvet, and spun around, bewildered, drawn swords in their hand. Ladies bellowed for pages. The falconer dashed from the mews, wearing a doublet of white satin slashed over crimson, the peregrine on his wrist fitted with gold-trimmed jesses with ivory bells.

Rose hobbled to the stableyard. The king's roan pawed and snorted. Men ran to and fro. A serving wench lowered the bucket into the well, on her head a coif sewn with gold lace.

Only Corwin noticed Rose. He stood a whole head taller than she—surely it had only been a half head difference, once? He glanced at her, away, and then back again, puzzlement on his fresh, handsome face. His eyes, she saw, were gray.

"Do I know you, good dame?"

"No," Rose said.

"Did you come, then, with the visitors?"

"No, lad."

He studied her neat black dress, cropped hair, wrinkled face. Her eyes. "I thought I knew everyone who lived in the castle."

She didn't answer. A slow flush started in his smooth brown cheeks. "Where do you live, mistress?"

She said, "I live nowhere you have ever been, lad. Nor could go." His puzzlement only deepened, but she turned and hobbled away. There was no way she could explain.

There was shouting now, in the high tower, drifted down on the warm summer air. Through the open windows of the Long Gallery, Rose saw the queen rush past, her long velvet skirts swept over her arm. A nearly bald woman in a lace nightdress rushed from the north bedchamber, screaming. Soon they would start to search, to ask questions, to close the drawbridge.

She hobbled over it, through the place where the Hedge had been, now a bare circle like a second, drier moat. And they were waiting for her just beyond, half concealed in a grove of trees, seven of them. Old women like her, power in their glances, voices like the spinning wind.

Rose said, "Is this all there is, then, for the life I have lost? This magic?"

"Yes," one of them said.

"It is no little thing," another said quietly. "You have brought a prince back to life. You have clothed a fiefdom. You have seen, as few do, what and who you are."

Rose thought about that. The woman who had spoken, her spine curved like a bow, gazed steadily back.

The first old woman repeated sharply, "It is no little thing you have gained, sister."

Rose said, "I would rather have had my lost life."

And to that there was no answer. The women shrugged, and linked arms with Rose, and the eight set out into the world that hardly, as yet, recognized how badly it needed them. And perhaps never would.

STRONGER THAN TIME

by
Patricia C. Wrede

The keep rose high above the brush and briars that choked the once-clear lawns around its base, and cast a cold shadow across the forest beyond. Arven hated walking through that somber dimness, though it was the shortest way home. Whenever he could, he swung wide around the far side of the keep to avoid its shadow. Most people avoided the keep altogether, but Arven found its sunlit face fascinating. The light colored the stone according to the time of day and the shifting of the seasons, now milk-white and shining, now tinged with autumn gold or rosy with reflected sunset, now a grim winter-grey. The shadowed side was always black and ominous.

Once, when he was a young man and foolish (he had thought himself brave then, of course), Arven had dressed in his soft wool breeches and the fine linen shirt his mother had embroidered for him, and gone to the very edge of the briars that surrounded the keep. He had searched all along the sunny side for an opening, a path, a place where the briars grew less thickly, but he had found nothing. He had circled, reluctantly, to the shadowed side. Looking back toward the light he had just quitted, he had seen white bones hanging inside the hedge, invisible from any other angle. They shivered in the wind, and leaned toward him, and he had run away. He had never told anyone about it, not even Una, but he still had nightmares in which weather-bleached bones hung swaying in the wind. And ever since, he had avoided the shadow of the keep as much as he could.

Sometimes, however, he miscalculated the time it would take to fell and trim a tree, and then he had to take the short way or else arrive home long after the sun was down. It made him feel like a fool to hurry through the shadows, glancing up now and again at the keep looming above him, and when he reached his cottage he was always in a bad temper. So he was not in the best of humors when, one autumn evening after such a trip, he found a young man in a voluminous cloak and a wide-brimmed hat sitting on his doorstep, obviously waiting.

"Who are you?" Arven growled, hefting his ax to show that his white hair was evidence of mere age and not infirmity.

"A traveler," the man said softly without moving. His voice was tired, bone-tired, and Arven wondered suddenly whether he was older than he appeared. Twilight could be more than kind to a man or woman approaching middle age; Arven had known those who could pass, at twilight, for ten or fifteen fewer years than what the midwife attested to.

"Why are you here?" Arven demanded. "The road to Prenshow is six miles to the east. There's nothing to bring a traveler up on this mountain."

"Except the keep," said the man in the same soft tone.

Arven took an involuntary step backward, raising his ax as if to ward off a threat, though the man still had not moved. "Go back where you came from," Arven said. "Leave honest men to their work and the keep to crumble. Go!"

The man climbed slowly to his feet. "Please," he said, his voice full of desperation. "Please, listen to me. Don't send me away. You're the only one left."

No, I was mistaken, Arven thought. *He's no more than twenty, whatever the shadows hint. Such intensity belongs only to the young.* "What do you mean?"

"No one else will even talk about the keep. I need—I need to learn more, I need to find out how it is. You live on the

76

mountain; the keep is less than half a mile away. Surely you know something about it."

"I know enough to avoid it," Arven said mendaciously. He set his ax against the wall and looked at the youth, who was now a grey blur in the deepening shadows. "Stay away from the keep, lad. It's a cursed place."

"I know." The words were almost too faint to catch, even in the evening stillness. "I've... studied the subject. Someone has to break the curse, or it will go on and on and... Tell me about the keep. Please."

"No."

"But you must! I can't—" The young man stopped. "You're the only one who... who might help me."

Arven shook his head. "And I won't help you kill yourself. Didn't those books you read tell about the men who've died up there? The briars are full of bones. Don't add yours to the collection."

There was a moment of silence, then the youth raised his chin. "They all went alone, didn't they? Alone, and in daylight, and so the thorns killed them. I know better than that."

"You want to go up to the keep at *night*?" Arven stared into the growing darkness, willing his eyes to penetrate it and show him the expression on the other's face.

"At night, with you. It's the only way left to break the curse."

"You're mad." But something stirred within Arven, a longing for adventure he had thought buried with Una, and the image of the keep, shining golden in the autumn sun, rose temptingly in his mind. He shook his head to drive away the memories and pushed open the door of his cottage.

"Wait! I shouldn't have said that, I know, but at least let me explain."

Arven hesitated. There was no harm in listening, and perhaps he could talk the young fool out of his suicidal resolve. "Come in, then, and explain," he said at last.

The young man held back. "I'd rather talk here."

"If you want to talk at all, you'll have to do it indoors,"

Arven growled, regretting his momentary sympathy. "I'm an old man, and I want my dinner and a fire and something warm to drink."

"An old man?" The other's voice was startled, and not a little dismayed. "You can't be! It didn't take that long—" He stepped forward and peered at Arven, and Arven saw the outline of his shoulders sag. "I've been a fool. I won't trouble you further, sir."

"My name is Arven." Now that the younger man was turning to go, he felt a perverse desire to keep him there. "It's a long walk down the mountain. Come in and share my meal, and tell me your story. I like a good tale."

"I wouldn't call it a good one," the young man said, but he turned back and followed Arven into the cottage.

Inside, he stood uneasily beside the door while Arven lit the fire and got out the cider and some bread and cheese. Una had always had something warm ready when Arven came in from the mountain, a savory stew or thick soup when times were good, a vegetable pottage when things were lean, but since her death he had grown accustomed to a small, simple meal of an evening. The young man did not appear to notice or care until Arven set a second mug of warm cider rather too emphatically on the table and said, "Your story, scholar?"

The young man shivered like a sleepwalker awakened abruptly from his dreams. "I'm not a scholar."

"Then what are you?"

The man looked away. "Nothing, now. Once I was a prince."

That explained the world-weariness in his voice, Arven thought. He'd been raised to rule and then lost all chance of doing so before he'd even begun. Probably not too long ago, either, or the boy would have begun to forget his despair and plan for a new life, instead of making foolish, gestures like attempting the keep. Arven wondered whether it had been war or revolution that had cost the young prince his kingdom. In these perilous times, it could have been either. Not that it mattered; the result was the same.

"Sit down, then, prince, and tell me your tale," Arven said

in a gentler tone.

"My tale isn't important. It's the keep—"

"The keep's tale, then," Arven interrupted with a trace of impatience.

The prince only nodded, as if Arven's irritability could not touch him. "It's not so much the story of the keep as of the Counts who lived there. They were stubborn men, all of them, and none so stubborn as the last. Well, it takes a stubborn man to insult a witch-woman, even if he was unaware as some have claimed, and then refuse to make apology for the offense."

Without conscious thought, Arven's fingers curled into the sign against evil. "That's what the Count did? No wonder the keep is cursed!"

The prince flinched. "Not the keep, but what is within it."

"What?" Arven frowned and rubbed the back of his neck. Trust a young nobleman to make hash of things instead of telling a simple, straightforward tale. "Go on."

"You see, the Count's meeting with the witch-woman occurred at his daughter's christening, and the infant suffered as much or more than the father when the witch-woman laid her spell of revenge. Before the assembled guests, the witch declared that the girl would be the last of the Count's line, for he would get no more children and his daughter would die of the pricking of a spindle before she turned sixteen. The guards ran up then, but the witch laughed at them and vanished before they could lay hands on her.

"The Count made fun of the curse at first, until he found that half of it at least was true. Then he raged like a wild man, but it did him no good. His daughter was the only child he would ever have. So he became wary of the second half of the curse, more because he did not wish his line to end than out of love for the girl.

"He was too stubborn to take her away, where the witch's power might not have reached. For seven generations, his fathers' fathers had lived in the keep, and he would not be driven away from it, nor allow his daughter to be raised anywhere else. Instead, he swore to defeat the curse on his own ground. He ordered every spindle in the castle burnt and banished spinners and weavers from his lands. Then he forbade his daughter to wander more than a bowshot from the outer wall of the keep. He was confident that he had beaten the witch, for how could his daughter die of the pricking of a spindle in a keep where there were none?

"The Count's lady wife was not so sanguine. She knew something of magic, and she doubted that the Count's precautions would save her child. So she set herself to unravel the doom the witch had woven, setting her love for her daughter against the witch-woman's spite."

"Love against death," Arven murmured.

"What was that?" the prince asked, plainly startled.

"It's something my wife used to say," Arven answered. His eyes prickled and he looked away, half out of embarrassment at being so openly sentimental, half out of a desire to cherish Una's memory in private.

"Oh?" The prince's voice prodded gently.

"She said that time and death were the greatest enemies all of us must face, and the only weapon stronger than they are was love." Arven thought of the grave behind the cottage, with its carpet of daisies and the awkward wooden marker he had made himself. He had always meant to have the stonemason carve a proper headstone for her, but he had never done it. Wood and flowers were better, somehow. Una would have laughed gently at the crooked marker, and hugged him, and insisted on keeping it because he had made it for her, and the flowers—she had always loved flowers. The shadows by the wall wavered and blurred, and Arven rubbed the back of his hand angrily across his eyes. Love might be stronger than death or time, but it had won him neither peace nor acceptance, even after five long years.

"Your wife was a wise woman," the prince said softly.

"Yes." Arven did not trust his voice for more than the one short word. The prince seemed to understand, for he went on with his story without waiting for Arven to ask.

"The Countess was not skilled enough to undo the witch's

curse completely, but she found a way to alter it. Instead of death, the prick of the spindle would cast her daughter into an enchanted sleep, never changing. The witch's curse would turn outward, protecting the girl for one hundred years by killing anyone who sought to do her harm. One hundred years to the day after the onset of the spell, a man would come, a prince or knight of great nobility, who could pass through the magical barriers without harm. His kiss would break the spell forever, and the girl would awake as if she had slept but a single night instead of a hundred years."

"And meanwhile men would die trying to get to her," Arven said, thinking of the bones among the briars. "It was a cruel thing to do."

"I doubt that the Countess was thinking of anything but her daughter," the prince said uncomfortably.

"Nobles seldom seem to think beyond their own concerns," Arven said. The prince looked down. Arven took pity on him, and added, "Well, it's a fault that's common enough in poor folk, too. Go on."

"There isn't much more to the story," the prince said. "Somehow, on the eve of her sixteenth birthday, the girl found a spindle and pricked her finger, setting the curse in motion. That was over a hundred years ago, and ever since, men have been dying in the attempt to break it."

"*Over* a hundred years? You said the curse would last a hundred years to the day."

"That's why I need your help." The prince leaned forward earnestly. "The curse was only supposed to last for a hundred years, but the Countess wasn't as skilled in magic as she thought she was, and mixing spells is a delicate business. She was too specific about the means of breaking the curse, and now there is no way I can do it alone."

"Too specific?"

"She tied the ending of the curse to a precise day and the coming of a particular man. It would have worked well enough, if the right prince had been a steadier sort, but he was... impetuous." The prince looked down once more. "He arrived a day too soon, and died in the thorns."

"And thus the curse goes on." *The young are so impatient,* Arven thought, *and it costs them so much.* "How do you know all this?"

"He was... a member of my family," the prince replied.

"Ah. And you feel you should put his error right?"

"I must." The prince raised his head, and even in the flickering firelight, naked longing was plain upon his face. "No one else can, and if the curse is not broken, more men will die and the Countess's daughter will remain trapped in the spell, neither dead nor alive, while the castle crumbles around her."

"I thought the girl would come into it somewhere," Arven muttered, but the image touched him nonetheless. He and Una had never had a child, though they had wanted one. Sixteen—she would have been full of life and yearning for things she could not name. He had known children cut off at such an age by disease or accident, and he had grieved with their parents over the tragedy of their loss, but now even the cruelest of those deaths seemed clean and almost right compared to this unnatural suspension. He shuddered and took a long pull at his mug. The cider had gone cold. "How do you hope to break the curse, if the right time and the right man both have come and gone?"

"I've studied this spell for a long time," the prince replied. "Two men can succeed where one must fail."

"How?" Arven insisted.

"The curse is complicated, because it is really two spells muddled together. A single man, if he knows enough of magic, might hold it back for a few hours, but he couldn't do that and clear a path through the briars at the same time. Sooner or later, his spell would falter and the thorns would kill him. With two men—"

"One can work the spell and the other can clear the path," Arven finished. He gave the prince a long, steady look. "You didn't really come looking for me to get information about the keep."

"No." The prince returned the look, unashamed. "But you

82

wouldn't have listened to me at all if I'd begun by saying I wanted you to help me get inside."

"True enough." Arven considered. "Why at night?"

"I can only work the spell then."

Arven glanced sharply at the prince's face. He knew the sound of a half-truth, and that had been one. Still, there had been truth in it, and if the prince had additional reasons for choosing night over day they could only strengthen his argument. Arven realized with wry humor that it did not matter any longer. He had already made up his mind; all that remained was to nerve himself to the act he had decided upon. That being so, hesitation would be a meaningless waste of time. He looked down and saw with surprise that his plate was empty; he had finished the bread and cheese without noticing, as they talked. He drained his mug and set it aside, then rose. "We'd best be on our way. Half a mile is a far distance, in the dark and uphill."

The prince's eyes widened. He stared at Arven for a long moment, then bowed his head. "Thank you," he said, and though the words were soft they held a world of meaning and intensity. Again Arven wondered why this was so important to the younger man, but it made no real difference now. Whether the prince was trying to make up for the loss of his kingdom, or had become infatuated with the sleeping girl of his imagination, or truly wanted to repair the harm his unnamed uncle or cousin had done, Arven had agreed to help him.

"You take the lantern," Arven said, turning to lift it down from the peg beside the door.

"No," the prince said. As Arven looked back in surprise, he added a little too quickly, "I need to... prepare my mind while we walk. For the spell."

"Thinking won't keep you from a fall," Arven said, irritated. "There's no moon tonight."

The prince only looked at Arven. After a moment, Arven gave up. He took the lantern down, filled and lit it, and carried it outside himself. He was half-inclined to tell the young prince to go on alone, but each time the words rose in his mouth he bit them back. He shifted the lantern to his left hand and picked up his ax, then glanced back toward the door. The prince was standing on the step.

Arven jerked his head to indicate the direction of the keep, then turned and set off without waiting to see whether the prince followed him or not. If the prince wanted a share of the lantern light, let him hurry; if not, it would only be justice if he tripped and rolled halfway down the mountain in the dark.

Thirty feet from the cottage, with the familiar breeze teasing the first fallen leaves and whispering among the beeches and the spruce, Arven's annoyance began to fade. It was not the prince's fault that he was young, nor that he was noble-born and therefore almost certainly unaware of the perils of a mountain forest at night. Arven paused and looked back, intending to wait or even go back a little way if necessary.

The prince was right behind him, a dim, indistinct figure against the darker shapes of the trees. Arven blinked in surprise, and his opinion of the young man rose. Prince or not, he could move like a cat in the woods. Arven nodded in recognition and acceptance of the other man's skill, and turned back to the trail. He was annoyed at having been inveigled into misjudging the prince, but at the same time he was grateful not to have to play the shepherd for an untutored companion.

The walk up to the keep seemed to take longer than usual. The prince stayed a few steps behind, moving so quietly that Arven glanced back more than once to assure himself that his companion was still there. Mindful of the prince's comment about preparation, Arven did not try to speak to him.

At the edge of the briars, Arven halted. Though the keep was all but invisible in the darkness, he could feel its presence, a massive pile of stone almost indistinguishable from the mountain peaks, save that it was nearer and more menacing. "What now?" he asked as the prince came up beside him.

"Put out the light."

With more than a little misgiving, Arven did so. In the dim starlight, the briars reminded him of a tangle of sleeping snakes. Frowning, he untied the thongs and stripped the leather cover from his ax, feeling foolish because he had not done so before he put out the light. A breath of wind went past, not strong enough to ripple the prince's cloak but more than enough to remind Arven of the clammy fear-sweat on the back of his neck. *I'm too old for this*, he thought.

"Hold out your ax," the prince said.

Again, Arven did as he was told. The prince extended his hands, one on either side of the blade, not quite touching the steel. He murmured something, and a crackle of blue lightning sprang from his hands and ran in a net of thin, bright, crooked lines across the ax-blade.

Arven jumped backward, dropping the ax. The light vanished, leaving a blinding after-image that hid the ax, the briars, and the prince completely. Arven muttered a curse and rubbed at his eyes. When the dazzle began to clear, he bent and felt carefully across the ground for his ax. When he found it, he picked it up and slid a slow finger along the flat of the ax-head toward the cutting edge, brushing off leaves and checking for nicks. Only when he was sure the ax was in good order did he say, "Prince?"

"I'm sorry," the prince's voice said out of the night. "I should have warned you."

"Yes."

"It will help with the briars."

"It had better." Arven wiped one hand down his side, then transferred the ax to it and wiped the other. "What else do you have to do?"

"I will restrain the thorns so that they will not harm you while you cut a path through them. I must warn you; I can only affect a small area. Beyond that, the briars will remain...active. The sight may be disturbing."

"This whole venture is disturbing," Arven grumbled. "Very well, I'm warned."

"One other thing: do not look back until you reach the

castle gate. Your concentration is as important as mine; if you are distracted, we may both be lost."

"You're a cheerful one." Arven paused. "Are you sure you want to do this? I'm an old man..." *And you are young, with a long life, perhaps, if you leave this lunacy undone*, he thought, but did not say because it was the same advice his elders had given him when he was young. The prince would probably pay as much attention to it as Arven had, which was none at all.

"You're the only one who would come with me," the prince said, misinterpreting Arven's question and confirming his opinion at the same time.

"You've about as much tact as you have sense," Arven said under his breath. He twisted the ax handle between his hands, feeling the smooth wood slide against his palms, and his fear melted away. He had worked these woods all his life; he knew the moods of the mountain in all times and seasons, and the moods of the keep as well; he had cut every kind of tree and cleared every kind of brush the forest had to offer, over and over. This was no different, really. He turned to face the briars, and said over his shoulder, "Tell me when you are ready."

"Go," said the prince's voice softly, and Arven swung his ax high, stepped forward, and brought it down in a whistling arc to land with a dull, unerring thump an inch above the base of the first briar.

The stems were old and tough, and as thick as Arven's forearm. He struck again, and again, and then his muscles caught the familiar rhythm of the work. A wind began to rise as he hacked and chopped and tossed aside. A corner of his mind listened intently for the warning creak of a tree about to fall in his direction, but otherwise he ignored the growing tempest.

All around, the briars shifted and began to thrash as the wind ripped their ends from their customary tangle to strike at air, straining against their roots. Where Arven stood, and for thrice the length of his ax in all directions around him, the air was calm and the briars inert. The only motion within the charmed circle was the rise and fall of his arm and the shifting of the cut stems as he pushed them aside. The sound of the wind and the thrashing briars were clear but faint, as if they came from a great distance or from outside the walls of a sturdy house. The thud of his ax, the rustle of the briars as he passed, and the crunch of his boots against the mountainside were, in contrast, clear and precise, like the sound of crystal singing in silence.

Dream-like, Arven glided steadily onward, moving surely despite the gloom. His ax, too, never missed a stroke, though as the keep drew nearer the night thickened until the faint light of the stars no longer penetrated its blackness.

Arven had no idea how long he spent carving his path through the snarl of briars. His arms grew tired, but his strokes never lost their rhythm and his steps never faltered. Even when he came to the ditch that surrounded the castle, three man-heights deep and nearly as wide, and so steep-sided that a mountain goat might have had difficulty with the climb, his progress slowed only a little. The briars grew more sparsely in the thin soil that veiled the rocky sides of the ditch, and now and again Arven left a stem in place, to catch at his sleeves and the back of his coat and help keep him from slipping.

He reached the bottom of the ditch at last and paused to catch his breath. He could feel the keep looming above him and hear the rushing wind and the thrashing of the briars, though he could see none of them. He wondered what would happen if he lost his direction, and was suddenly glad of the ditch. It was a landmark that could not be mistaken, even in such blackness; if he climbed the wrong side, his mistake would be obvious as soon as he got to the top, and he would only have to retrace his steps.

"Go on," the prince's voice whispered in his ear.

Arven jumped, having all but forgotten the other's presence. There was exhaustion in that voice, a deeper exhaustion by far than the world-weary undertone it had had when Arven first heard it, and in his concern he almost turned to offer the prince his arm. Just in time, he remembered the prince's warning.

"Put your hand through my belt," Arven said, forgetting his own fatigue. "We've a climb ahead, and you'll keep up better if I tow you a way."

The prince did not answer. Arven waited, but he felt no tug at his belt. "Stubborn young fool," he muttered. Holding back the briars must be more tiring than the prince had expected. Arven tried not to think of what might happen if the prince's magic failed before they got to the keep. Well, if the prince was too proud to admit he needed help, the only thing Arven could do was finish his part of the business as quickly as he could. He raised his ax and started forward once more.

Climbing out of the ditch took even longer than climbing into it had done. Arven's weariness had taken firm hold on him during the brief rest, and his arms were nearly too tired to swing his ax. His back ached and his legs felt as if his boots were weighted with lead. He let himself sink into a kind of daze, repeating the same movements over and over without thinking.

The jolt of his ax striking unyielding stone instead of wood brought Arven out of his trance. He cursed himself for a fool; that stroke had blunted the ax for certain. He probed for a moment with the flat of the blade and realized abruptly that this was no random protruding rock. He had arrived at the outer wall of the keep.

Arven felt along the wall a few feet in both directions, but found no sign of a gate or door. He also discovered that the briars grew only to within two feet of the wall, leaving a narrow path along the top of the ditch. Without looking back, he called an explanation to the prince, then turned left and started to walk sunwise around the keep, one hand on the wall.

He had not gone far when the wall bulged outward. He followed the curve, and as he came around the far side he felt the ground smooth out beneath his feet. The wind that whipped the briars ceased as though a door had been shut on it, and silence fell with shocking suddenness. A moment later, the prince said, "This is the gate. We can rest here for a few minutes, if you like."

Arven looked over his shoulder. The night seemed less dense now; he could just make out the prince's silhouette, charcoal grey against midnight blackness. He stood squarely in the center of an arched opening through which Arven had passed without noticing. Though the prince's voice was tireder than ever, Arven could see no trace of weariness in his stance.

"What else must we face?" Arven asked, leaning against the crumbling wall.

"Only finding the Count's daughter and waking her," the prince said. "Whatever is left in the keep is not dangerous, though it may be unpleasant."

"Then there's no point in lingering," Arven said. "Light the lantern, and we'll start looking for the girl."

There was a long pause. "I didn't bring the lantern."

"Young idiot," Arven said without heat. He should have thought to mention it himself; he was old enough to know better than to rely on an untutored and romantically inclined youth to think of practical matters. He smiled. He was old enough to know better than to try and penetrate the briars around the keep, too, but here he was. "I suppose we could just wait for dawn."

"No!" The prince took a quick step, as if he would shove Arven on by main force. "I can't—I mean, I don't—"

Knowing that the prince could not see him, Arven let his smile grow broader. "Well enough," he said, trying to keep the smile from showing in his voice. "I can understand why you'd be eager to have this finished. But while we look for your girl, keep an eye out for a torch or a lamp or something. I've no mind to come this far just to break a leg on the stairs for lack of light."

"As you wish," the prince said. "Are you rested?"

Arven laughed. "As much as I'm likely to be." He pushed himself away from the wall and started off. He kept one hand on the stone as he walked, feeling the texture change as he passed under the supporting arches. Despite his care, he stumbled and nearly fell a moment later. When he felt for the obstruction that had tripped him, he found a well-rotted stump of wood leaning against a heavy iron bar—all that was left of the first door. With a shrug, he rose and entered the outer bailey.

As he did, something brushed his face. He jerked and swiped at it one-handed, and found himself holding a handful of leaves.

"Ivy," said the prince from behind him, and Arven jumped again. "It's not the climbing sort; it grows in the cracks between the stones above, and hangs down."

"I know the plant," Arven said shortly. He threw the leaves away and looked up. A few yards ahead, the curved sides of the inner gatehouse rose dizzily above him and flattened briefly into the inner wall before bulging out into the round corner towers. This close, the gatehouse blotted out even the shapes of the mountains. Its dark surface was broken only by the darker slots of the arrow loops and a few irregular clumps of ivy, swaying gently.

Arven blinked and realized that the darkness was beginning to fade. He could see the stars behind the towers, and there was a faint, pale haze in the sky that hinted at the coming of dawn in an hour or two. Somewhere a bird chirped sleepily.

"We must hurry," the prince said. "Come." He started for the twin towers of the inner gatehouse, and Arven followed. His part in this adventure might be over, but he had earned the right to see the end of it.

"There is work for your ax here," the prince called from the tunnel that led between the towers to the inner part of the keep.

Arven snorted at himself and quickened his step. When he reached the prince's side, the difficulty was clear. The first portcullis was down, but closer examination showed that the iron bands had rusted and sprung apart and the wooden grate was all askew and rotten besides. A few careful ax strokes cleared the way with ease. The second portcullis, at the far end of the tunnel-like entrance, had fallen and jammed partway. Arven ducked under the spikes and stepped out into the inner bailey.

Another bird chirped from somewhere on the wall above his head, and another. Arven had never understood why birds insisted on chattering at each other from the moment the night sky began to lighten. Surely dawn was early enough! He turned to point out the perversity of birds to the prince, and did not see him.

"Prince?"

"Here." The prince waved from the door of the gatehouse. "There are candles."

"Good." The door was half ajar. Arven shoved it wide and peered in, then recoiled. Two skeletons lay sprawled across the table in the center of the room, their white bones protruding from the rotting shreds of their livery. Arven looked reproachfully at the prince. "You might have warned me."

"I didn't think." The prince sounded as much worried as apologetic. "They are only dead, after all."

"Next time, get the candles yourself, then," Arven snapped. He went in and retrieved two fat, stubby candles and a rusty iron holder, fixed one of the candles in place, and lit it with some difficulty using the flint striker he always carried.

The prince was waiting for him in the bailey. "The Count's daughter will be somewhere in the great hall, I think," he said, pointing. "I... expect there will be more such as those."

"Dead men, you mean."

The prince nodded. "The spell—the curse—should have protected the whole of the keep, but it has gone on too long. I doubt there is anyone living, except the girl."

"Let's find her, then, and leave this place to the ghosts."

The prince winced, then nodded again. "As you say. Lead on."

"I?"

"You have the light."

Arven shot a glare at the prince, though he knew the effect would be mostly lost in the darkness. There was nothing he could say to such a reasonable request, however, so he did as the prince had suggested.

The door to the great hall was made of solid oak planks, a little weathered but still more than serviceable. It took most of Arven's remaining strength to wrestle it open. He threw another glare in the prince's direction; the man couldn't be any tireder than Arven, no matter how wearing magic was. The prince did not seem to notice.

Inside, the main room was eerily still. On the far side, the window-glass had shattered, letting in starlight and the small noises of wind and birds. Closer by, long tables filled the center of the room and the candlelight struck glints from gold and silver plate. Around the tables, and sometimes over them, lay a collection of black, shapeless figures. A faint, sweetish odor of decay hung in the air, and Arven grimaced. He skirted the edge of the room, avoiding the tables and taking care to shield the candle so that he would not see the details of the anonymous forms.

"There will be stairs in the corner," the prince said.

Arven found them: a narrow stone spiral built into the wall of the keep itself. He started up, his shoulders brushing the wall on one side and the central pillar on the other. The steps were as steep as the rocks of the upper mountain, and the climb was awkward. More than once, Arven wished he could lean forward a few inches more and climb on all fours, as if he were going up a ladder or scaling a cliff. He wondered how castle folk felt about it. Did they become accustomed to the tight, circular ascent, until they thought no more of it than Arven did of shinning up a tree to cut away an inconvenient branch that might affect its fall? He supposed they must. The prince, at least, did not seem bothered.

Around and around they went, passing one door after another, until Arven lost track of how far they had come. At each door, Arven stopped to ask, "This one?" Each time, the prince shook his head and they went on. Finally, they reached the top of the stairs. This time, Arven pushed the door open without asking; there was, after all, no other place to go.

He found himself in a narrow hall. "The far end," the prince said, and Arven went on. He found a door and pushed it open, and stopped, staring.

The chamber was small and cluttered. Broken boards leaned against one wall, some of them carved, others plain. A stool with a broken leg was propped on a circular wash-tub; next to it was a chair with only one arm. A stack of table-trestles filled one corner, and a pile of rolled-up rugs and tapestries took up another. Old rope hung in dusty loops from a peg beside the window, and the window ledge was full of dented pewter and cracked pottery.

The center of the room had been cleared in haste by some-one unconcerned with niceties of order. In the middle of the open space stood a broken spinning wheel. One leg was miss-ing and two of the spokes were broken; the treadle dangled crookedly on a bent wire and the driving cord was entirely gone. Only the spindle shone bright and sharp and new. Be-side the spinning wheel, a girl lay in a crumpled heap, one hand stretched out as if to catch herself and a tumbled mass of black hair hiding her face.

Arven set the candle holder on top of the stack of table-trestles and bent over the girl. Gently, he slid an arm under her. His work-roughened fingers caught on the heavy, old-fashioned brocade of her dress as he lifted her and turned her shoulders so that he could see her face.

She was beautiful. He had expected that; noblemen's daughters were nearly always beautiful, protected as they were from the ravages of sun and illness and general hard-ship. But he had not expected to find such determination in the pointed pixy chin, or such character in the fine bones of her face. Arven tore his eyes away and turned to the prince.

The prince stood in the doorway, watching the girl with such love and longing that Arven almost averted his eyes to keep from intruding on what should be private. "Well?" Ar-ven said gruffly.

"Kiss her," said the prince, and looked away.

"What?" Arven stared, astonished. "Do it yourself. That's why you came, surely."

"I can't." The prince's voice was hardly more than a whisper.

"Can't? What do you—" Arven broke off as the prince raised his hand and stretched it toward the candle. Suddenly the pieces came together and Arven knew, even before he saw the candle gleaming through the translucent flesh, even before he watched the prince's hand grasp the holder and pass through it without touching. *No wonder he would not carry the lantern*, Arven thought, *no wonder he could only work the spell at night*, and marveled that he could be so calm.

"Please, it's almost dawn," the prince said. He gestured toward the window. The sky beyond was visibly paler. "Kiss her and break the curse, so that I can see the end of this before I must go." His eyes were on the girl's face again, and this time Arven did look away.

"Please," the prince repeated after a moment.

Arven nodded without looking up. Awkwardly, he bent and kissed the girl full on the lips.

For a long moment, nothing seemed to happen. Then there was a grinding sound from somewhere below, and a loud crash, and the girl heaved a sigh. Her eyelids flickered, then opened. She looked at Arven, and an expression of puzzlement crossed her face. She sat up, and glanced around, and saw the prince. Their eyes locked, and she stiffened, and Arven knew that, somehow, she understood.

"Thank you," the girl said.

"Thank him," said the prince. "He is the one who broke the curse. I did nothing."

Arven made a gesture of protest that neither of them saw. "You came back," the girl told the prince with calm certainty. "That is a great deal more than nothing."

The prince went still. "How did you know?"

"I know." She rose and brushed her skirts, then gave the prince a deep and graceful curtsey. The prince stretched out a protesting hand, and the girl smiled like sun on morning dew. "And I thank you for it."

"You should rather blame me. If I had done it right the first time, there would have been no need for these shifts."

"True." The girl's smile vanished and she looked at him gravely. "I think perhaps you owe me something after all, for that."

The prince gave her a bitter smile. "What is it you want of me, lady?"

"Wait for me."

The prince stared, uncomprehending, but Arven understood at once. It was what he had asked of Una, at the last. *Wait for me, if you can.*

"It won't be long," the girl continued. "I can feel it."

"You have a lifetime ahead of you!" the prince protested.

"A lifetime can be two days long, if there is a birth at the beginning and a death at the end," the girl said. She smiled again, without bitterness. "By any usual reckoning, I have had more than my share of lifetimes."

"The spell..."

"Was unraveling. If you had not come, I should have slept another hundred years, or two, dying slowly with no company but dreams. I have learned a great deal from my dreams, but I prefer waking, if only for a week or a month."

"I see." The prince reached out as if to stroke her hair, but stopped his hand just short of its unattainable goal. Arven could see the curve of the girl's shoulder clearly through the prince's palm. He glanced at the window. The sky was lightening rapidly.

"Then, will you wait?" the girl asked again.

"I will try," said the prince. He was almost completely transparent by this time, and his voice was as faint as the distant breeze that rustled the trees outside the keep.

"Try hard," the girl said seriously.

Arven had to squint to see the prince nod, and then the sky was bright with dawn and the prince had vanished. The girl turned away, but not before Arven caught the glitter of tears in her eyes. He rose and picked up the candle, unsure of how to proceed.

"I have not thanked you, woodcutter," the girl said at last, turning. "Forgive me, and do believe I am grateful."

"It's no matter," Arven said. "I understand."

She smiled at him. "Then let us go down. It has been a long time since I have seen the dawn from the castle wall."

WORDS LIKE PALE STONES

by

Nancy Kress

The Greenwood grew less green as we traveled west. Grasses lay flatter against the earth. Brush became skimpy. Trees withered, their bare branches like crippled arms against the sky. There were no flowers. My stolen horse, double-laden but both of us so light that the animal hardly noticed, picked his way more easily through the thinning forest. Once his hooves hit some half-buried stone and sparks struck, strange pale fire slow to die away, the light wavering over the ground as if alive. I shuddered and looked away.

But the baby watched the sparks intently, his fretful body for once still in the saddle. I could feel his sturdy little back pressed against me. He was silent, although he now had a score of words, "go" and "gimme" and "mine!" that ordinarily he used all day long. I couldn't see his face, but I knew how his eyes would look: wide and blue and demanding, beautiful eyes under thick black lashes. His father's eyes, recognizing his great-great-grandfather's country.

It is terrible for a mother to know she is afraid of her infant son.

I could have stabbed the prince with the spindle from the spinning wheel. Not as sharp as a needle, perhaps, but it would have done. Once I had used just such a spindle on Jack Starling, the miller's son, who thought he could make free with me, the daughter of a village drunkard and a washerwoman whose boasting lies were as much a joke as her husband's nightly stagger. *I have the old blood in me. My father was a lord! My grandmother could fly to the moon!* And, finally, *My daughter Ludie is such a good spinster she can spin straw into gold!*

"Go ahead and spin me," Jack leered when he caught me alone in our hovel. His hands were hot and his breath foul. When he pushed both against my breasts, I stabbed him with the spindle, square in the belly, and he doubled over like scythed hay. The spindle revolved in a stone whorl; I bashed him over the head with that and he went down, crashing into the milk pail with a racket like the end of the world. His head wore a bloody patch, soft as pulp, for a month.

But there was no stone whorl, no milk bucket, no foul breath in the palace. Even the spinning was different. "See," he said to me, elegant in his velvets and silks, his clean teeth gleaming, and the beautiful blue eyes bright with avarice, "it's a spinning wheel. Have you ever seen one before?"

"No," I said, my voice sounding high and squeaky, not at all my own. Straw covered the floor, rose to the ceiling in bales, choked the air with chaff.

"They're new," he said. "From the east." He lounged against the door, and no straw clung to his doublet or knee breeches, slick with embroidery and jewels. "They spin much faster than the hand-held distaff and spindle."

"My spindle rested in a whorl. Not in my hand," I said, and somehow the words gave me courage. I looked at him straight, prince or no prince. "But, my lord, I'm afraid you've been misled. My mother... says things sometimes. I cannot spin straw into gold. No mortal could."

He only smiled, for of course he was not mortal. Not completely. The old blood ran somewhere in his veins, mixed but there. Fevered and tainted, some said. Only the glimmerings of magic were there, and glimmerings without mastery were what made the cruelty. So I had heard all my life, but I never believed it—people will, after all, say anything—until I stood with him in that windowless room, watching his smile as he lounged against the door, chaff rising like dusty gold around me.

"*I* think you are completely capable of spinning straw into gold," he said. "In fact, I expect you to have spun all the straw in this room into gold by morning."

"Then you expect the moon to wipe your ass!" I said, and immediately clapped my hand over my mouth. Always, *always* my mouth brings me trouble. But he only went on smiling, and it was then, for the first time, that I was afraid. Of that bright, blue-eyed smile.

"If you don't spin it all into gold," he said silkily, "I will have you killed. But if you do, I will marry you. There—that's a sweet inducement, is it not? A prince for a husband for a girl like you. And for me—a wife with a dowry of endless golden fingers."

I saw then, as if in a vision, his fingers endlessly on *me*, and at the expression on my face his smile broadened.

"A slow death," he said, "and a painful one. But that won't happen, will it, my magical spinster? You won't let it happen?"

"I cannot spin straw into gold!" I shouted, in a perfect frenzy of loathing and fear, but he never heard me. A rat crept out from behind the bales and started across the floor. The prince's face went ashen. In a moment he was gone, whirling through the door and slamming it behind him before the rat could reach him. I heard the heavy iron bar drop into its latch on the other side, and I turned to look at the foreign spinning wheel, backed by bales to the rough beams of the ceiling.

My knees gave way and I sank down upon the straw.

There are so many slow and painful ways to die.

I don't know how long I shrank there, like some mewling and whimpering babe, visioning horrors no babe ever thought of. But when I came back to myself, the rat was still nosing at the door, trying to squeeze underneath. It should have fit; not even our village rats are so thin and mangy. On hands and knees, I scuttled to join the rat. Side by side we poked at the bottom of the door, the sides, the hinges.

It was all fast and tight. Not even a flea could have escaped.

Next I wormed behind the bales of straw, feeling every inch of the walls. They were stone, and there were no chinks, no spaces made rotten by damp or moss. This angered me. Why should the palace be the only sound stone dwelling in the entire damp-eaten village? Even Jack Starling's father's mill had weak stones, damn his crumbling grindstone and his scurrilous soul.

The ceiling beams were strong wood, holding up stronger, without cracks.

There were no windows, only light from candles in stone sconces.

The stone floor held no hidden trapdoors, nor any place to pry up the stone to make a tunnel.

I turned to the spinning wheel. Under other circumstances I might have found it a pretty thing, of polished wood. When I touched the wheel, it spun freely, revolving the spindle much faster than even I, the best spinster in the village, could have done. With such a thing, I could have spun thread seven times as fast. I could have become prosperous, bought a new thatch roof for our leaky cottage, a proper bed for my sodden father...

The rat still crouched by the door, watching me.

I fitted straw into the distaff. Who knew—the spinning wheel itself was from some foreign place. "From the east," he'd said. Maybe the magic of the Old Ones dwelt there, too, as well as in the west. Maybe the foreign wheel could spin straw. Maybe it could even spin the stuff into gold. How would I, the daughter of a drunkard and a lying braggart, know any different?

I pushed the polished wheel. It revolved the spindle, and the straw was pulled forward from the distaff, under my twisting fingers, toward the spindle. The straw, straw still, broke and fell to the floor in a powder of chaff.

I tried again. And again. The shining wheel became covered with sticky bits of straw, obscuring its brightness. The straw fell to the stone floor. It would not even wind once around the spindle.

I screamed and kicked the spinning wheel. It fell over, hard. There was the sound of splintering wood. "By God's blood," I shouted at the cursed thing, "damn you for a demon!"

"If it were demonic, it would do you more good," a voice said quietly.

I whirled around. By the door sat the rat. He was a rat no longer but a short, ratty-faced man, thin and starved-looking and very young, dressed in rags. I looked at his eyes, pale brown and filmy, like the floating colors in dreams, and I knew immediately that I was in the presence of one of the Old Ones.

Strangely, I felt no fear. He was so puny, and so pale. I could have broken his arm with one hand. He wasn't even as old as I was, despite the downy stubble on his chin—a boy, who had been a rat.

What danger could there be in magic that could not even free itself from a locked room?

"You're not afraid," he said in that same quiet voice, and if I *had* been, the fear would have left me then. He smiled, the saddest and most humble smile I have ever seen. It curved his skinny mouth, but it never touched the washed-out brown of his eyes. "You're a bold girl."

"Like my mam," I said bitterly, before I knew I was going to. "Bold in misfortune." Except, of course, that it wasn't *her* who would die a slow and painful death, the lying bitch.

"I think we can help each other," he said, and at that I laughed out loud. I shudder now, to remember it. I laughed aloud at one of the Old Ones! What stupidities we commit from ignorance!

He gave me again that pitiful wraith of a smile. "Do you know, Ludie, what happens when art progresses?"

I had no idea what we were talking about. Art? Did he mean magic arts? And how did he know my name? A little cold prickle started in my liver, and I knew I wouldn't laugh at him again.

"Yes, magic arts, too," he said in his quiet voice, "although I was referring to something else. Painting. Sculpture. Poetry. Even tapestry—everything made of words and colors. You don't weave tapestry, do you, Ludie?"

He knew I did not. Only ladies wove tapestries. I flushed, thinking he was mocking me.

"Art starts out simple. Pale. True to what is real. Like stone statues of the human body, or verse chanted by firelight. Pale, pale stone. Pale as straw. Simple words, that name what is true. Designs in natural wool, the color of rams' horns. Then, as time goes on, the design becomes more elaborate. The colors brighter. The story twisted to fit rhyme, or symbol, or somebody else's power. Finally, the designs are so elaborate, so twisted with motion, and the colors so feverish—look at me, Ludie—that the original, the real as it exists in nature, looks puny and withered. The original has lost all power to move us, replaced by a hectic simulacrum that bears only a tainted relation to what is real. The corruption is complete."

He leaned forward. "The magic arts are like that, too, Ludie. The Old Ones, our blood diluted by marriage with men, are like that now. Powerless in our bone-real paleness, our simple-real words."

I didn't have the faintest idea what he was talking about. His skin was so pasty; maybe a brain pox lay upon him. Men didn't talk like that, nor boys either. Nor rats. But I wanted to say something to cheer him. He had made me forget for a few minutes what awaited me in the morning.

"*A slow and painful death*"... the rack? The red-hot pincers? The Iron Maiden? Suddenly dizzy, I put my head between my knees.

"All you have to do," the Old One said in his thin voice, "is get me out. Of this room, of the palace, of the courtyard gate."

I didn't answer. *A slow and painful death...*

"Just that," he said. "No more. We can no longer do it for ourselves. Not with all this hectic... all this bright..." I heard him move wearily across the floor, and then the spinning wheel being righted. After a long moment, it whirred.

I raised my head. The wheel was whole, with no break in the shining wood. The boy sat before it on a bale of straw, his ashen face sad as Good Friday. From under his fingers, winding around the spindle turning in its wheel-driven whorl, wound skein after skein of feverishly bright gold thread.

Toward morning, I slept, stretched out on the hard stone floor. I couldn't help it. Sleep took me like a drug. When I woke, there was not so much as a speck of chaff left in the room. The gold lay in tightly wound skeins, masses and masses of them, brighter than the sun. The boy's face was so ashen I thought he must surely faint. His arms and legs trembled. He crouched as far away from the gold as possible, and kept his eyes averted.

"There will be no place for me to hide," he said, his voice as bone-pale as his face. "The first thing they will do is paw through the gold. And I... have not even corrupted power... left." With that, he fell over, and a skinny rat lay, insensible, on the stone floor.

I lifted it gingerly and hid it in my apron. On the other side of the door, the bar lifted. The great door swung slowly on its hinges. He stood there, in turquoise silk and garish yellow velvet, his bright blue eyes under their thick lashes wide with disbelief. The disbelief changed to greed, terrible to watch, like flesh that has been merely infected turning dark with gangrene. He looked at me, walked over to finger the gold, looked at me again.

He smiled.

I tried to run away before the wedding. I should have known it would be impossible. Even smuggling out the rat was so hard I first despaired of it. Leaving the room was easy enough, and even leaving the palace to walk in the walled garden set aside for princesses, but getting to the courtyard gate proved impossible. In the end I bribed a page to carry the rat in a cloth-wrapped bundle over the drawbridge and into the woods, and I know he did so, because the child returned with a frightened look and handed me a single stone, pale and simple as bone. There was no other message. There didn't need to be.

But when I tried to escape myself, I couldn't. There were guards, pages, ladies, even when I went to bed or answered the call of nature. God's blood, but the rich were poor in privacy!

Everywhere, everyone wore the brightest of colors in the most luxurious of fabrics. Jade, scarlet, canary, flame, crimson. Silks, velvets, brocades. Diamonds and emeralds and rubies and bloodstones, lying like vivid wounds on necks brilliant with powder and rouge. And all the corridors of the palace twisted, crusted with carving in a thousand grotesque shapes of birds and animals and faces that never were.

I asked to see the prince alone, and I came at him with a bread knife, a ridiculous thing for bread, its hilt tortured with scrollwork and fevered with paint. He was fast for so big a man; I missed him and he easily disarmed me. I waited then for a beating or worse, but all he did was laugh lazily and wind his hands in my tangled hair, which I refused to have dyed or dressed.

"A little demon, are you? I could learn to like that..." He forced his lips on mine and I wasn't strong enough to break free. When he released me, I spat in his face.

"Let me leave here! I lied! I can't spin gold into straw—I never could! The Old Ones did it for me!"

"Certainly they did," he said, smiling, "they always help peasants with none of their blood." But a tiny line furrowed his forehead.

That afternoon a procession entered my room. The prince, his chancellor, two men carrying a spinning wheel, one carrying a bale of straw. My heart skittered in my chest.

"Now," he said. "Do it again. Here. Now."

The men thrust me toward the wheel, pushed me onto a footstool slick with canary silk. I looked at the spinning wheel.

There are so many different kinds of deaths. More than I had known just days ago.

I fitted the straw onto the distaff. I pushed the wheel. The spindle revolved in its whorl. Under my twisting fingers, the straw turned to gold.

" 'An Old One,' " mocked my bridegroom. "Yes, most certainly. An Old One spun it for you."

I had dropped the distaff as if it were on fire. "Yes," I gasped, "yes ... I can't do this, I don't know how ... "

The chancellor had eagerly scooped up the brief skein of gold. He fingered it, and his hot eyes grew hotter.

"Don't you even know," the prince said, still amused, disdaining to notice the actual gold now that he was assured of it, "that the Old Ones will do nothing for you unless you know the words of their true names? Or unless you have something they want. And how could *you*, as stinking when I found you as a pig trough, have anything they wanted? Or ever hope to know their true names?"

"Do you?" I shot back, because I thought it would hurt him, thought it would make him stop smiling. But it didn't, and I saw all at once that he did know their true names, and that it must have been this that gave his great-great-grandfather power over them for the first time. True names.

"I don't like 'Ludie'," he said. "It's a peasant name. I think I shall call you 'Goldianna'."

"Do it and I'll shove a poker up your ass!" I yelled. But he only smiled.

The morning of the wedding I refused to get out of bed, refused to put on the crimson-and-gold wedding dress, refused to speak at all. Let him try to marry me bedridden, naked, and dumb!

Three men came to hold me down. A woman forced a liquid, warm and tasting of pungent herbs, down my throat. When I again came to myself, at nightfall, I was standing beside a bed vast as a cottage, crusted with carvings as a barnacled ship. I wore the crimson wedding gown, with bone stays that forced my breasts up, my waist in, my ass out, my neck high. Seventeen yards of jeweled cloth flowed around my feet. On my finger was a ring so heavy I could hardly lift my hand.

The prince smiled and reached for me, and he was still stronger, in his corrupted and feverish power, than I.

The night before my son was born, I had a dream. I lay again on the stone floor, chaff choking the air, and a figure bent over me. Spindly arms, long ratty face... the boy took me in his arms and raised my shift, and I half stirred and opened my legs. Afterward, I slept again to the whirring of the spinning wheel.

I woke to sharp pain in my belly. The pain traveled around to the small of my back, and there it stayed until I thought I should break in two. But I didn't shriek. I bit my tongue to keep from crying out, and when the pain had passed I called to the nearest of my ladies, asleep in my chamber, "Send for the midwife!"

She rose, rubbing her eyes, and her hand felt first for the ornate jewels in which she slept every night, for fear of their being stolen. Only when she found they were safe did she mutter sleepily, "Yes, Your Grace," and yawn hugely. The inside of her mouth was red as a wound.

The next pain struck.

All through that long morning, I was kept from screaming by my dream. It curled inside me, pale and wispy as woodland mist in the morning. If... maybe... God's blood, let it be true! Let the baby be born small, and thin, and wan as clean milk, let him look at me with eyes filmy as clouds...

Near the end, the prince came. He stood only inches inside the door, a handkerchief over his mouth against the stench of blood and sweat. The handkerchief was embroidered with gold and magenta threads. Above it his face gleamed brightly, flushed with hope and disgust.

I bit through my lip, and pushed, and the hairy head slid from between my legs. Another push, and he was out. The midwife lifted him, still attached to his bloody tether, and gave a cry of triumph. The prince nodded and hastily left, clutching his handkerchief. The midwife laid my son, wailing, on my belly.

He had a luxuriant head of thick bright hair, and lush black eyelashes. His fat cheeks were red, his eyes a brilliant, hectic blue.

I felt the dream slide away from me, insubstantial as smoke, and for the first time that morning I screamed—in fury, in despair, in the unwanted love I already felt for the vivid child wriggling on my belly, who had tethered me to the palace with cords as bloody and strong as the one that still held him between my legs.

I walked wearily down the palace corridor to the spinning room. My son toddled beside me. The chancellor met me outside the door, trailing his clerks and pages. "No spinning today, Your Grace."

"No spinning?" There was always spinning. The baby always came with me, playing with skeins of gold, tearing them into tiny bits, while I spun. Always.

The chancellor's eyes wouldn't meet mine. His stiff jeweled headdress towered two feet in the air, a miniature palace. "The Treasury has enough gold."

"Enough gold?" I sounded like a mockingbird, with no words of my own. The chancellor stiffened and swept away, the train of his gown glittering behind. The others followed, except for one courtier, who seemed careful not to touch me or look at me.

"There... is a woman," he whispered.

"A woman? What woman?" I said, and then I recognized him. He had grown taller in three years, broader. But I had still the stone he gave me the day he carried the stricken rat beyond the courtyard gate.

"A peasant woman in the east. Who is said to be able to spin straw into diamonds."

He was gone, his rich velvets trembling. I thought of all the gold stacked in the palace—skeins and skeins of it, filling room after room, sewn into garment after garment, used for curtain pulls and fish nets and finally even to tie up the feet of the chickens for roasting. The gold thread emerged blackened and charred from the ovens, but there was always so much more. And more. And more.

Diamonds were very rare.

Carefully I took the hand of my son. The law was clear—he was the heir. And the raising of him was mine. As long as I lived. Or he did.

My son looked up at me. His name was Dirk, but I thought he had another name as well. A true name, that I had never been allowed to hear. I couldn't prove this.

"Come, Dirk," I said, as steadily as I could. "We'll go play in the garden."

He thrust out his lip. "Mama spin!"

"No, dearest, not today. No spinning today."

He threw himself full length on the floor. "Mama spin!"

One thing my mother, damn her lying soul, had never permitted was tantrums. "No."

The baby sprang up. His intense blue eyes glittered. With a wild yell he rushed at me, and too late I saw that his chubby fist clutched a miniature knife, garish with jewels, twisted with carving. He thrust it at my belly.

I gasped and pulled it free—there was not much blood, the aim of a two-year-old is not good. Dirk screamed and hit me with his little fists. His gold-shod feet kicked me. I tried to grab him, but it was like holding a wild thing. No one came—*no one*, although I am usually surrounded by so many bodies I can hardly breathe. Finally I caught his two arms in one hand and his two flailing legs in the other. He stopped screaming and glared at me with such intensity, such hatred in his bright blue eyes, that I staggered against the wall. A carved gargoyle pressed into my back. We stayed like that, both of us pinned.

"Dirk," I whispered, "what is your true name?"

They write things down. All of them, all things. Births, deaths, recipes, letters, battles, buyings and sellings, sizes, stories—none of them can remember anything without writing it down, maybe because all of it is so endlessly complicated. Or maybe because they take pride in their handwriting, which is also complicated: swooping dense curlicues traced in black or gold or scarlet. They write everything down, and sometimes the ladies embroider what has been written down on sleeves or doublets or arras. Then the stonemasons carve what has been embroidered into designs across a lintel or mantel or font. Even the cook pipes stylized letters in marzipan across cakes and candies. They fill their bellies with their frantic writing.

Somewhere in all this was Dirk's true name. I didn't know how much time I had. Around a turn of the privy stairs I had overheard two ladies whisper that the girl who could spin straw into diamonds had already been captured and was imprisoned in a caravan traveling toward the palace.

I couldn't read. But I could remember. Even shapes, even of curlicued letters. But which curlicues were important? There were so many, so much excess corrupting the true.

The day after the privy stairs, the prince came to me. His blue eyes were cold. "You are not raising Dirk properly. The law says you cannot be replaced as his mother... unless, of course, you should happen to die."

I kept my voice steady. "In what way have I failed Dirk?"

He didn't mention the screaming, the knives, the cruelty. Last week Dirk cut the finger off a peasant child. Dirk's father merely smiled. Instead, the prince said, "He has been seen playing with rats. Those are filthy animals; they carry disease."

My heart leaped. Rats. Sometimes, in the hour just before dawn, I had the dream again. Even if it wasn't true, I was always glad to have it. The rat-boy bending over me, and the baby with pale, quiet eyes.

The prince said, "Don't let it happen again." He strode away, magnificent in gold-embroidered leather like a gilded cow.

I found Dirk and took him to the walled garden. Nothing. We searched my chambers, Dirk puzzled but not yet angry. Nothing. The nobility have always taken great care to exterminate rats.

But in the stable, where the groom lay drunk on his pallet, were holes in the wall, and droppings, and the thin sour smell of rodent.

For days I caught rats. I brought each to my room hidden in the ugly-rich folds of my gown, barred the door, and let the rat loose. There was no one to see us; since the rumors of the girl who can spin diamonds, I was very often left alone. Each rat sniffed the entire room, searching for a way out. There was none. Hours later, each rat was still a rat.

Dirk watched warily, his bright blue eyes darting and cold.

On the sixth day, I woke to find a pale, long-nosed girl sitting quietly on the floor. She watched me from unsurprised eyes that were the simplest and oldest things I'd ever seen.

I climbed down from my high bed, clutching my nightshift around me. I sat on the floor facing her, nose-to-nose. In his trundle Dirk whimpered.

"Listen to me, Old One. I know what you are, and what you need. I can get you out of the palace." For the first time, I wondered why they came into the palace at all. "No one will see you. But in return you must tell me two things. The true name of my son. And of one other: one like yourself, a boy who was here three years ago, who was carried out by a page because he taught a washerwoman's daughter to spin straw into gold."

"Your mother is dead," the rat-girl said calmly. "She died a fortnight ago, of fire in the belly."

"Good riddance," I said harshly. "Will you do as I ask? In

exchange for your freedom?"

The rat-girl didn't change expression. "Your son's true name would do you no good. The blood is so hectic, so tainted"—she twitched her nose in contempt—"that it would give you no power over him. *They* keep the old names just for ritual."

Ritual. One more gaudy emptiness in place of the real thing. One more hope gone. "Then just tell me the name of the Old One who taught me to spin gold!"

"I would sooner die," she said.

And then I said it. Spare me, God, I said it, unthinking of anything but my own need: "Do it or you will die a slow and painful death."

The rat-girl didn't answer. She looked at me with bone-white understanding in her pale eyes.

I staggered to my feet and left the room.

It was as if I couldn't see; I stumbled blindly toward my husband's Council Chamber. This, then, was how it happened. You spun enough straw into gold, and the power to do that did not change you. But when that power was threatened, weakened by circumstance—*that* changed you. You turned cruel, to protect not what you had, but what you might not have.

For the first time...I understood why my mother lied.

The prince was at his desk, surrounded by his councillors. I swept in, the only one in the room whose clothes were not embroidered with threads of gold. He looked up coldly.

"This girl who can spin diamonds," I said. "When does she arrive?"

He scowled. The councillors all became very busy with papers and quills. "Escort the princess from the Council Chamber," my prince said. "She isn't feeling well."

Three guards sprang forward. Their armor cover was woven of gold thread.

I couldn't find the young page of three years ago, who at any rate was a page no longer. But in the stable I found the stablemaster's boy, a slim youth about my height, dressed in plain, warm clothing he probably thought was rags. "In my chamber, there is a rat. If you come with me I will give it to you wrapped in a cloth. You will take it through the courtyard gate and into the forest. I will watch you do this from the highest tower. When you're done, I'll give you doublet and hose and slippers all embroidered with skeins of gold."

His eyes shone with greed, and his color flushed high.

"If you kill the rat, I'll know. I have ways to know," I told him, lying.

"I wouldn't do that," he said, lying.

He didn't. I know because when he came to my chambers from the forest, he was shaken and almost pale. He handed me a stone, clean and smooth and light as a single word. He didn't look at me.

But nonetheless he took the gold-embroidered clothes.

That night, I woke from the old dream. It was just before dawn. The two pale stones lay side by side on my crimson-and-gold coverlet, and on each was writing, the letters not curlicued and ornate but simple straight lines that soothed the mind, eased it, like lying on warm rock in the elemental sunshine.

I couldn't read them. It didn't matter. I knew what they said. The words were in my mind, my breath, my bone, as if they had always been there. As they had: *rampel*, the real; *stillskin*, with quiet skin.

The forest disappeared, copse by copse, tree by tree. The ground rose, and Dirk and I rode over low hills covered with grass. I dismounted and touched some stalks. It was tough-fibered, low, dull green. The kind of grass you can scythe but never kill off, not even by burning.

Beyond the hills the forest resumed, the trees squat but thick-bodied, moss growing at their base, fungus on their sides. They looked as if they had been there forever. Sometimes pale fire moved over the ground, as no-colored as mist but with a dull glow, looking very old. I shuddered; fire should not be old. This was not a place for the daughter of a washerwoman. Dirk squirmed and fretted in front of me on the saddle.

"You're going to learn, Dirk," I said to him. "To be still. To know the power of quiet. To portion your words and your makings to what is real."

As my mother had not. Nor the prince, nor his councillors, nor anyone but the rat-boy and rat-girl, who, I now knew, crept back into the corrupted palace because the Old Ones didn't ever let go of what was theirs. Nor claim what was not. To do either would be to name the real as unreal.

Dirk couldn't have understood me, but he twisted to scowl at me. His dark brows rushed together. His vivid blue eyes under thick dark lashes blinked furiously.

"In the real, first design is the power, Dirk."

And when I finished those words he was there, sitting quietly on a gnarled root, his pale eyes steady. "No," he said. "We don't teach children with fevered and corrupted blood."

For just a second I clutched Dirk to me. I didn't want to give him up, not even to his own good. He was better off with me, I was his mother, I could hide him and teach him, work for him, cheat and steal and lie for him...

I couldn't save my son. I had no powers but the tiny, disposable ones, like turning straw into gold.

"This time you will teach such a child," I said.

"I will not." The Old One rose. Pale fire sprang around him, rising from the solid earth. Dirk whimpered.

"Yes, you will," I said, and closed my eyes against what I was about to do: Become less real myself. Less powerful. For Dirk. "I can force you to take him. *Rampel stillskin* is your name."

The Old One looked at me, sadness in his pale eyes. Then Dirk was no longer in my arms. He stood on the ground beside the boy, already quieter, his fidgeting gone. The pale fire moved up from the ground and onto my fingers, charring them to stumps. A vision burned in my head. I screamed, but only from pain: Dirk was saved, and I didn't care that I would never spin again, nor that every gold thread in the kingdom had suddenly become stone, pale, and smooth and ordinary as a true word.

EVERY WORD I SPEAK

by

Cindy Lynn Speer

My husband is gone. I can be silent today, tomorrow, and until his return. There's freedom in that, knowing that I can go and sew by the lake, perhaps, or take meals in my room by myself.

In my dressing table there is a secret compartment. In it I have hidden slips of paper, even though paper and ink are forbidden. They are one of my rare rebellions, a way to make my wishes known in silence.

"Please bring my dinner."

"Please fetch my maid."

"Please prepare a coach."

Please. A habit, from my destitute youth when I believed sweet words were more precious than pearls.

I'll do anything not to speak, these days. In my youth I could not speak enough.

"Your majesty?" I turn, slips ready in my hands, fingers light without jewels. I nod for her to speak.

Deirdre, my lady in waiting, gives me a sad look.

"A diplomat from Andovia is here to see you."

I nod again, put aside my papers. Together we go to meet him.

"Queen Sarah," the diplomat murmurs over my hand. I recognize him, though to my knowledge we have never been formally introduced. He is Amon, the Grand Duke of Andovia.

I look at him, his dark hair tied smoothly back, his carefully fitted clothes expensive. He smiles charmingly, and I remember what I have heard about the way he uses his handsome looks to good advantage.

"Amon," I say, and with that one word, a pearl, perfect and creamy, iridescent, rolls from my mouth, falling from the curve of my lower lip, and into the bosom of my gown. I blush, but he is watching with such avid interest that he does not seem to notice.

"So it is true," he whispers, amazed. "You have been enchanted by the fairies."

"Every word I speak," I reply, and one rose, pink as a blush, another pearl and two diamonds cascade from my mouth.

A page hurries forward, a basket in his hand. He ignores the flower, going straight for the treasure. The diamond lands next to Amon's feet. Before the page can pick it up, it is in his hands, being rolled thoughtfully, tested for reality. He pinches it between thumb and forefinger and peers at me through its fractured light. He laughs a little, a man playing at a boy's mischief, and hands the jewel to the page. He smiles at me, inviting me to share in his silliness, but I do not smile back. I do not trust handsome men.

I find myself thinking in the ensuing silence of the old woman at the well. She looked so weary, (as weary as I now feel, staring at this man) that I fetched a drink of the coolest, cleanest water I could find for her. In return, she confessed to be one of the Fair Folk, and granted me this gift.

This gift. I say it over and over, to remind myself, to convince myself. This is the gift that gave me my husband, who in turn saved me from my family, who has professed to love me deeply. Love me, I fear, only as long as I continue talking.

The duke knows the story well. I can see in his eyes that he has speculated long upon it, and I realize that the timing of his arrival is no coincidence.

"Your husband, I hear, is fond of Andovian cherry wine. It has come to my attention that he might wish to own some of our orchards for himself."

My heart sinks. The negotiation for land and the rights to sell the produce from it will make for a long and tricky process. Talking makes me so hungry and my mouth so dry, and my lips cannot always form words properly, even though I have had plenty of time to learn how to talk around the jewels. I am tempted to send him away, but my husband would be ill pleased to lose such an opportunity.

"Is this of interest to you, milady?" He mocks me, I think.

"I shall be honored to discuss terms with you, sir, but perhaps you would be better pleased to speak with my husband? He will return in a few days."

He kneels to pick up an orchid, which he tucks behind my ear. I allow my eyes to tell him how I feel about this familiarity. My skirts rustle as the page goes through them, looking for lost jewels, anxious not to miss one pearl.

He smiles a little. "You'll do, my lady queen."

A gentle rejoinder forms in my mind, but I smother it, the first word sounding in my throat. Something else forms, a diamond from the feel of it. I tuck it behind my teeth and smile.

"If you can't say something nice," my mother told me once when I was very little, "say nothing at all." She'd told me this with a gentle slap. My sister received no such advice, nor treatment. She did not believe in the magic of kind words.

He turns and leaves without asking my permission. As I signal a guard to lead him to his chambers, I wonder if he is really so confident of his charms.

I spit the diamond at the wall.

"I have traveled far, Queen Sarah, to hear from your lips the story of your gift," Amon says as we sit at dinner. I nod to Deirdre.

"My lady queen prefers not to speak at supper. Sometimes

the flowers and the jewels get into her food. And her diamonds are of such fine, clear quality that she might drink one accidentally."

I look down at my plate, wanting to scoop the food down as quickly as possible, for I am starving from speaking so much, but I force myself to dawdle. Once dinner is over, I will doubtless need to talk.

"Perhaps she fears a poison flower will land on her plate?"

"No, my lord, nothing poisonous has ever come from my lady's mouth." Deirdre looks at him, truly hurt and angry, despite her breeding, which is far better than mine.

"Perhaps so," he whispers, then smiles. He looks around the chamber at the gilded torches with their dwarf stones, glowing constantly without need for fire, at the tapestries and paintings. There is too much gold for my taste, and the mirrors that I had once loved, enjoying their reflected colors, horrify me. I avoid them for fear of seeing myself speak.

"You gift has provided well for your husband. But what has it done for you?"

I know what he's about. He says such things to make me speak, to leave me no choice. I lift a napkin to my mouth. I choose my words carefully. "We have been most fortunate. And it will serve you, as well, should my husband decide he wants your orchards."

He shakes his head and sighs, "Ah, for shame, to begin negotiations already, before we've even been served dessert. Is this how you've been taught?"

His words sting. "I know you're not here to discuss the orchards, and I will not play the dancing bear to a swaggering opportunist." I collect my words in the napkin, amazed at their power, their strength.

"Sarah." He stands and approaches me, stares down at me with eyes as black as a basilisk's, and I am frozen, the words I sought gone.

"Sir!" Deirdre protests. "Perhaps you should..." She falls silent as he looks at her, his face expressionless and somehow all the more intimidating for it.

I place the napkin again in front of my mouth. "It's all right, Deirdre."

"You are right," he confesses quietly. "I didn't come to talk about orchards, though I'm willing to. I came out of curiosity, for magic has long left my lands. I wanted to see proof of it for myself."

He takes a chair beside me, lowers his eyes with his voice. "I have not meant to be unkind, but you are so guarded I knew flowery words would not force you to speak."

"Deirdre, please tell the cook that we're ready for dessert."

Deirdre looks at him suspiciously, but does what I ask.

"I forgive you." My eyes do not leave my plate. I am aware of him as he sits so close, his warmth, the smell of his soap and of leather. Against my better judgment, I lay the pearl and two roses on the table before him.

"I am honored," he says, taking the roses. The pearl, ignored, rolls to a stop against the knife. I search his face, his eyes, for mockery, but there is none.

He stands again, looks down at me with a tenderness I haven't t known in a very long time.

"With your permission, I'll be off to bed."

I nod and offer him my hand.

He bends to kiss it. His warm lips send a pleasant shiver through me. "Who needs to speak?" he asks, and I allow him the tiniest of smiles.

He takes a step away, and I sit bemused. His hand touches my shoulder gently, and I feel his breath against my cheek as he leans close again. "Would that I did not, that by some other eloquence I could convince you to come to me tonight." His thumb touches my cheek, gently tracing a path down. "You wouldn't have to say a word."

I shiver again as I watch him leave, thinking of my husband. Even in bed, he encourages me to speak, to whisper inconsequential things. I soon learned that the content of the words did not matter, as long as I spoke, as long as the jewels came tumbling out.

Another hand falls upon my shoulder, and I jump. "Are

you all right? I don't trust that man, duke or no." I squeeze Deirdre's fingers, grateful for her friendship.

"He's all right." I say. "He'll be gone, once he gets what he wants." I gather up the stray jewels and put them beside the plate. I smile at her. "I can fend for myself this night, and you deserve some rest. I bid you sweet dreams."

I climb the stairs, alone for once, and think of Fanchon, my older sister. She met the fairy, too. But Fanchon didn't fetch water when she was asked. In fact, she was so rude in her refusal that she, too, was touched by fairy magic. A darker kind that turned her words to vipers and toads. I now fear what will happen if I say anything too unkind.

I am about to push open my chamber door when I hear Amon's voice.

"If I offer him half my lands, will he give you to me in exchange?"

I turn to face him.

He stands in a pool of light, his shirt open at the throat, his coat gone. His smile is soft and lazy; his hair glistens in the golden light.

I step closer.

"Are you lost?" I ask. His rooms are further down the hall.

"You didn't answer my question."

"No," I say, and the resulting pearl joins my other words in their pouch.

"Your husband has already asked for those lands. You're the only thing I'll take for them."

"Then he will not have them." I catch two diamonds, a pearl, and three violets in my hand. I drop the flowers to the floor.

"Then he will also have no cherry wine," Amon teases. "I will refuse to sell it to him at any price."

I wince, for cherry wine is my husband's favorite drink aside from ambrosia, the only fitting liquor for a king.

"What will he say to that?" He takes a diamond from my hand and places it on top of my head. He laughs as my lips press together, annoyed. The stone slips off and is lost in the darkness. I bend to look for it.

"Leave it. There's more where that came from."

I shake my head furiously, fearing what my husband will say if he finds an unattended diamond in the hall.

"You are inexplicable. Kind one moment, cruel the next." My hand fills with stones and pearls.

"Are you any less so?" Amon asks. "What am I to think of a woman who hates jewels?"

A nervous laugh escapes me despite myself.

"What am I to think of a woman so beautiful and so sad?"

I have no words for an answer, nor does he expect them. His hands slip round my waist. His lips press softly into mine. He is so gentle that it feels like affection, and I eat it up, take it like a starving woman. His rooms are not so far away from mine.

True to his promise, he doesn't ask me for a single word.

In the morning, early, I look upon his profile in the light. "Thank you," I whisper, and leave the roses on his pillow.

I wander the halls, reproaching and justifying myself. He has given me hope, but I know it cannot be true. My husband has encouraged me to talk until words have become unbearable, but would Amon really turn out to be any different? Would any man?

I push back my bedcovers, and undress, put on my nightgown. Bitterness and hope wage their own wars inside me, but above all I know that I am desperate to believe. I laugh at myself, and ring for a maid.

Sometimes I envy Fanchon, who died alone in the woods. No, not alone. She had her stinging vipers, her little red toads. You always knew where you stood with them.

When I finally go down to him, Amon greets me with a conspiratorial grin. He has two roses tucked into his belt. I refuse to be charmed.

"I cannot bargain with you in this matter," I say, spilling gems at his feet. "You'll have to deal with my husband when he returns."

"As you wish," Amon says, a pained expression on his face.

I nod and leave. I am done with him, I tell myself, and I refuse to recognize any regrets.

I pass that same room later in the day. I pause, and then go in. The stones, all eighteen of them, are arranged in a heart, two roses lie in its center. I touch the arrangement carefully, smiling a little.

"Do you like it?" His voice comes from the gloom of the curtains hung against impending night.

I want to believe in him, but I can't. I know better. "Don't trifle with me!" I nearly choke on the pearls as they rise on anger in my throat.

He steps into the light. "Trifle?" he says, and has the gall to look confused.

"Yes! I'm not falling for this nonsense you've concocted."

"What nonsense?"

"I know what you truly want."

His eyes narrow, and he rocks back on his heels. His arms fall away. "Even if I give your husband half of my lands, my greater wealth will remain untouched."

"But you know he'll mismanage it. That you'll get it back in the end, anyway."

He nods, thoughtful. "Without you, it won't be so easy for him to repay his debts."

"I knew it."

"Believe what you want."

And I do. In his room that night, I believe. His touch is gentle, and with his mouth always on mine, words become meaningless.

When I dress in the morning to leave, he whispers, "Side with me. I will take you away to my home in Andovia, and take care of you."

He smiles up at me, boyish and sweet in the sweep of predawn light that erases all lines. I sit on the edge of the bed, lean in to kiss him, and against his lips I whisper, "I love you. I should not, but I do."

Pearls and diamonds tumble from my lips to his, and down the counterpane to the floor, untouched.

I back away, smiling, holding my dress closed. He rolls on his side to watch me, his eyes unreadable in the darkness.

My husband returns that same day. I dress carefully, fingers trembling as I pick the right things to wear.

I stare out the window, trying to be invisible. Behind me, husband and lover discuss my future.

As expected, my husband does not like the idea of giving me away, but neither is he pleased with the prospect of losing his supply of cherry wine. Amon offers the most ridiculous things, much more than half his wealth. I listen to them, pleased with Amon's attempts.

"Come on, man," he says, anger and frustration finally taking hold. "Everyone knows that you do not care for her. You make it plain at every inn and gambling hall you visit." He stops abruptly, looks at me.

I hadn't known.

Wait, that's not true. I had known but I'd tried to believe it wasn't so.

My husband orders guards to escort Amon to the border. King though he is, he does not dare order an execution. I am taken to the north tower, where I now sit, my husband in the doorway. He wants me to explain the flowers and jewels that were found in Amon's room.

"Perhaps he took them. I spoke to him at great length, trying to negotiate the cherry orchards for you."

"He took the flowers, too? Don't be stupid, woman."

"Maybe he thought they were pretty." I smile, but it is brittle. "I would really have no idea."

"Which is why he wanted you so badly. Because you're a fool."

He hands me a basket as deep as my arm and as round as a serving platter. "You will not leave this room. All things that you require will be brought to you. This basket is to be filled every day."

I nod, not surprised.

"Starting today."

"But it's late, already," I protest. The diamonds clatter together as they fall in.

He smiles. "Whatever you have to do."

I smile back. I think I know what I have to do.

And so I sing. I stand with the basket resting on the window ledge and sing to the night air. I sing to the stars and to the moon and to the trees. I sing to the forest I grew up in, to the well I had so often drawn water from. I sing to the fairy who thought she had rewarded a good heart.

People gather, and I sing to them.

I sing as if my heart is breaking, and it is.

Eventually, the basket fills, and then I collect the jewels in my hands and throw them to the people below.

"Do you love me?" I call, leaning out the window, my basket set aside. The jewels fall to the ground.

The people below cheer, and say they do.

I raise my voice in one final song. There is silence as the notes fade and die, pearls and gems and flowers dropping to the ground.

I back away, and close the shutters.

I try to break the spell. I whisper obscenities I have heard the grooms use in the barns. I mutter every mean and miserable thing I can think of, over and over. The clutter of my attempts marks a trail as I pace.

At last, I fumble for the knife Deirdre sewed into my hem when I begged her to hide it for me.

I know what I have to do.

Nothing but misery follows for days after the first cut, the swelling, the fever. I want to die, but I live.

My husband laughs when sees what I had done.

"Heal her," he commands. "I don't want pain to distract her from the coldness of the nights."

He refuses to look at me. "I want you to truly know what it's like to be completely alone."

I felt bad for him, almost, for a moment. After all, he had a freak for a wife.

I cannot speak now, as I wander the edge of the forest between my old land and Andovia. Perhaps, though, there is nothing to say.

When I healed, he sent me here. He says it's justice for me to die as my sister did. Alone and unwanted in the woods.

I don't believe in fairies anymore. I believe in devils, and sometimes in angels, but not in fairies. I sit with my back to a tree, the palace of the Grand Duke of Andovia decorating the slope above me.

I wonder if Amon would want me, now that I have cut out my tongue.

REMAINS

by
Siobhan Carroll

We hear on the radio that a body has been found. A young woman lies facedown in a drainage ditch near Shimpling Park. Instantly, a cold tightness in the stomach. *Is that her?*

And so we listen, as though the radio's thin crackle were the oracular voice of the dead.

Those of us who live nearby drive to the muddy field and stare at the horrible line of police tape. Together we stand in the cold, and wait. The fathers of the missing pace the field. Some call out names, the faint ghost-echoes of unfamiliar faces. Their voices spiral up into the dark. We imagine the things the radio leaves out. We imagine her as pale Ophelia, tangled up in pondweed, goldfish darting in and out of her mouth. In terrible moments we imagine her bloated like a pig. We imagine that much-loved face swollen beyond recognition, save for something we remember: A tattoo. An earring. That terrible clue.

Sooner or later word gets out: it isn't her. In the field the fathers press their ruined shoes harder into the mud. The mothers stand like husks of people, old grief on their faces. The friends and the sisters and the step-brothers and the ex-boyfriends—whoever else came—we look where we need to, so that we do not see each other's faces.

Eventually we drift back to the cars and the long drive. In

other, farther places, we reach over and turn the radio off.

My great-grandmother had a friend who was a sleepwalker. As girls, they took a trip to the grey-blue sea. They rented a house on the hill. Window boxes trailed red geraniums down the sunlit walls.

They first saw the man at twilight. They were walking up from the village; the air smelled of ocean and storm-tossed weeds.

He tipped his hat to them as they passed the graveyard. That was the first time my great-grandmother noticed him. The man was sitting on the bench by the greening stones in the graveyard wall. Perhaps he had been there awhile.

The young women giggled and walked faster; her friend looked back. But that was all my great-grandmother saw. That was all she glimpsed pass between them.

Ten days later her friend was dying, stretched out shrunken and bloodless on a thin mattress. The doctors did what they could for her, but medicine could not do much in those days. When they lifted her body, my great-grandmother said, it was as light as a dead butterfly on the tip of a pin.

They buried her in one of those beautiful old tombs with carvings of knights on the door. Seven days later they had to open it again. Someone had seen her stumbling across the moors with blood on her face.

What they did in there, her family will never say. *One cannot speak ill of the dead*, my great-grandmother said, *nor the undead neither*. She shook her head over her crochet needles, her face grey and empty like a dandelion after the wind comes.

Sometimes newspapers run blurred photos of women in foreign countries, women stepping off cruise ships or caught in fuzzy profile on a busy street. Their barely-seen features are dwarfed by sunglasses; they clutch fashionable hats against the wind. We peer at the photos as though we can make these half-imagined figures resolve into the girl we remember. *Could it be?*

We show these photos to acquaintances, to friends of the family, passing them casually over dinner tables. We want their dispassionate eyes to see for us. We hope one day someone will look up in amazement and say, it's her. Definitely her.

Photographs are the worst. Doubts seep through us: were her wrists that narrow? Was her chin that round? Is the woman in the photograph a couple inches too tall?

If only we'd spent more time studying her angles when she lived among us, committing to memory every possible pose. Then we would not lie awake at night, fearing we have forgotten what she really looked like.

Everyone knows someone. Often we don't hear these stories until it affects us directly, and then people come forward, catching us by the arm in hallways and streets. *My cousin*, they say. *My sister's friend.* Sometimes they give us a searching look, as though they are hoping we can explain it to them.

There was a girl at my school who fell in love with a vampire. She knew what he was from the start; she claimed she found him beautiful. Like a statue, she told her friends. Like a Greek god.

Her friends hoped she was joking. They'd seen him, some of them, lurking at the edge of parking lots, a wolf with eyes like fossils. They could not imagine themselves kissing that face, touching skin white and strange as bone, tongue flicking past teeth like broken glass.

When she disappeared, people blamed her friends. *They should have said something.* The girls themselves stood at the memorial service with their heads down, nursing emotions too large for words.

Girls aren't the only ones who disappear. I heard of a middle-

128

aged woman, someone's mother, who walked into the night with one of Them and was never seen again. And then there was that boy in Sweden, so young you'd never think it. We watched his mother on television, weeping and wailing into the camera, begging for her child's return. We didn't know the language she was speaking, but we understood every word.

The hardest part is not knowing. Why did they do this? Was there a reason? Something that could have been avoided, or prevented, or fixed? Did some unseen maggot turn in their brain, driving them to an act of insanity? Did they really understand what they were doing?

Was it our fault? Theirs?

In the days that follow, those of us who remain search for answers. We don't find any.

Most of them do not even leave a note.

The last time I saw my sister was at the window of her bedroom, overlooking the lawn.

I'd got up to get a drink of water. Something had disturbed me; a noise, a dream. I walked to the bathroom in a fog of sleep, and saw the wind had pushed her door ajar. A low murmur of voices came from inside.

To this day I wonder if I knew. Something made me open the door.

I saw her in her nightdress, framed by the window. I saw Him as a black shadow, eyes like the collapsed pits of stars.

She turned. Saw me. Her face went taut with fear.

She raised a finger to her lips. *Shhh.*

Here is the part I do not understand. I could have shouted, raised the house. I could have asked her to stay.

I looked at her and saw she wanted to go.

My unwilling feet made their way back to my room. I lay down in my bed of guilt and fear and thought, *tomorrow it will all be okay. It will all turn out okay.*

I have never thought that since.

We all have our stories: the stories we tell; the ones we never share. Lying awake, I listen to the thin voice of the radio and try to take comfort that somewhere, others are doing the same.

Some nights I catch myself thinking that I too could go out into the night. I could find answers.

But I do not think They would be interested in me anymore. It is life They want to taste, hot and bright-flowing. Not this endless, suspended existence.

We hear on the radio that a body has been found. Some of the unliving rise, put on thick woolen gloves, get ready for the drive. In other, farther places, we lie hoping for an ending that never comes.

FRAYED TAPESTRY

by

Imogen Howson

The first time it happened was almost a year after he'd married her. They were giving a drinks party, and the spacious top-floor apartment was filled with sleek, beautiful people in immaculately cut trousers, or little black dresses and the discreet glint of gold jewelry.

Candy had been busy since the first guests arrived. Clym liked her to keep the canapés coming and make sure he was supplied with ice for the drinks. With that, as well as welcoming new guests and trying to make sure she remembered everybody's names, she'd scarcely sipped her own glass of wine.

So, afterwards, although she tried to blame the alcohol, she knew she couldn't.

She was in the kitchen, cutting up more lemons for the gin and tonics. She had a gleaming steel bowl of them, glossy polished yellow next to the duller green globes of limes, and a neat little serrated knife to slice them into perfect rounds. But then, of course, she had everything. She'd seen it reflected in her guests' eyes. Her, this nineteen-year-old, already with a beautiful apartment, a handsome, adoring, powerful husband...

The knife slipped. It shouldn't have—she was holding it carefully; its edge had already bitten into the yellow rind,

131

sending the sharp fragrance up to her nose. But it did: slipped downward sharply and sliced into the side of her left thumb.

The pain was instant and shocking. She gasped, dropping the knife, and clamped her right hand over her left. Such a small cut—it shouldn't hurt so much. But after a second she realized the pain came from the lemon juice seeping, acidic, into the wound.

"Oh, you *stupid...* " With her uninjured hand, she twisted the tap on the sink next to her. It stuck a moment and, the pain unendurable; she put her thumb in her mouth to soothe it.

Water poured into the sink so hard it splashed up against the matt black tiles above the taps, spattering the worktop. She thrust her thumb under the water, swallowing against the tears coming to her eyes.

And it happened. All at once her hand was submerged in a rush of water so cold it instantly numbed the pain. Her other hand was grasping not the tap but the rough bark of a twisted, moss-covered tree branch. Her bare toes clung to damp, gritty stone and cold air struck her skin, raising goose bumps on her bare arms.

And it was familiar. She knew where she was, knew if she turned away from the waterfall she'd see the cliff rising to the sky, and knew the tree was an oak, ancient and craggy, home to thousands of tiny creatures. She'd stood here before, feet cold on the stone, stood here with—

"Candy? Are you in the kitchen?"

She jumped, lost her grip on the branch, grabbed for another handhold, feet slipping on the wet—On the wet kitchen floor.

"*Candy!*" Arms came around her. For a moment she didn't recognize them, didn't know who was holding her. "What are you doing?"

Clym's voice. *Oh, of course*—Clym's hands. She stood in his arms, her thumb streaking watery blood all over his shirt, the front of her dress drenched.

He reached past her and turned off the tap. "What happened? What did you do?" His voice roughened with bewilderment and exasperation. "You've got the tap on so that it's splashing all over the floor—no wonder you slipped." Then his voice went cold and suddenly his hands seemed cold too, sending ice into her bones. "Where are your shoes?"

She looked down, her breath already coming short at that tone in his voice. "I don't—I was *wearing* them." But sure enough, there were her feet, bare and brown against the white tiles, their toenails neat and straight, shiny with pale gold nail polish.

"Sit down."

He moved her backwards and she sat on one of the kitchen stools. From the sitting room behind him came the jumble of conversation, laughter, the click of high heels as someone stepped out onto the balcony, the ripple of the low music she'd spent an hour selecting. Clym reached over her head and pulled the first aid box off its shelf. "Give me your hand." He wiped the cut with a disinfectant wipe, not roughly, but not bothering to be gentle either, and then stretched a plaster over it.

She sat motionless, still feeling that bite of cold in his fingers as he touched her. He always had cold hands. Sometimes she teased him about it—but only in bed. She'd learned early on not to seem to make fun of him anywhere else—and never, ever in front of other people.

He pressed the plaster down to seal it firmly over the cut. Pain jabbed through her thumb. "You know I don't like you not wearing shoes. Especially on this floor. If you'd been wearing them you wouldn't have slipped."

Well, that was ridiculous. The shoes she'd put on for the party were dainty, strappy things with smooth soles—plenty more slippery than bare feet. And where were they, anyway? If she'd taken them off in the kitchen wouldn't they be around here somewhere?

"*Candy.*"

Her attention jerked back to him. He was looking down at her, his eyes very dark. "Go and dry your dress and put some shoes on. No—not that way." This as she got off the stool and took a step toward the sitting room. "Do you think I want our guests to see you like that?"

This time the anger came clear through his voice. She turned and went through the little corridor at the other end of the kitchen—narrow and lined with shelves, it was normally only used as a store cupboard—then into the entrance hall, and from there into their bedroom.

She rubbed her dress and feet with a towel, found some other shoes. Grit and a dusting of earth came off on the towel. She shook it into the bath, rinsed it away, and stuffed the towel into the laundry bag. Hopefully he wouldn't ask her to find the missing shoes. The grit on her feet had only confirmed what she already, really, knew. Wherever she'd left her shoes, it wasn't in the apartment.

The next morning she woke with a headache and lay still, eyes shut against the sunlight that turned red as it came through the curtains. Clym liked red. To her, though, it seemed the wrong color for curtains. Curtains should be pale gold, leaf green, letting through dappled light that moved like sunspots on water...

She felt her thoughts pause. Where had that image— huge trees filtering the sunlight, a wide milk-calm lake—come from? Nowhere in the city, where she'd lived her whole life—

And at that she paused again, stuttered as if she'd met a break in the track of her thoughts. *My whole life? But where was I before I married Clym?*

"Wake up, baby."

She eased her eyes open. Clym stood, a shadow against the sunlit curtains, holding a tray. She moved to prop herself up on her elbows, trying to clear her mind of the weird jumble of thoughts that made no sense.

"I don't think I should have had those other glasses of wine," she said. "I feel like death."

Clym laughed, setting the tray down on the bedside table.

"Baby doll, a few glasses of wine won't have done you any harm. Like I said, you needed it after cutting your thumb so badly. Now, you need a good breakfast, that's all. Sit up."

She wriggled up to lean against the bank of huge, marshmallow-soft pillows. Clym passed her a mug of tea—gentle, pale brown, with plenty of milk. The scent of honey drifted up with the steam and she breathed it in.

"Oh, that's heaven. Thank you."

"Here." He moved the tray over onto her duvet-covered lap. "Chilled melon slices. And—you need protein—scrambled eggs on toast."

He sat on the bed next to her, moving carefully so as not to tip the tray. She bit into the melon slice and cold, sweet juice filled her mouth. Its fragrance seemed to travel up through the roof of her mouth into her head, clearing it of the ache, smoothing the jagged tracks of her thoughts.

Clym had cut the thick slices of white toast into fingers, golden with a shimmer of butter. He leaned forward to put one into her mouth and it crunched deliciously between her teeth.

"Last night," she said. "I don't know why I took my shoes off. Are you still angry?"

"No, baby. I know you didn't mean to worry me. Just"—he leaned forward, brushed a kiss over her nose—"be more careful next time, okay?"

"Okay." She smiled at him, feeling warm, relaxed, floating on the pillows as if they were clouds. She reached for the fork and his hand came down on hers, stopping her. She blinked at him. "Hey, I need protein, remember?"

He laughed. "I'll feed you, sweetheart. Here, open wide."

She really wanted to feed herself. She was hungry now, and he was clumsy, and buttery crumbs and bits of egg got spilled on the crimson satin duvet cover. But it was worth it, to know he wasn't angry with her, that he'd forgiven her. And while he was with her, laughing, spooning eggs into her mouth, leaning over to kiss her, then eventually putting the tray on the floor so he could join her under the duvet, she knew her thoughts were safe. While he was here her thoughts wouldn't go jagged, they wouldn't hiccup and pause and shoot strange familiar images into her head. They'd be safe, and so would she.

Clym went to work six days a week and she didn't yet know many of their neighbors, but she had plenty to do. It was only a short walk to the avenues of shops, and Clym had accounts at all of them. It was fun to try on slinky little outfits, then, if she especially liked one, walk out dressed head to toe in all new clothes.

This time, she found a chiffon dress in different shades of green, beech-leaf to moss, fastened with a gold belt that hugged her rib cage, just under her breasts. Pulling the dress on over her head, she imagined she smelled cut grass, the drifting sweetness of honeysuckle.

They knew her here; she told them she'd take it, asked them to send her clothes home, and stepped out of the shop, lifting her face to the warmth of the sunlight.

And stopped. It was—it *was* sunlight, but what had she been expecting? She looked up into the arc of indigo sky, from which the sun shone, golden-red and familiar—and wrong. In her head was an image of something different, something brighter, cleaner... *higher*, although that was ridiculous.

She shook her head as if to clear it. She needed to buy new shoes. She looked down at herself, and her shoulders slumped a little. This was exactly the sort of dress that didn't even *look* good with shoes. Which was probably, really, why she'd bought it. She *missed* going barefoot.

Well, you should have thought about that before you married him, she told herself severely, beginning to walk again. *If you marry a man who thinks bare feet look slutty, then you know very well what you're getting into.*

Except—*had* she known?

Her feet stuttered on the pavement. The sun—the odd, wrong-colored sun—blazed down at her. She felt sick, a little dizzy.

She was just passing the cool, dim doorway of a coffee shop. She turned in to it, and sat at a small round table. Its metal surface was patterned with irregular diamond shapes that seemed to run into each other, making the surface look as if it were warped. She spread her fingers on it, and of course it was perfectly flat. Her heart was pounding horribly, down next to her stomach so she felt nausea pulse through her.

She couldn't remember. She couldn't remember deciding to marry him. She couldn't remember meeting him. She couldn't remember her *wedding* day. *What sort of freak can't remember her wedding day?*

"Can I get you anything?"

She looked up at the thin, dark-haired waitress and answered automatically. "Latte, please."

"Anything else?"

"No, thank you."

The waitress disappeared behind the counter. Candy pressed her hands hard on the table, watching the skin around her nails whiten. This was insane. What was wrong with her? For the past year she'd lived this idyllic life. She'd been wonderfully, dreamily happy. Clym adored her, all his friends treated her like a queen, and she had everything she could want. Then one slip of a knife, and she no longer even recognized her own *mind*. How could it have done that? How could it have affected her so much?

Her hand stilled. Slowly, she turned it over so she could see the ugly mark on her thumb, the flesh around it bruising as it healed. It hadn't happened when she cut herself. It had happened when she'd put her thumb in her mouth, when she'd tasted her blood.

Not that that made any more sense. But somehow, in those echoes in the back of her mind, she knew blood was important. It had... meaning, significance beyond the obvious. If she could just remember properly, pull the memories forward to look at, maybe something would start to make sense.

A saucer clinked gently on the table.

"One latte."

"Thank you." She stirred in sugar, picked the cup up and sipped, the foam soft on her upper lip. Her heartbeat slowed and the tightness in her chest eased. She shut her eyes for a moment and sipped again.

She was so silly. Sitting here, heart pounding, letting all sorts of thoughts into her head. She was hungry, that's all. She'd have lunch, and then she'd be much more able to work out why her imagination was suddenly getting the better of her like this.

She ordered a hot-smoked salmon salad and a freshly squeezed orange juice, and sat drinking her coffee, letting the warm sweetness travel down through her, easing her into relaxation, until the food arrived.

The salmon broke into thick flakes under her fork, and the curly lettuce and slices of translucent green cucumber tasted of olive oil, lemon juice and black pepper. It came with a split ciabatta roll, dusty with flour, and a pat of butter, golden and oily from being next to the warm roll.

The orange juice glowed in its tall frosted glass, thick with specks of orange pulp, sweet and sharp. She sipped the last of it as she used the ciabatta crust to mop up the remnants of the salad dressing, and although she knew something had been bothering her, she could no longer remember what it was. So she signed the bill—she was so lucky, Clym had accounts everywhere—and went out again into the sunshine to buy the sexiest shoes she could find.

The sunlight was lovely today, and after buying her shoes she decided to walk home through the meadows. They called them meadows, but it was a park really, with wide paths. The flowers grew neatly in flowerbeds as well as straggling, skimmed-milk white, amongst the faded green of the dry grass in the fields stretching down to the river.

Across the river was where Clym worked. But she didn't let

her feet drift toward it. "I have to deal with people who aren't very nice, baby," he'd said, months ago, when they were first married. "So when I'm at work I'm not very nice, either. If you saw me there"—and he'd laughed, rubbing the tip of his nose on her forehead—"maybe you wouldn't like me any more."

"Oh, *Clym*," she'd said, laughing with him, but partly shocked that he'd ever think such a thing, "as if that would make any difference!"

Still, the subject had dropped, and somehow she hadn't liked to raise it again.

But all the same it was nice to sit in the long, prickly-soft grass, letting the sun warm her hair, knowing she wasn't far away from him. And that maybe, if she sat here long enough, and if he decided to walk home this way, she might meet him and they could walk home together.

In the distance, she caught sight of other visitors. There were so many coming back and forth, strolling down the paths and wandering through the tall grass, that it was odd that, in all the times she'd visited the meadows, she'd never come close enough to speak to any of them. Nor, in almost a year, had she ever seen the same face twice.

Idly, she plucked a few of the flowers' thin stems. Their petals were soft—she could hardly feel them where they touched her skin—but their leaves were long and tough, coming to spiky points. She'd thought she could take them home, arrange them in a vase, but looking at them now, she realized they'd fade to invisibility against the blacks and reds of the apartment. And even as she held them, they drooped, their petals melting into nothing, leaves shriveling, the stalks drying, twisting into something like hair between her fingers that, released, floated away over the nodding grasses.

She hadn't thought they'd die so quickly. She pushed her fingertips down into the earth, wondering what their roots were like, that, once severed from them, they died so fast.

Except there was no earth. She dug her nails into the ground, looking down, bewildered, and met nothing but the faded, springy stuff she sat on, that she'd thought was the tangled lower stems of the grasses, the growth of new plants, a layer of dry soil that would crumble under her fingernails... It wasn't. It was fibres, woven tightly together, a tapestry of ochre, sand-color and faded brownish-green. Completely convincing until you touched it.

Candy snatched her hand back. No, she wasn't going to do this. Her world was perfect, *perfect*. She wasn't going to go prying and poking beneath the surface. She wasn't going to try and think back, try and remember how or when things had changed. She wasn't going to ask questions. She wasn't going to let the panic come back in.

She got to her feet, brushing broken bits of the flowers off her skirt. She wouldn't wait for Clym after all. She'd go home, have a shower, and put wine to chill. Then later, he'd come home and she'd let his hands and his mouth blot out the day, take her down into dark oblivion with him.

She gathered up her bags. Dust from the dead flowers clung to her dress, a thin pale sheen like the skin of a soap bubble. She shook her skirt, hoping it wouldn't stain... but of course it wouldn't. She was thinking of pollen. The asphodel didn't pollinate, they were just *there*. That's why they had no smell, why there were no insects, no bees, in the long grass. The meadows didn't grow, or change—that wasn't what they were there for—

"*Stop it*," she said aloud, and her own voice made her jump. "Go home. Go *home*."

She walked home fast, her heels clicking on the pavement, the skin between her shoulder blades damp with sweat. She was feeling dizzy again, as if her eyes couldn't focus properly, as if the world were too small, then too large. At the corner of her eye things moved, shimmered—in the *heat haze*, that was all.

Her key slipped in her fingers as she put it into the lock, and the door swung open onto the dim hallway. Cool, definite lines, the black marble floor cold and solid under her feet. She pushed the door shut behind her, and let her eyes fall closed for a moment, breathing in the chill of the air, the scent of polish.

"Mrs Rich, are you all right?"

Candy's eyes snapped open. "Oh, Mari—I'd forgotten it was your day! I'm fine, just hot. I'll just get a drink and get out of your way."

The maid, pale as narcissi in her black top and trousers, moved back against the wall as Candy went into the kitchen. Candy took a glass from the cupboard and ran water, making sure it was cold. Mari made her uncomfortable. She looked so thin, tired—it seemed wrong that she was here to do Candy's housework, to clean Candy's bathroom, and all Candy did was shop and have showers and prepare delicious little meals for when Clym came home.

She turned the tap off, hitched her bags onto her wrist, and turned to go back through the hall to her bedroom. "I'll just be in my room, Mari. You carry on." The discomfort, the edge of unreasonable guilt, made her direct a smile—slightly too wide—at the maid as she opened her bedroom door. Mari was already turning away. The hem of her trouser leg drew up over one white, bony ankle, and Candy froze.

Mari wore chains.

A metal band circled her ankle. Heavy, rough edged, splotched with rust: it was no ornament. The chain snaked down from it, then over the floor and out through the door. *How did I not see it when I came in? How did I never see it before?*

"Mari—" She stopped as the maid looked back toward her. Fear weighed her tongue, made her throat go cold. Mari had been the maid for the apartment before Candy came here, when it was just Clym's. Clym knew about this.

She swallowed. "Mari, don't worry about the kitchen. I'm going to go in there and cook and I'll just make a mess anyway."

The maid's eyes widened. Before they'd just been tired, dull. But now fear came into them as it had into Candy's voice. Too late, the thought came: *She's not here for me. It*

141

doesn't matter if I excuse her. It's Clym. It's what he wants. It's what he says.

"I'm sorry," she said. "Take no notice of me. I know you need to clean the kitchen."

Mari ducked her head—"Yes, Mrs Rich"—and turned away again. The chain slithered along the floor after her and, as she disappeared into the kitchen, Candy realized one last thing that struck cold not just into her throat but all the way through her, numbing her fingers, making her legs feel as if they didn't belong to her. The spots on the ankle cuff weren't rust. They were blood.

It seemed ridiculous, now, to think she'd been afraid just of her world changing, of finding out things weren't quite how she'd thought. Standing in her bedroom, icy fingers clasped together, Candy knew it wasn't just that things weren't quite right. Things were terribly wrong.

She turned her hands over and stared down at the ragged cut on her thumb. If all this had started to happen when she tasted her own blood, she could make it happen again. Would it be worse, next time? Already the skin of her beautiful world was unraveling, coming apart, showing things underneath that she'd never wanted to see—if she revealed even more, what would it be like?

She scratched at the healing wound with her fingernail, and it twinged, a precursor of pain. She could make it bleed again—but her stomach clenched and, again, her head swam with dizziness. She was scared, scared of the pain and scared of what she'd discover.

But wait. That first time, the sudden flash of oak tree, crashing waterfall, the scent of cold damp leaves—that hadn't been frightening. Okay, so it had opened her up to all this other stuff, the scary bones protruding through her world, but that moment, that feeling of stepping out of her life into something wonderful—and wonderfully familiar—that had been a good thing.

And you're not really a coward.

She blinked. The thought had come from nowhere, words whispered through a space in the world. She stood here, shivering, dressed like an expensive doll in clothes her husband let her choose, ashamed to look her own maid in the eye—just as the world wasn't the way she'd thought it, maybe this wasn't who she really was, either.

She clenched her jaw and marched across the room to the en-suite bathroom. Catching a glimpse of herself in the mirror as she went past, she didn't recognize her own reflection and checked, disoriented for a moment.

Clym's razor lay by the side of the sink, its reflection like a smudge of shadow in the shining white porcelain. She shut and locked the door, then picked up the razor and flipped the head so she could remove its sliver of blade. She wouldn't think about it, she wouldn't look. She turned her head away, biting her lip, and drew the blade across the back of her arm. It stung, sharp and brief, and she looked down—expecting to see nothing but the faintest scratch—to find she'd cut deeper than she'd realized and blood was oozing in a fat crimson line an inch long across her skin.

It was automatic to suck the wound, and the blood was in her mouth before she'd made the conscious decision to do so. But then her stomach heaved—what was she *doing?*—and she had to fight against the impulse to spit it out, had to force herself to swallow it.

She swallowed, and the world changed.

Trees stood all around her—oak trees and silver birches, their leaves a rustling whisper in the air—but not close enough to prevent the sunlight streaming down onto the knee-high grass in which she stood. Real grass, tall and living, spiky with seed-heads, scent rising from the crushed stalks under her bare feet. Midges rose around her, tiny specks of life, a bee blundered past her leg, and somewhere, invisible, grasshoppers chirped.

Oh. She found herself crying, without meaning to, almost without realizing. She knew this place. It was like a bereavement, to stand here and not know why she recognized it, not know why it felt like home in a way the apartment—oh, the apartment had *never* felt like this.

It was the memories that made this place precious, memories she couldn't remember, and yet she knew they were there.

Was it Clym who'd taken them, stolen her memories and left her with nothing but blankness, like looking into mist so thick it made you feel you'd gone blind? But why? And *how?*

She swallowed again, the taste of the blood a metallic layer in her mouth, overlaying the traces of salmon and orange juice—*the food.* That was how he was doing it, using the food he gave her, drugging it. Or no, that didn't seem quite right, it didn't seem like a drug, and it wasn't just the food he gave her. She remembered how she'd gone into the coffee shop, panicking, needle-sharp aware of something being wrong, and how the first sip of coffee, thick with sugar and foamed milk, had smoothed down all the edges of fear, pushed her back into dreamy forgetfulness.

She drew in a long breath, trying to think, and breathed in the scent of grass and leaves and the dusty, moss-damp bark of the oak trees. And with the scent came clarity.

Oh Candy, you're being stupid. This isn't just Clym—it's the whole world. The sky being the wrong color, the asphodel flowers growing out of something more like fabric than earth—if this was Clym's doing, then Clym controlled a lot more than just their apartment.

She breathed in again. Grass, and bark... then coconut-scented bathroom soap, and shampoo, and bleach. The meadow blurred, like a reflection in a lake, fell apart into ripples, and disappeared.

She was back. She looked down and saw grass seeds stuck to her new skirt, solid and real, quite different from the ephemeral sheen of the asphodel earlier. And again, her shoes were missing.

Okay, Candy, think.

She sank to her knees on the bathroom floor, hands pressed so tightly against her eyes that phantom lights flickered against the insides of her eyelids.

The food—the food of this whole world—that was what made her forget, overlaid her memories like the haze of smoke over glass. And when she'd swallowed some of her own blood... she ran her fingers up into her hair, hard against her scalp, as if trying to force her thoughts to the surface of her mind... it had cut through the haze, shown her gleams of hidden memory.

But why? Why blood?

Her fingers stilled against her scalp. Of course. It wasn't because it was *blood*—it was because it was the only thing that didn't belong to this world, didn't carry Lethe's power.

What's Lethe? Never mind. Think. Think about the food.

Oh. For the first time anger crashed down through her and surged up again, boiling. *That* was why Clym had kept refilling her glass last night, why, this morning, he'd fed her melon and eggs and toast.

She got to her feet, the anger filling her, simmering. Spoon-feeding her, calling her baby names—it wasn't love, it was control.

From back through the apartment, the front door slammed. All Candy's muscles tightened, pulling her upright. He was back, and she was supposed to have cooked dinner. She was supposed to *eat* dinner. And the moment she did... What if she lost this new awareness? What if she went back to that dreaming, cloudy existence where she was nothing but Clym's wife, his baby doll, his little docile sweetheart?

"Candy?"

He'd come into the bedroom—she heard the wardrobe door open and the clink of him unhooking a hanger for his suit jacket.

She relaxed her hands—up until this moment she hadn't realized they were so tightly clenched her nails had left deep crescents in the skin. "Coming!" she called through the door, and then drew in a breath, trying to let it flow through her body, trying to force the tension down so it wouldn't show.

She unlocked the door and stepped out.

There was the strangest moment, then, as Clym turned, smiling, from the wardrobe—tall, dark, handsome, utterly familiar, the husband she'd lived with for a year—and she looked at him with no more feeling than if she were seeing a statue.

She had loved him—or she had thought she loved him. She'd slept with him and teased him and begged to go to work with him; had glowed with pleasure when he'd bought her something cute to wear or taken her out to dinner or shown her off to his friends.

And now she looked at him and didn't even feel pain at realizing their whole relationship had been false, or regret at what had never really been. Not even disappointment that she'd thought she was in love and found that that was false, too.

She did feel anger, though. Oh yes, she felt enough anger to make up for the lack of everything else.

She smiled at him, teeth hidden behind her lips, deliberately crinkling her eyes so he wouldn't see the fury in them. "I'm so sorry, Clym. Dinner's not ready. I was shopping, then I walked home through the park, then I got distracted looking at my new dress."

He was staring at her, and sudden fear iced over her anger. Could he tell? Did it, after all, show in her eyes, in her tone of voice? She stood still, not daring to speak.

He pushed the wardrobe door and it shut with a slam that would have made her jump if she hadn't been holding herself tight against any betraying movements. He didn't speak, just dropped his gaze to her feet.

Oh no—her shoes. *Again.*

She forced herself not to look down, not to react. Relaxed, calm, her stomach in knots, she strolled across to the bed and reached into the bag for the shoes she'd bought that afternoon. Pulling them out, she turned back to Clym.

"Look, aren't they beautiful? They go perfectly with my dress."

His voice was heavy, cold as stone. "And yet you're not

wearing them."

She smiled again, rolled her eyes a little. "Well, of course not. Didn't I say—I walked through the park, my feet were all dusty. These shoes"—she dangled them at him—"they're not having anything but sparkly-clean feet in them."

His gaze lightened a little. Not much, but Candy instantly felt her muscles sag as some of the tension left them. "You have slippers."

"Yes, but I can't wear them when I'm washing my feet!" She sat on the bed to slip the shoes on, fastened the slim golden ankle straps, and then smiled up at him. "I wasn't going to parade up and down the hall barefoot, honestly, Clym."

"Okay." His face relaxed into a smile. "So, no dinner, huh?"

"I'm *sorry*. It'll only take half an hour—"

"No, baby, it's just as well. I thought we'd go out for supper—I told Dem and Adriano we'd meet them at Nino's in an hour. Fix your face, doll, and we'll go."

Baby. Doll. She clamped down on a shudder—how weird, only this morning she hadn't minded him calling her that— and got to her feet, balancing on the high golden heels. "Of course, Clym. I'll get ready." Halfway into the bathroom, she checked, biting her lip against another shudder—this one for a very different reason. "Did you notice, has Mari gone?"

He nodded. "By the time I came in. Do your make-up in the bedroom, okay, darling? I want a shower."

The restaurant stood in a loop of the river, surrounded by a veranda of clean, white stone flags. Squat amber candles burned on the tables, a tiny shimmer of heat haze rising from each one.

Dem and Adriano had turned into Dem and Adriano and Ebon and Calla, plus Hy and Phira and Gray who turned up halfway through the meal. Tall, elegant people with long fingers and beautiful angular cheekbones, who tore heads off prawns and stabbed up olives on cocktail sticks and opened bottle after bottle of wine.

Distracted, still confused, Candy felt as if her head were swelling with the need to be alone, the need to think. She made a show of sipping her wine, put a few olives on her plate and pushed them back and forth. How much could she eat before all her thoughts would get wiped out again? And how long before they would come back? She was terrified of going back into that state of vague, unfocused fear—and even more terrified of going back to two days ago, when she hadn't been afraid, hadn't even known she should be afraid.

"Candy, *sugar*, you're not eating. Aren't you feeling well?"

It was one of the tall, dark, beautiful women. Calla? Adriano? Candy forced her face into a smile, hoping Clym hadn't heard.

"I'm fine. I am eating."

"But you're *not*. Clym, your little wife—she can't be feeling well."

From across the table, Clym looked at her. "Candy?"

"I'm fine. I *am* eating." And to prove it, she posted one of the stuffed olives into her mouth. Her throat closed, her body—now it knew what the food would do—reacting against the threat. She'd never be able to swallow it. But now half the table was looking at her, and she had to.

She made herself swallow it, and immediately felt her body relax—forced relaxation, like being swaddled, like being held down. *No. Oh no.* But she had no choice. Someone passed her the bread, someone else scooped salad onto her plate. And Clym was watching. She didn't know yet exactly what was wrong, but she knew it came from him, and she knew there was danger, and he mustn't find out that she knew.

Slowly, her hand heavy, her throat choked with fear and anger, she spiked tomato and cucumber and feta cheese, put it into her mouth, chewed, swallowed, felt the sweet, floating lethargy take her. She smiled across the table at Clym—and realized she wasn't entirely acting. Under cover of the table she dug sharp fingernails into her thigh. *Stay awake! Don't let this happen.*

The evening ground onward. Candy tried, unobtrusively,

to eat as little as possible. She talked a lot, deferring to Clym, directing others' attention to him as he liked her to do.

Memory ebbed and flowed. Sometimes, she couldn't remember why it was so important not to eat, couldn't remember why her fingernails were biting through her skirt. Sometimes, it all came back to her in a shuddering rush that turned her stomach upside down, and which she had to conceal.

After one of these moments, cold with sweat, she slipped away from the table and escaped to the toilets. Inside one of the cubicles, she sat down and let her head drop into her hands. It swam with jumbled thoughts, flickers of disconnected memory. The food sat like poison in her stomach, and she felt her throat pulse with the urge to vomit.

Her head jerked up. She listened. No one had followed her in, no one would hear her. Maybe, if she could expel the food, some of this woozy, cloudy feeling would clear. Maybe she'd get through the rest of dinner without feeling terrified she was losing her mind again.

She stood up, lifted the lid of the toilet and leaned over it. Her stomach heaved but the food stayed down. And, once again, familiarly, horribly, her mind started to cloud. What was she doing here? What was she thinking? And—*oh*—she felt awful. Why did she feel so sick?

Her sense of balance went askew. She swayed heavily sideways, knocking into the cubicle wall. She clutched the hard cold metal of the toilet-roll holder, all her thoughts vanishing as nausea and dizziness overwhelmed her.

The shoes weren't helping. Clym didn't like her to take them off, but no one was going to see. And the cold, solid floor would feel good beneath her bare feet. She leaned against the wall, one hand braced against the door, the other fumbling with the tiny buckle on the inside of her ankle. The shoe fell to the floor and, thankful, she put her bare foot down, steadying herself while she undid the other strap.

Oh, that was better. She didn't dare shut her eyes—she'd fall—but she lowered her head, breathing the scent of disinfectant and pseudo-pine air freshener. She'd just stay here a moment until she recovered, then she'd be able to go back to the restaurant—

No! Memory raced up through her. She felt it like a blow to her stomach. The *food*. The food was killing her thoughts.

This time she didn't stop to think it through. She leaned over the toilet, and slid her index finger along her tongue, right to the back where, if you touched it, it would make you retch...

The vomit came boiling up her throat, all the undigested food and wine she'd forced into her body, turned sour and vile. She heard herself make a horrible croaking noise and her hand clenched on the toilet-roll holder as she was sick and sick and sick.

It left her empty. Empty and—once again—aware. She spat into the toilet, wiped her mouth with the tissue paper, breathing shallowly though her teeth, waiting for the prickle of cold sweat, the goose bumps all over her skin, to disappear.

So, that had helped. And—oh, taking her shoes off had helped, too. She'd remember that. And now, for the first time, it came home to her that she had to do something. She couldn't live like this, not daring to eat, trying to pretend to Clym that she knew nothing.

Although I still feel as if I know nothing. Something's wrong, that's all I know. My husband is controlling me and I don't remember why, or how it started, or who I was before.

Outside the cubicle, the door to the restaurant opened. "Candy? Are you all right?"

One of the women—Adriano, Calla? Candy put a hand against the cubicle wall, bracing herself, trying to think. "I'm okay! I just felt a bit faint. Give me a minute."

A moment's silence. The woman wasn't leaving. *I can't go back out there yet. I have to think what to do.*

Then a clink in the next-door cubicle—the toilet lid going down—and a scraping sound on the wall by Candy's head.

Adriano's face appeared over the top of the wall. "Candy! You've been *sick!* You're *not* okay. Just hang on, I'll tell Clym."

Her face disappeared. Candy heard the click of her heels

as she hopped down from the toilet, then the outer door open and shut. *I'll tell Clym.* Yes, of course she would.

They'd been married for a year, and still, all their friends were really just Clym's friends. His colleagues, actually—no, not just his colleagues, but his *employees*. Was that part of their job, too, to notice if she wasn't eating or was hiding in the toilet making herself vomit, and to report back to him?

The door opened again, banging against the wall. The sound vibrated through Candy's head. Several heels tap-tapped across the floor. Two pairs of them, now.

"Candy? Clym is so worried. He's going to take you home. He's bringing the car round. Candy? Are you all right?"

Well, hardly. But she was stuck now. She pulled back the bolt and let the door swing open.

Adriano and Calla peered in at her, tall and gauntly elegant, with smooth olive-skinned cheekbones and sleek dark hair. Calla, though... had her coiled hair always had that scaly sheen, as if it were not hair but the entwined bodies of snakes? And had tiny flames always flickered within the pupils of Adriano's eyes?

I have to deal with people who aren't very nice, Clym had said.

Calla moved forward. "Come on, Candy. Do you need to take my arm?" From behind her ear, something like the tip of a scaly tail curled and clung.

"*No,*" said Candy, then, habits of courtesy too familiar to break, "Thank you. I'm okay."

As she went out of the cubicle, Adriano swooped down behind her. "Candy, your *shoes*. Don't you want them on?"

She'd been vomiting in the toilets, her husband was having to take her home early, they were worried she needed help *walking*, and Adriano thought she wanted to put her wobbly high heels back on?

"No," she said, firmly.

"Oh, but Candy, you know that Clym—"

Candy stopped walking. "Clym what? Clym doesn't like me to go barefoot? How would you know that?"

Adriano looked taken aback. "Oh—well, Clym, everyone

knows he—"

Calla cut in. "You don't want to upset him, do you, sweetie? Here, let me steady you, and Adriano will just slip them on..."

They were doing it almost before she realized. Adriano had stooped and put a slim, cool hand on Candy's ankle, raising her foot so she could slide the sandal on.

"I said *no!*" Candy snatched her foot back and Adriano overbalanced, landing inelegantly on the floor.

Calla looked appalled. "But *Candy.* You *know* Clym likes—"

Candy shook herself away from her. "*Clym likes.* Well, for once Clym can just do without what he *likes.*"

Adriano came to her feet. Her eyes were flickering blue now, the flames larger, licking outside the edges of her pupils. "That's enough. Calla, hold her."

"Don't you dare!" Candy flung off their arms. "Touch me again and I'll—" *What? Tell Clym? Run away? I don't even know where I am.* Desperate, she fell back on playground tactics. "I'll *bite* you."

Calla laughed, coming closer, smiling into Candy's face. "Oh sweetie. You're not the only one who can bite." From the back of her head, something gave a dry rustle. Something hissed.

"No," said Adriano. "Clym would be furious. Let's just get her to him. Let him deal with her."

Calla laughed again, a dry rustle to match her hair. "You're so sensible, Adri. Come on, then, little girl. Let's get you to your... husband."

They kept close beside her as she went back out into the restaurant. It seemed unnaturally quiet. The candles burned steadily, reflected and multiplied in the dark windows all around the restaurant.

By the door, car keys dangling from his hand, Clym waited for her. In the low light of the candles, she couldn't read his expression.

The women fell behind her, but she had to walk toward him all the same. Where else would she go?

But what will I do? What am I going to do? He's the ruler here—how can I possibly not end up doing exactly what he tells me?

"Put your shoes on."

She'd reached him. She stared up into his face, feet firmly on the floor, and didn't move. The shoes—they really mattered. Maybe even as much as the food. Why else, for a year, would he insist she wore them, get angry if she forgot? Okay, he could probably force her to put them back on—he had plenty of support, after all—but she was damned if she was going to do it for him.

"Candy. Put your shoes on."

"Why?" she said, standing straight, feeling, oddly, taller than she had in all the high heels he'd ever bought her.

He stared at her a moment, unblinking, and she felt her face screw up slightly as if she were bracing herself for a blow.

"Because you look cheap." The words came with a sharp-edged emphasis, a twist like the lash of a whip. Intended to strike her, intended to make her flinch.

She didn't flinch. Not this time. Not anymore. She lifted her chin, keeping her eyes on his. "I do not. I look powerful. You know that, and that's what you don't like."

"*Powerful?* With your shoes off, like a streetwalker, like some cheap nymph—"

That word did strike her, but with a shock like a dash of water, like a leafy branch springing up against her face, cool and green-scented.

"A what?" she said.

He faltered. She saw him hear his last word, saw—for the first time—something like fear enter the dark face.

"A streetwalker. A *whore*—"

"That's not what you said. You said a *nymph*." And as she spoke the word, more words came, unexpectedly pattering into her mind like falling, rain-drenched blossom. "A dryad. A nature goddess. *That's* what you don't want me to look like. Why? What are you scared of? What are you hiding?"

Fury rose in his face, swamping the fear. "You don't get to

speak to me like that. I'm hiding nothing—"

"Oh, you so are. There's no point, Clym. I know you've done something to me. It's why you insist I eat, it's why you're trying to make me put my shoes on. Tell me—why don't I remember our wedding? Why does our maid wear chains?"

He hadn't realized she'd noticed that. She saw his face freeze a moment, as shocked as if she'd thrown something at him. The sight sent courage shooting into her veins, bright, intoxicating.

She went closer to him, walking tall in her shoeless feet, feeling as if she drew strength through the bare soles. "I wasn't supposed to notice, was I? What else is there, Clym? What other nasty secrets am I not supposed to see? What *is* your work, that I have to be kept away from it? Who are these friends of yours you get to follow me and spy on me? Who are *you*?"

She was staring into his eyes now—*up* into his eyes. She'd forgotten how tall he was, and the bright wave of courage ebbed a little, leaving her feeling too weak, too small.

Without stepping away, without taking his eyes off her, he snapped his fingers. Except... no, he couldn't have, because there was a glass in them. A glass filled with red liquid. She'd seen something like that before and, although she couldn't remember when or where or what it had done to her, she started to shiver.

She should have stayed out of reach. She made to take a step away and his free hand shot out and grabbed her arm, fingers closing around her wrist. His eyes bored down into her.

"I'm your husband. That's all you need to know."

He brought the glass to her lips. The liquid swam in it, a brighter, sharper colour than blood. And, unlike her blood, this wouldn't cut through the clouds, wouldn't shred the tapestry and let her step through, back into her own world. It smelled very sweet, like fruit and syrup. The scent woke a half memory. She had seen this before. She'd drunk this before, nearly a year ago, and that was when the world had dimmed and faded and turned into something she didn't want.

She pulled away, lips tight shut, head averted, but he wouldn't let go of her arm. He jerked her back, pinned her between him and the nearest table edge.

"Drink it, Candy. You're not happy fighting with me like this. Drink it, and we can go back to being happy."

"I don't want that kind of happy!" she flashed, then tried to clamp her lips shut. Too late. His hand came up, forced the edge of the glass between her teeth, tilted it so the liquid ran into her mouth.

No. *No.* This was how it had started. She wasn't going to let it start again.

She twisted in his arm, closing her throat against the sweet, sliding liquid, and thrust her hand, fingers clawed, at his face. His head snapped back. His grip slackened and the glass tilted, the dark liquid spilling down her chin and onto the breast of her dress. She spat after it, tried to push away sideways, get out from under his arm, but he was too strong.

He yanked her back and jammed the glass up into her mouth. Bright pain splintered into her lip, her tongue, the gums at the base of her lower teeth.

She shrieked. The blood flooding into her mouth drowned the noise, turning it into a gargled sound, and her body lost its fight, went loose against the table.

"*Candy,*" he said, and let her go. She felt herself start to slide toward the floor, and reached out to grip the table, fighting the blur in her eyes, fighting to stay upright.

"I'm sorry. Oh Candy, I'm sorry. I didn't mean..."

His voice became a garbled background noise with no sense to it. She put up a hand to her mouth and pulled a wicked sliver of glass, slick with moisture, out of her lip. The skin around it clung, dragging, and the pain shot along every nerve, razor blades turning her skin to prickling ice. Liquid—sickly, salty liquid—flooded into her mouth and she swallowed instinctively, not thinking any more about what the drink would do to her, blind to everything but the pain and the fear of broken glass—*broken glass*—stuck in her mouth.

Another shard of glass in her lip, one in her tongue. She drew them out too, trying not to think how much damage they'd done, trying to do it while she was still brave with shock. More liquid slid over her tongue—warm, salty, metallic—and she swallowed again.

His voice came through the pain, pulsing, loud then soft, as if something had gone wrong with her ears. "Candy. Candy, let me help you." And his hands over hers—so cold they felt as if they burned her skin.

She jerked away, felt the floor shift under her feet, and fell. Her teeth came down hard onto her lower lip and fresh blood spurted from the open cuts. She cried out, choked on it—

"Spit it out! *Don't swallow.* Candy—"

She heard the panic in his voice—*don't swallow*—and a last bit of stubbornness rose within her like steel through her spine. She swallowed.

The pain cleared, not much, but enough so her eyes unblurred. She put her hand to her mouth and felt no more splinters of glass. She looked up.

She was facing the wall of windows that faced out onto the river, the meadows beyond it. All over them shone the reflections of the candle flames, a multitude of little amber petals suspended in darkness.

She focused on the flames, trying to pull herself together, trying to brace herself to fight, and saw the color bleach out of them, saw them go cold and bright, tiny points like specks of twinkling glass. The window lost its reflected gleam, darkened, melted away into the...

...into the sky. It was no longer the familiar landscape of river and meadow, but sky: high, clear sky, stretching away farther and farther, endlessly into the distance. And the lights were no longer candles, but stars.

The windows had gone. She was looking out of the mouth of a cave. Below her, the hillside fell away. In the starlight she could see the short, scrubby mountain grass. Wind swept in at her, scoured clean with the scent of snow.

"Stop! Stop—Candy, don't!"

But he was too late. She was already scrambling to her feet, and as he grabbed at her she flung herself out of the cave, out across the rock ledge at its entrance, onto the grass. It was sparse, now, in wintertime, and her hands brushed through the blades, straight onto the frozen-hard earth beneath.

The shock hit her like lightning, driving up her hands, her arms, all the way through her body. And memory came back, starkly lit—one flash after another.

She'd wandered here, farther and farther up the mountain, gathering narcissi, singing, and the chariot had come, its wheels shaking the mountainside. The driver had glanced at her as it thundered past, and then dragged on the reins, bringing his horses to a slithering, screaming halt.

"Candy. . . "

Clym came out of the cave. Behind him the restaurant, the candles, the people—all had slid away, melted into the darkness. She looked up at him and recognized the face of the chariot driver. Memory flashed again—the feel of his hand, icy on her bare arm. The sound of his cold voice.

She sprang to her feet. Even that short contact with the earth had done its work. She could feel her cuts healing, feel the power that was her inheritance pouring up through her, like tree sap wakening in the springtime.

"I said *no*," she said. "I said *no* and you took me *anyway*."

"I couldn't help it. Candy, I fell in love with you, and you wouldn't come—"

Another lightning flash. She had struggled, screaming, the narcissi falling in a scatter all around her. He'd clamped one cold hand across her mouth and nose, crushing the screams back down her throat, cutting off her breath. Bundled her into the chariot and careened down, into the darkness—darkness blacker than she, an earth goddess, could have ever known, blacker than she could bear.

"That wasn't love," she said.

"It was. It is. Candy—"

"You poisoned me! You gave me that juice—from fruit grown next to Lethe's waters—you wiped out my mind!

You—" She stopped as another thought came. "You *changed my name*. You called me *Candy*. What the hell sort of name is that?"

"I couldn't let you keep a tie to who you really were. I couldn't lose you—"

"That was the shoes, too, wasn't it? Even in your damned fake kingdom, you couldn't risk me touching the earth with bare feet, couldn't risk it recognizing me and calling me home. Well, you lost. It reached me anyway. Twice I lost my shoes, did you know? The wall broke down and the earth took them, held onto them, let me know something was wrong."

He didn't speak, just stood still, looking at her.

"Does my mother know? Does she know where I am?"

He said nothing, and she read the answer in his eyes.

"She doesn't, does she? She doesn't know. She must think I'm—" She looked around, seeing as if for the first time the dry, wintry grass, the bare-branched trees, stark in the cold light of the stars. "And this—I've been gone for a year. This should be springtime. Is that what this is? Does she think I'm *dead?*"

He lifted one shoulder. "She'll know by now."

"But a *year!* A year of mourning!" She spun away from him, every moment feeling stronger; the earth's strength rising through her.

His voice came from behind her, heavy as earth on a dead man's eyes, cold as the coins they paid to cross the Styx. "Better than eternity."

She knew perfectly well he meant himself, but she didn't care. All those others—his sycophantic colleagues, the shop girls and waitresses, poor Mari with the chain on her ankle— Lord of Death, it was his right to keep them. He'd never had a right to her. She was going home.

She began to walk down the mountain. In the distance she could see the waterfall in the sacred grove, from here nothing but a shining starlit thread, apparently motionless against the cliff face. Farther still, down in the meadow, her mother was waiting for her. Mourning, but holding onto enough hope that summer had stayed there, only there, in the meadow where their house stood.

With every step the earth welcomed her. The grass softened under her feet, grew lush with spring growth. The wind lost its cold bite, threading gentle fingers through her hair. Sweet night-time scents rose around her.

"Candy..."

He was following her. She didn't look back at him. "That's not my name."

She heard him swallow. "Persephone. Please understand. I love you."

You do not. She turned, the furious words rising to her lips. He was standing behind her, on the new grass she'd left in her wake, the entrance to his dark kingdom behind him. And his eyes, his face—they were so bleak he looked like one of his own damned souls.

She didn't say those words after all.

"I know," she said. "But you did it wrong."

And this time, when she turned away, he didn't follow her.

THE COLD BLACKNESS BETWEEN

by

Lucy A. Snyder

Mary Keller was exhausted but elated when Karl's eyes finally flickered open. He rose up a little on his one good elbow, the plastic sheet crinkling beneath him.

"Mary?" he rasped. "Where'm I? Throat...hurts. Feel like...crap."

She smiled. His voice was rough, but it worked. His head had been torn off when he lost control of his motorcycle and wrapped it around a tree up in the mountains. She'd not been sure she'd gotten his vocal cords reconstructed properly.

"Rest now. You don't need to worry about a thing. You just need to get your strength back."

She leaned down over the antique feather bed and kissed his still-cold forehead. At least the sleet that had slicked the roads that night had also meant he'd been wearing his helmet with the visor down. He hadn't gotten anything worse than a bloody nose when his head went skittering down into the rocky ravine.

Shattered bones, punctured lungs, crushed organs and severed spines she could handle; damaged brains were hard. It was like trying to put custard back together. If she'd had to bring him back from a crushed skull, chances were she'd end up with a zombie on her hands that was only the barest revenant of the man she loved.

"What happened?" he asked, his eyes already fluttering into the sleep of the living.

She kissed him again, then straightened up and re-checked the position of the I.V. needle in his arm. Her hands were trembling; it was definitely time for breakfast. The saline-and-glucose drip was still three-quarters full. She'd put two units of O-negative blood into him during the night. He needed far more than that, but even if she'd replaced all his blood, he'd still be more dead than alive. It would be several days before his system recovered from the shock. For now, it was most important that she not let him dry out while she slept.

That the transfusion needle was steel was unfortunate but unavoidable; she'd made sure to put it in his good arm, where the steel's interference with the life magic would cause the least damage to her work. Nothing else in the room contained inorganic iron; the I.V. stand was aluminum, the furniture put together with wooden pegs, the light fixtures bronze, the wiring copper. That floor of the mansion had its own breaker switch, and she'd turned its electricity off before she'd started work. Electricity had an unpredictable effect on resurrections.

She snuffed out the candles surrounding the bed and set her tray of bandages, sutures and ceramic surgical instruments up on the vanity. In the old days, she'd had to use instruments made from wood, ivory, and glass. Her mother had taught her how to chip scalpel blades from broken window panes, which Mary had always found a deeply tedious task. Modern ceramics were a wonderful invention.

Mary's skills as a witch kept her in high demand as a healer, but she'd never hoped to work on Karl. Soon after they started seeing each other, she cast a ward on him to keep him from harm. Dogs would not bite him, bees would not sting him, drunks would not pick a fight with him. But the spell couldn't protect him from the laws of physics, so she added a divination element to warn her when he was getting into danger.

She'd been downstairs reading a potboiler mystery when she had a vision of Karl sliding sideways on the icy highway.

She sped out to Pineytop Road to try to intercept Karl before he crashed... but she couldn't get there quite fast enough. At least she was able to get his body into her trunk before anyone else passed by and saw the wreck. The bike was a total loss, and far too heavy for her to lift; she rolled it down out of sight in the ravine.

Mary pulled the covers up to Karl's bandaged neck and stumbled to the bedroom door. She locked it behind her to keep her lover from prying eyes and started down the stairs.

Yolanda, their housekeeper, came through the back door just as Mary got down the stairs. The younger woman's eyes widened when she saw Mary.

"My God, are you okay?" Yolanda exclaimed.

Mary looked down at herself. Her sweatshirt and jeans were smeared with Karl's blood. She'd been so focused on saving Karl that she hadn't noticed.

"I'm fine," Mary replied. "Some friends from the gym took me out to Lake Zurich for a party last night. We hit a deer on the way back, and I helped Joe pull it off the grille and carry it off the road. The car was wrecked; I only got home a little while ago."

"Mr. Barrington doesn't like you going out partying." Yolanda's tone was matter-of-fact.

Mary shrugged. "He knew who I was when he married me. He knows I won't stay at home by myself. If he wants me here, he can stop going off on so many business trips."

She brushed at the crusty stains on her sweatshirt. "I need to put on something clean—I'll be back down in a minute."

Mary trudged up to her bedroom on the third floor to change. She wondered how she was ever going to break the news of her affair to William. He was still more her employer than her husband. She'd started as his personal nurse, but when sex became a part of their relationship, he decided they should be married. She was fond of him... but he was not a passionate man and never had been. And he had grown increasingly cold over the past year; he hardly spent time with her anymore.

Karl was passionate, and sweet, and damn fine company. She first laid eyes on him at the gym; he was tall and lean and the smell of him made her blood sing. Karl had been reluctant to get involved with a married woman, but he was just as attracted to her as she to him.

At first she told herself it was just a casual fling, but the more time she spent with him, the more she knew in her heart that she couldn't bear to be without him. And she could tell how uncomfortable he was about having to sneak around.

Karl deserved better than to be her dirty little secret. And William deserved her honesty. She didn't know how she could do right by both men, so for now all she could worry about was keeping Karl alive.

"Is Mr. Barrington still coming back from Mexico City next Wednesday?" Yolanda asked when Mary returned.

"That's his plan, last I heard." Five days would suffice to get Karl strong enough to move to his apartment for the remainder of his recuperation. She shuffled into the kitchen and got a few slices of sourdough from the breadbox.

"I'm starving, and I'm exhausted." Mary said. "Would you mind fixing me some breakfast?"

"Not at all." Yolanda set a skillet on the stove to heat.

Mary got a butter knife from the draining rack, found her jar of herb paste in the refrigerator, and sat down at the blond oak breakfast table. Yolanda made a face as Mary spread the thick, green-black paste on the bread.

"I don't see how you can eat that stuff." Yolanda carried a bowl of oranges to the juicing machine. "It smells like shit."

"It's full of flavonoids and antioxidants and it's just the thing for a killer hangover." Actually, it was just the thing for keeping Mary from aging rapidly and drastically as a result of the resurrection she'd performed. "A little rosemary for the brain, valerian for the nerves, ginseng for strength, ginko for the circulation, garlic for the heart..."

...and a little consecrated silver to fortify my spiritual strength, ground oak leaf to center my soul, and dried blood from my mother to preserve my flesh, she finished to herself.

163

Mary set the half-eaten bread aside and laid her head on the cool wood table. Her skull felt like it was filled with sloshing quicksand. God. She'd really pushed it this time. She'd done a rejuvenation on her husband only two weeks ago—she had no business doing a full resurrection so soon afterward.

But what else could she do? The longer she waited to raise Karl, the more decomposition set in, the bigger the risk he'd come out a twisted, soulless monster.

She worried about the effect her rejuvenations had on her husband. He'd been in his late sixties when they met and was recovering from a quadruple bypass. All the signs indicated he wasn't going to see the end of the decade. But he'd heard about her special services through a spiritualist he'd consulted for stock advice, and he offered her more cash than she'd seen before to cast a spell to add a few years back onto his life.

She'd done twelve rejuvenations on him in the four years since then. He'd recently celebrated his seventy-first birthday and looked a fit forty-something. But with each rejuv she'd cast, he'd grown a little colder in manner and mind. He still smiled, still laughed, still took care in his foreplay with her, but when she looked in his eyes, she sometimes felt she was staring out into the cold blackness between the stars. Once upon a time, she was sure she'd seen something like love in those dark eyes of his. Now she wondered if it hadn't been a figment of her imagination, if she'd never really been anything more than a favorite investment to him.

Or maybe she'd stopped letting herself see anything but his natural coldness to justify her affair with Karl.

Yolanda set a glass of fresh juice on the table beside Mary's head.

"Now, don't you fall asleep before I get breakfast ready," Yolanda admonished.

"Don't worry, I'm awake." With effort, Mary sat up and took a sip of her juice.

Mary admired the graceful curve of Yolanda's neck as the younger woman turned back to the fridge. They'd been friendly enough the past four years, but weren't really friends.

Mary had held Yolanda at arm's length because she felt she had to keep too many secrets to cultivate a real friendship with her. Maybe that had been a mistake.

"William hired you right out of high school, so you've been his housekeeper for, what, ten years now?" asked Mary.

Yolanda nodded as she cracked two eggs into the hot skillet. "Yes, about ten years."

"Did you two ever...? You know. Get involved."

Yolanda gave her a sharp look. "What kind of girl do you think I am?"

"A young and pretty one. And don't tell me he's too proper to sleep with his employees, because I'm still on the payroll." She paused. "Look, I'm not going to get mad; I'm just asking."

Yolanda sighed, staring down at the coagulating eggs.

"I was nineteen," she said quietly. "I couldn't say no to him. I didn't *want* to say no. I dreamed that he might fall in love, and make me his wife. But it was just sex to him, and he lost interest after a few weeks. Afterward, I felt like I'd been his whore, and thought about quitting... but jobs that pay this well aren't easy to find. Not for girls like me, anyway. So I stayed."

Yolanda gave her a quick, worried glance. "He hasn't tried to touch me since he brought you here, if that's what you thought."

Mary shook her head. "No, it's not that. I just wondered how well you knew him. Sometimes I don't think I know him at all."

"Why do you say that?" Yolanda turned the eggs and put two pieces of sausage in a separate pan.

"Yolanda... do you think he loves me?" Mary asked.

"He *ought* to love you, after all you've done for him."

"I haven't done that much. I'm just a nurse." The savory smell of the frying sausage made her mouth water.

"Mary, I have *eyes*. I've seen the change in him. He was an old, sick man, and now he's back in the prime of his life."

"But do you think he loves me?"

Yolanda spoke carefully. "I think men like him know how

to possess things and take care of things. They don't know how to love as women need to be loved."

Mary quietly sipped her juice while Yolanda grated sharp cheddar onto the eggs.

"Speaking theoretically," Mary finally said, "how angry do you think he'd be if I took a lover?"

"He'd be furious. Mr. Barrington doesn't like to share." Yolanda brought the steaming breakfast plate to Mary.

"Oh, this looks yummy, you're a lifesaver!" Mary picked up her knife and fork and started digging in.

"Mary... you've been going out an awful lot. Mr. Barrington might not have noticed yet, but... just please be careful. I would miss you if you were gone."

The phone rang.

"If that's William, please tell him I'm asleep," Mary said.

Yolanda hurried over to the phone in the corner.

"Yes? Oh, hello, Mr. Barrington," Yolanda said. "Is everything okay? Yes. She's still asleep upstairs. Tonight? Yes, I'll tell her. Are you sure everything is okay? Fine. Goodbye."

Yolanda hung up and walked back to the table. "Mr. Barrington wants to talk to you about something. He'll call back at 10, and he wanted me to make sure you'll be here."

"I'm not going anywhere." Even if she had the energy to go out, she wasn't about to leave Karl by himself. "I wonder what he wants?"

Mary speared another piece of sausage. Mid-lift, her hand began to shake, and the hairs rose on the back of her neck and arms. Her heart began to pound, faster and faster.

"Are you okay?" Yolanda asked.

Mary's chest felt constricted; it was hard to breathe, and harder to talk. "I—I don't know—"

Suddenly, Mary was floating disembodied above Karl's bed in the upstairs bedroom. The walls and curtains were on fire, but the flames were the wrong color, deep red and purple and green. The air was filled with thick red smoke and the stench of black magic. Karl was coughing and weakly calling for help. He looked *old*, his face sunken. He almost looked like William. Through the smoke, she saw a corpse lying in a wide pool of blood beside the bed. Her horror deepened as she realized the body was *hers*...

Mary came out of the vision and found that she'd fallen out of her chair and lay crumpled on the floor. Yolanda was beside her, trying to help her up, but her legs weren't cooperating.

"What's the matter? Should I call for a doctor?"

We're going to die, Mary tried to say, shaking her head, but the words wouldn't come. Her vision clouded, and everything went black.

Mary came to a few minutes later as Yolanda hoisted her onto the bed in the first floor guest suite.

"What—" Mary began, still disoriented.

"Shh, be still. I'm going to...call you a doctor," Yolanda said between gasps, winded from the effort of carrying Mary down the hall.

"No, don't. Don't need a doctor. Just need to rest," Mary slurred. She couldn't keep her eyes open. "I'm fine...just need a nap. Please don't let me sleep too long..."

Mary was running up the stairs of the mansion. Her legs moved too slowly, as if the staircase were covered in a foot of sticky tar that was sucking her down. The air stank of brimstone. From Karl's bedroom, she could hear a low, slithery voice chanting in a language older than mankind. The sound chilled her to the core. Something terrible would happen to Karl if she didn't stop it.

Mary finally got to the second floor and ran to the bedroom. The door was ajar, and a deep red light glowed from within. She pushed inside. The red light flared bright, blinding her, and the serpentine voice rose to a roar—

"Mary!" Yolanda was shaking her. "Wake up!"

"Oh God!" Mary jerked fully awake, breathing hard.

"Shh, shh, it's okay, it's just a nightmare. Everything's

okay," Yolanda soothed, laying a cool hand against Mary's forehead. "I heard you call out in your sleep, and I thought I should wake you."

"Thanks." Mary sat up. A pain like someone had shoved an icepick behind her eyes lanced through her skull.

"God, what time is it?" Mary asked, clutching her head.

"Nine p.m."

"Twelve hours?" Mary threw off the thin quilt. "That's your idea of not letting me sleep too long?"

She rolled out of bed and staggered into the adjoining guest bathroom, turned on the faucet and splashed cold water on her face.

Yolanda followed her into the bathroom. "I tried waking you earlier, but you wouldn't get up. I didn't want to push you."

Mary found a bottle of aspirin in the medicine cabinet, and gulped down four tablets along with a handful of water. Her nerves were still humming from the alarm his ward spell had set off. "You've got to get out of here. Something really bad's going to happen."

"Mary, what's going on?"

Mary shook her head. "I can't explain. There's no time."

She stepped back into the bedroom and stuck a hand in her pocket to find the key to Karl's bedroom. Her fingers found nothing but lint. She'd left the key in her dirty jeans upstairs.

"You didn't happen to bring the dirty clothes down to the laundry, did you?"

"I put them in the wash." Yolanda reached into the breast pocket of her apron and pulled out the key. "Are you looking for this?"

"Yes."

Mary reached for the key. Yolanda dropped it back in her pocket.

"No. Not until you explain," Yolanda said. "*I* am responsible for this house when Mr. Barrington is away, and if there's a danger here, I need to know exactly what it is. 'Something bad' isn't a good explanation."

"Dammit, I can't—"

"When I was upstairs, I heard a noise in the second-floor bedroom. I was surprised the door was locked, but not half as surprised as when I found a strange man in there." Yolanda paused. "The blood on your shirt wasn't from a deer, was it?"

Mary took a deep breath. "No. It's wasn't. The man in the bedroom is... my boyfriend Karl. He wrecked his bike, and I brought him here."

"That boyfriend of yours is a real cutie. But he has an awful lot of stitches in him. I'm no doctor, but I think I can tell when a guy's had his head sewn back on.

"So how come your boyfriend is still breathing when he should be in a morgue?"

"I'm... a healer. A white witch. That's why William hired me. I could keep him alive when the doctors couldn't."Mary took another deep breath, trying to steady her nerves. "Last night, I had a vision that Karl had an accident. He was dead when I found him, so I brought him here to bring him back. Since then, I've had... bad premonitions. Something very evil is coming here, and I honestly don't know what it is. I *do* know that if we don't get out of here, it's going to kill me and Karl, and probably you, too."

Yolanda considered this information. "Maybe all this is happening because you helped Karl cheat Death?"

"No. I've done resurrections before, and nothing like this happened. Besides, by that logic, the spells I cast on William should've brought evil down on us, too. Heart failure is just as fatal as decapitation. Neither of the men in my life should be alive right now."

Yolanda stared at Mary. "I knew of a Santeria witch woman once. She claimed she did white magic, too, but there was a blood price for everything she did. There was a balance. If she cured a cold, a chicken or a lizard had to die. If she helped someone stay alive, someone else had to die."

"There has to be a balance, yes. You can't generate magic out of nothing. Healing requires a lot of spiritual energy, and the easy way to get it is to take it from another life. But my mother taught me a better way: I can generate the energy myself, if I stay fit and eat right and all that good stuff."

"So you don't kill people?"

"Not unless they're trying to kill *me*."

Yolanda considered this, then pulled the key out of her pocket and tossed it to Mary. "Let's get your boyfriend and get out of here. If something happens to the house... well, that's why Mr. Barrington has insurance."

After checking on Karl and replacing his I.V. bag, the two women went up to Mary's bedroom. Mary quickly laced on her old hiking boots and threw a few changes of clothes and some toiletries into an overnight bag.

"We've got to be really careful with Karl." Mary shook her head. "He shouldn't be moved at all, but we have no choice. There's an old wheelchair up in the attic. We can use that to take him out to the car."

Mary left her bag on her dressing table and knelt down beside her bed. She reached under it and pulled out a battered steel case.

"First things first," Mary said. "We've got to be able to defend ourselves."

Mary undid the combination locks and opened the case. She pulled out a large revolver, flipped open the cylinder and checked the contents. Satisfied, she closed the cylinder and held the pistol out to Yolanda. "Here, take this. It's loaded with consecrated silver bullets half-jacketed in cold iron. Ammunition against most anything, dead or alive."

Yolanda stared at the gun as if it were a very large spider. "I have never fired a gun in my life."

"It's easy: just point the gun at the thing you want to kill and squeeze the trigger." When Yolanda didn't reach for the gun, Mary added, "Look, you've *got* to take it. It's iron; I can't have it on me, or it'll screw up any spells I try to cast."

Yolanda reluctantly took the pistol and stuck it in one of the deep side pockets of her apron.

Mary lifted an ancient silver-bladed bronze dagger in a red leather sheath from the case. It was an Irish priest's scían, made sometime in the fourth century. She stuck the holy weapon in the waistband of her jeans under her pullover. "Please get the wheelchair, and I'll prep Karl for the trip."

Mary grabbed her overnight bag and hurried down the stairs. The aspirin had only blunted the pain in her head, and her stomach was growling unpleasantly. At least her overlong sleep had given her most of her energy back. Once they had Karl squared away at a motel someplace, she could order a pizza and cast a divination to figure out what the hell was causing her visions.

Her stomach growled again, loudly. God, she was so hungry! If she didn't get more food soon, she'd lose what little concentration she had left. Mary dropped her bag beside Karl's bedroom door on the second floor landing and headed down to the kitchen.

As she was hunting for a Powerbar in the pantry, the back door opened.

"Who's there?" she called, putting a hand on the hilt of her dagger.

"It's just me, dear." William Barrington stepped out of the darkened entry hall into the light from the kitchen. He looked alert and cheerful, despite his long flight. "I'd have called to let you know I was returning early, but that would have spoiled the surprise. Please meet Nala, my new nurse."

A tall, beautiful model in a tailored green suit stepped up beside William. Her silken auburn hair cascaded down over her shoulders, and her eyes—Mary blinked, and did a double-take.

The woman's lovely high cheeks, pouting lips and green eyes seemed *transparent*, and behind the beautiful mask of a face Mary could just barely see the visage of something ugly and gray, something with skin that writhed and eyes like molten lead.

"I met Nala in Mexico City a few months ago," William said. "I appreciate all you've done, but the fact is, it's not enough. Nala can give me eternal youth. I've got to say her magical skills are quite impressive. Did you know she can pull a man's guts out through his mouth, and keep him alive indefinitely? She can also make the dumb son-of-a-bitch who's been fucking my wife wreck his motorcycle. Neat, huh?"

Mary's stomach dropped as she remembered her visions.

"But you *can't* be young again and remain William Barrington, can you?" she said. "So you have to become someone else. I get it. You planned to have *her* magic Karl's bones and teeth to look like yours, then kill me and burn the place down."

She took a step toward him. "The police would find the skeletons and think we'd both died in a freak fire. And then you'd take over the identity of whoever inherits the estate and the insurance money."

She paused, trying to remember the latest rewrite of his will. "It's your nephew George, isn't it? You're gonna kill him and Rita. Damn you, those kids just got married."

"You're a sharp girl; I always liked that about you." William's expression didn't change.

Mary swallowed nervously, trying hard not to look at Nala. "You didn't have to do this. I could've made you young again, and arranged a new life for you—"

"Bullshit." His eyes gleamed with fury. "How am I supposed to trust you after you've cheated on me? Do you think I can't smell that bastard's stink on you?"

"The only stink you're smelling is coming from your new girlfriend. Christ, she's not even *human*! The only eternal life you're gonna get out of this is the one she's booked you in Hell."

He smiled thinly. "I doubt I'll die to see it anytime soon. So be sure to send me a postcard when you get there."

Out of the corner of her eye, Mary saw Yolanda creeping down the stairs with the gun in her hands.

"This is taking too long," Nala announced. She had a voice like a nestful of copperheads sliding through the strings of a bass violin. "I need to get on with the boyfriend's transformation if we're going to be finished by dawn."

"Right," William said. "Kill her."

Nala hissed and made a grasping gesture with her left had. Mary gasped as invisible claws raked her innards and closed around her heart. Her whole body began to shake. She tried to speak a protective charm, but her tongue was paralyzed. She could only emit a thin moan as the agony became unbearable—

Fire flashed from the muzzle of Yolanda's revolver. The twin Magnum booms were deafening. Two bullets exploded through Nala's belly, leaving behind raw, saucer-sized craters that oozed black ichor.

The spectral claws abruptly released Mary. Nala roared, enraged and in pain, and turned on Yolanda. The demoness raised her hands and made a sharp push in the air.

An invisible force slammed into Yolanda's chest. She was flung backward into the stairs. Mary heard the crack of bone against wood. Yolanda bounced forward and tumbled down to the ground floor like a rag doll.

Mary was already whispering an incantation as she drew the silver dagger. She tackled the demoness, pinning her arms to the tile floor.

"With the power of the Goddess I cast thee, foul creature, from this house and from this living plane!" Mary shouted.

She grabbed the shrieking demoness by the hair and carved into her neck until she felt the metal grinding against bone. She whispered the ancient Gaelic words of banishment into Nala's ear.

"*Immee gys Niurin!*" she finished with a shout.

Mary gave a hard yank, and heard a wet popping. She wrapped both arms beneath Nala's chin and yanked again, hard as she could. Nala's head tore free.

The decapitated demoness shuddered, then fell limp. Her flesh and bones smoked, collapsed and disintegrated as if her body had been little more than a shell of flash paper. In seconds, there was nothing left but a sulphurous stink and a film of ash on the floor and on Mary's jeans.

William was still standing there, dumbfounded. "What—what have you done?" he finally stammered. "I already gave up my soul. Oh God. What the *fuck* is going to happen to me now?"

Mary stood up. "You're going to Hell, asshole."

She slugged him in the jaw with everything she had left. He tumbled backward and fell flat on his back, unconscious.

Mary looked around. Yolanda lay in an unmoving heap at the bottom of the staircase. Mary's stomach sank. She hurried to the housekeeper's side and gently rolled her over. Her neck was broken, and her eyes stared out at nothing. Mary couldn't find a pulse.

Tears welled in her eyes. "Goddammit, I don't have anything left. I can't help her. Unless..."

Mary stared at her husband.

"What I've given, I can take away."

She dragged him over to Yolanda's corpse, washed her hands, and began.

Three weeks later, the first snow of the winter fell. Mary finished her conversation with the coroner and hung up the phone. She cinched her thick terrycloth robe tighter, wiggled her feet back into her bunny slippers and padded into the library.

Yolanda and Karl were reading on a quilt they'd spread beside the roaring fireplace.

"Well, looks like you two are feeling better," Mary said.

"Yes, much better," Yolanda replied. "Was that the coroner?"

"Yep."

"What did he say?"

"That Mr. William Barrington the Third died of natural causes. Namely, arteriosclerosis and coronary failure due to a long life of smoking and drinking and being a general heartless prick. The police are no longer interested in anything that may or may not have happened here last month. And so

William's estate will officially become mine once the paperwork is sorted out."

"So what happens now?" Karl asked.

Mary sat down beside him and gave him a playful pinch. "What happens now is that *you* are going to give me a foot rub. A very *long* foot rub, because I am *beat*."

She lay back on the quilt and closed her eyes. "But please, be gentle. I'm in mourning."

SOLSTICE MAIDEN

by
Anna Kashina

The crowd by the village well watched in silence as my guards and I rode up to the house at the end of the muddy street. The chipped, moss-covered logs of its walls lay unevenly, as if placed by a drunken builder. The man and woman standing in the doorway eyed me sullenly. As I stopped my horse in front of their broken fence, their silence made me wonder if force was going to be necessary after all. Then the man turned and pulled somebody from the darkness beyond the doorway. A girl.

"Mistress, this is my youngest daughter, Alyona. Sixteen, this past week. She will make a fine Sacrifice." His voice wavered, and I heard sobs in the depth of the house, followed by hushing, and then silence.

I nodded, surveying my quarry. She wore a baggy linen dress, her head covered by a dirt-gray knitted scarf. Her pale face was swollen with tears as she eyed me from underneath her long eyelashes.

"Remove your scarf," I ordered.

Her fingers trembled as she hastened to obey, revealing a mass of dark blond hair. She had pulled it all back into a tight braid, and tucked it into her dress—a hairstyle that came in handy during housework. What showed of her braid, though, looked thick enough to promise a fine display, if combed and arranged properly. I leaned forward in the saddle to take a closer look at her face. She would have been pretty if her face wasn't so puffed up from crying. Instinct told me she was a virgin, as the villagers must believe her to be. My servants would check, of course. But so far, so good.

I straightened in the saddle, turning to look at the frightened faces all around me. The silence was almost palpable. I could feel their anxiety upon me as I turned to my guards and said: "Very well. Bring her along."

Amidst suppressed sighs of relief I turned my horse and left the village.

It is a tale, old as time, true as life. Every Solstice, a maiden must die to appease the god of the crops, to keep hunger out of our simple kingdom. And I, the Mistress of the Solstice, must be the one to sacrifice her. On that night, every one of our subjects gathers around a bonfire, consumed by the power of love. Of lust, really, for no love could possibly bloom for one night and fade into nothingness, like the elusive fern flower the shier couples pretend to seek when they wander into the woods. The rest hold an orgy right at the bonfire glade, and I, the Mistress of the Solstice, must preside over this feast of love and lust and sacrifice without letting it touch me with its vile clutches. I must be free of love, or everything will turn to doom.

Doom followed me that day as I rode out onto the palace plaza. He blocked my way—a slim young man with straw-colored hair, freckles, cornflower-blue eyes, and a smile of wonder that made him look daft as he stood in front of my horse, gaping.

A fool, really.

He didn't move as I rode up to him, so I was forced to pull my horse to a stop.

"You're in my way."

His smile widened, his eyes wistful as he stared. "You're so beautiful."

I swallowed. I had been told this many times by men much more impressive than him. And yet, these simple words never made me feel like this.

They never made me *feel*.

It was his eyes, I realized. Their cornflower blue held a warmth, a mischievous vigor I had never seen before.

I forced my gaze away, over the frozen crowd of onlookers, toward my guards.

"Get him out of my way," I ordered, urging my horse on.

As I rode, I heard a whiplash and gasps behind me, but I never turned to look.

I am Marya, daughter of Tzar Kashchey the Immortal.

People call him Kashchey the Undead. Not true. He does have a Death, at least one. It dwells on the tip of a needle, just like the legends say. Breaking this needle is the only thing that could kill my father, but he'd taken precautions to make sure it would never happen. He made the needle sturdy, so that no mortal hands could possibly break it. And, he made it look ordinary, like other sewing needles. No mortal could possibly tell them apart. The needle is quite safe, sitting among the others in my sewing box, in my room. My father trusts me, his only living daughter, with his own Death.

Legends depict Kashchey as a withered old man, a walking corpse, but what is the fun of being immortal if you have to spend eternity in such a miserable form? He looks young and handsome, a dark man whose charms leave no woman unfeeling. Not until he tires of them.

It is rumored that my mother had been one of them, the most beautiful woman in the world, a victim of his dark passions. It is rumored that she loved him more than life and that he betrayed her. I don't know and I don't care. I am the Mistress of the Solstice and I know no love. We are two of a kind, my father and I.

My room greeted me with its soothing calmness. Stepping quietly not to wake Raven, asleep on his perch, I walked straight to my Mirror.

"Show me the most beautiful woman in the world."

A stillness enfolded me as the Mirror settled into our familiar game. Its gray mist thinned, revealing my own face. I knew I would see myself, and I could have simply asked the Mirror to show my reflection, but what fun would that be?

I smiled, and my face in the Mirror smiled back at me.

"Show me my thoughts."

My face disappeared. The gray mist wavered beneath the smooth surface of the glass, and then. . .

I found myself staring into a pair of blue eyes, a freckled face bearing that idiotic child-like smile as if he had just encountered a miracle. *The boy from the plaza.*

I drew back from the Mirror, nearly falling over. "Stop!" I shouted, and his face faded into the gray mist. Raven shrieked on his perch, trying to get my attention, but I could see nothing except the cornflower eyes, could hear nothing except the words he had uttered so stupidly back on the plaza. *You're so beautiful. . .*

"How dare he," I whispered. "How dare he tell me I am beautiful!"

"Because you are, Marya," Raven said quietly. "The most beautiful woman in the world."

I swallowed, forcing the trembling out of my clenched hands, forcing the memory of his caressing gaze out of my head. *I must—remain—free. I will. Whatever the cost.*

I knew what I had to do.

I cannot be bonded by love. Even a fleeting attraction is dangerous and must be stopped before it could flourish out of control. I cannot let my thoughts dwell on one man.

When it happens, I know a perfect remedy.

I share my bed with another.

I chose my favorite disguise: an adventurous village girl who ran away from her parents to attend her first Solstice. Such maidens act under a perception that the coming Solstice breaks all boundaries, and they are common objects of protection for wandering knights, and easy prey for passionate men.

I changed my black hair into reddish brown and tinted my eyes brown at the edges, aiming for the subtle look of adventurous inexperience. Big, strong men fall for this kind of thing.

A brown dress over a green undergarment, its neckline low enough to show a bit of cleavage, completed the disguise. Enough to provoke, but not to reveal. Inspecting my appearance, I added some fullness and color to the cheeks and decided that this would do.

The tavern across the palace plaza was full. Its common room was alit with packs of lanterns and drowned in ale vapor and the smell of cheap stew hanging over the crowd like a thick curtain. The background hum exploded here and there with roars of thunderous laughter. Waves of smells and sounds enfolded me as I paused in the doorway, adjusting my assaulted senses to a new level of tolerance.

Gazes followed me like thick, oiled fingers as I walked down to the counter, scanning the crowd from the corners of my downcast eyes. The lust in their gazes brought inadvertent color to my cheeks.

And then I saw my man. Lean, muscular, not too young. Handsome enough to be pleasing, but not overly so. His alert dark eyes followed me with genuine interest and I returned his gaze, holding it with as much promise as a shy young maid would dare. Making sure he was firmly caught, I blushed and looked away.

A group of rogues dominated the bar, the redness of their faces suggesting that they had been here for a while. I chose a lonely chair nearby, in good view of my future hero. Then, I beckoned the servers with a hopeless gesture they were bound to miss. Sure enough, the thin, nervous lad pouring ale two tables over turned his back to me and disappeared behind the bar.

I raised my hand higher and finally got the attention of my noisy neighbors. One of them, a tall man with a red, boar-like face and beady eyes, turned and winked to me, then raised his huge hand.

"Barman!" he bellowed. "This beauty here needs a drink!"

I blushed, putting on a look of unease, turning around as if searching for possible help. I saw my hero in the corner watching, and I did my best not to show my awareness of him.

"Come here, wench!" the man continued, waving to me and struggling to get up. "Join us for some ale." He slurred, too drunk to speak clearly.

It's not going to work. They're all too drunk. But I wasn't about to give up. I pushed away in my chair, moving as awkwardly as I could, so that my scarf slid off the shoulders to the floor. As I bent to pick it up, I made sure to reveal a glimpse of my breasts to the rogue, looking up at him with the helplessness that this type of man finds inviting.

This finally gave him the necessary boost. He fought his way out of his chair and rushed toward me, bumping into tables, causing his drunken companions to laugh at his back. I pretended to struggle as he tore at my dress, leaving a gaping hole. The comb that held my hair slid out, freeing my curls to fall loosely down to the waist. I didn't resist as he savaged my carefully prepared outfit. The only thing I didn't let him do was leave any marks on me. I had to look my best for later.

I hadn't realized that the man I had picked for myself was such a good fighter. He jumped out of his corner, swift as a lightning, and struck down my attacker with a single blow. Three rogues came to the aid of the fallen man, and he knocked down each of them with quick punches, aimed so expertly that none of his opponents even let out a sound. Not bothering to see if any of them would rise, he turned to me as I was standing against the wall, trembling, tears running down my face.

"You are so brave... sir," I whispered, holding my scarf loosely over my torn blouse.

"You shouldn't be alone in such a place. Let me walk you home."

"Thank you, sir." I reached out for his offered hand and drew back again, as one of the holes in my dress opened wider from the movement.

"I suppose you are in no shape to go outside," he said in a fatherly tone.

"I have my needlework with me," I whispered. "If I could only find a place to repair my dress—"

He hesitated. "I am staying in this tavern. Would you consider using my room? I promise you'll be safe."

I looked into his eyes and smiled. A smile of trust. Of hidden promise.

"You are my savior," I said. "I trust you with my life and honor."

Seduction is the only love-game I am allowed, and I enjoy it very much. Nothing is more exciting than making a man want me more than anything, and then allowing him to court me and win my favor. I especially enjoy the way experienced men do it. They savor the contest itself, sparing no detail. And then, as you finally give in, they take over completely, inside and outside. Your body becomes a pure essence of ecstasy under their skillful hands. They worship you like a goddess who granted her mortal admirer a moment of her presence.

And then, when the lovemaking is over, they leave you forever. For they are the wanderers, the seekers, and a woman is interesting to them only if she is new.

But I never wait this long. I like to leave first, before the break of dawn, before the memory grows cold on my body. I turn into my bird form, and fly home, to my tower in the

Tzar's palace. I fly as a dove, above love. I fly free.

I landed on the windowsill and folded my dove wings, shaking off the dampness of the night air. My head still swam with memories as I stood before my Mirror, changing back into my human form. My darkening hair, growing to its normal length. My cheeks, losing their fullness and rosy color. My long black dress, its silky folds caressing my skin, enfolding me down to my bare feet. My chance lover would wonder when he wakes up and sees my peasant clothes still heaped at the foot of his bed. I smiled at the thought.

And then I froze as I saw a shape behind me, by the window.

A man.

He stepped from the shadows toward me, slowly coming into view. I watched as if in a dream his freckled face, his straw hair, his cornflower eyes smiling at me with such gentleness that my heart nearly stopped beating in fear of scaring it away. *The boy from the plaza.*

"Hello, Marya Tzarevna," he said, his gentle voice sending chills through my spine.

His clothes looked different, more appropriate for an audience with the Tzar's daughter. His pants were still baggy, but at least they looked new. His fine linen shirt was embroidered at the neck with an elaborate red pattern. As my eyes traced it, they inadverently slid down to his muscular neck, his arms, the width of his shoulders under the bleached linen. He bore no visible weapon, but his body was lean and fit like that of a warrior.

"Who are you?" I demanded. "How did you get here?"

"My name's Ivan."

His smile was hard to resist. I lowered my eyes not to get caught in it. *Names. Why did I let him tell me his name?*

He reached into his shirt and pulled out a slightly crumpled bouquet of purple and yellow flowers.

"I brought this for you," he said.

In my daze, I reached out to take it before realizing what it was.

The purple and yellow that caught my eye weren't two kinds of wild flowers, as it first seemed. They actually belonged to a single plant, one of the most common found in the nearby forests. In this strange plant, the purple leaves on top contrasted with the bright yellow flowers underneath, which made them look like flowers of two kinds, gathered into a single inflorescence. To reflect this duality, people gave the plant a double name.

Ivan-and-Marya.

My outstretched hand wavered and the flowers cascaded onto the floor.

He didn't seem to notice and continued to look at me, the warmth of his gaze sending shivers down my spine. "See? There's a flower named after us. You and me."

I must call the guards. This is going too far. "If you don't leave this instant—"

His eyes were dreamy. Clearly, he wasn't listening at all. "You're beautiful beyond belief."

I shrugged, struggling to keep my sanity. "Of course I am. Don't you know I'm the most beautiful woman in the world?"

"You are, indeed! And, yet, no legends could possibly do you justice." He reached over and took my hand.

It felt like a surge of fire. My hand melted into his touch like a drop of ice into a patch of spring sunlight. The warmth of his skin, the brush of his fingers against mine echoed through my body.

Blessed Kupalo, give me strength.

I saw a movement out of the corner of my eyes. Ivan's gaze wavered as he saw it too. He dropped his hand away from mine and spun around to face the newcomer. His body tensed up, graceful like a wolf posing for a leap.

A strange mix of relief and regret washed over me as I watched the tall, stately figure clad in black cross the room in a few strides.

My father, Kashchey the Immortal.

His eyes burned like coals in his pale face, framed by the dark, long hair. "Stand back, Marya."

I wanted to step aside, but a strange power pinned me to the spot. It opened my lips and shaped them into words I hadn't meant to say. "But, father..."

He looked at me in surprise. His gaze hardened as he saw me the way I was—shivering, dazed. Lost.

Step aside, foolish girl. Step aside, Marya Tzarevna. Let your father release you. Let him set things right for you before he suspects that you, Mistress of the Solstice, are so close to the feeling that must never touch your soul.

I ordered my feet to move, to leave the space open for my father's deadly powers. But Ivan didn't waste any time. He rushed straight to my sewing box and brought out a needle.

The needle. My father's Death.

"How did you know—" My breath caught in my throat. *How did he pick the right one?*

Only an Immortal could know this. A chill ran down my spine. *Who is this boy? Who is helping him?...*

"Stay where you are, Kashchey," Ivan said. "Or, I'll kill you." His voice was quiet, almost friendly.

My father frowned. "I doubt it. Only an Immortal can break this needle. And you don't look immortal to me. But in a moment we'll know for sure." He raised his hands.

Ivan held the needle in front of him, in the way of the upcoming blast. "*You* can break it, Kashchey, can't you?"

My father hesitated.

"You fool! Put the needle back!" I exclaimed. I meant it to sound threatening. It came out as a plea.

Ivan's gaze softened as he glanced my way. "I'm sorry, Marya. I know you love your father. I don't want to do anything to hurt you. It's just that—"

My father lowered his hands and crossed his arms on his chest. "It would seem that you've come here to play with things you don't understand, boy. Why don't you hand the needle back? I'd hate for it to get messy with your blood and all." He glared.

185

I'd known this look to send people into nervous fits. Yet, Ivan simply stared back. He showed no emotion, and his very calmness screamed caution at the back of my mind. Despite his youth, despite his mellow looks and plain clothes, he looked almost like a worthy foe.

Who *was* he?

"I'll give it back," Ivan said. "If you promise to give up the Solstice Sacrifice."

A smile creased my father's pale lips. "You're not an Immortal, I'm sure of it. From your simple looks I also assume you don't know what you're dealing with. Who put you up to this?"

"Everyone knows what the Solstice Sacrifice is really for," Ivan said quietly. "You use the virgins' souls to feed your power, Kashchey. I'm here to put a stop to it."

I stepped forward. "You're mistaken. People say all kinds of things about the sacrifice, but you shouldn't listen to rumors. The sacrifice is necessary to—"

My father's look stopped me. Something in his face made me feel weak in my knees. But I *knew* the rumors were wrong. The sacrifice was necessary to protect our lands, to prevent hunger and ensure good crops. People didn't know what they were talking about when they spread those foolish rumors.

Did they?

"Fine," Kashchey said with bloodcurdling quietness. "Be a good boy, tell me who put you up to this, give me back the needle, and I'll let you go. Just this once."

Ivan met his gaze. He still looked calm. Too calm for someone facing my father's fury. My skin crept as I heard his quiet voice:

"I challenge you, Kashchey."

My father lifted his chin, his stunned expression dissolving into disbelief, then a smile. "*Challenge* me?"

"I know the rules, Kashchey," Ivan said. "You must now give me a task, and if I fulfill it before the Solstice, you must do what I ask."

My father's smile widened. "Very well, if you insist. In fact,

I usually ask my daughter, Marya, to invent the challenges. She does it so well."

Both men turned to me. Eyes on my father, I stood up straight, feeling lightheaded.

I didn't want this boy to die. And yet, his foolishness left me no choice.

"The Solstice is in three days," I said. "Bring us the Water of Life from the Hidden Stream by that time. Then, my father will consider your claim."

I let out a breath, catching approval in my father's face. We both knew this was an impossible task to fulfill. To travel to the Hidden Stream from our kingdom took months. *No one* could make it in three days, even if he had my Midnight Horse, the fastest horse in the world. And, even if by some miracle Ivan found himself in the right place at the right time, the Hidden Stream would never reveal itself to a mortal.

I was leaving Ivan no chance at all. He was going to die, like many before him. But he didn't seem to care. He just smiled, the innocent vigor in his eyes making my heart ache.

"Very well. See you in three days." His face became gentle as he looked my way. Warmth washed over me, but I forced it away. Whatever this boy made me feel didn't matter anymore.

"I'll see you soon, Marya," he said.

"I don't think so," I mumbled under my father's sarcastic gaze.

With slow, deliberate movements, Ivan wrapped the needle in a piece of leather and stuck it into a pouch at his belt. Then he jumped over the window sill and disappeared.

"It wasn't true what he said about the sacrifice," I said. "Was it?"

My father shrugged. "Come now, Marya, you've never been the one to listen to silly rumors."

"No."

Kashchey nodded, then glanced out the window. "Someone's helping the boy. Someone powerful enough to challenge me."

"Powerful enough to fulfill my task?"

"Let's hope not."

The surface of the lake was still as a mirror, reflecting the light blue and pink of the sunset sky. Flat wisps of evening mist spread low over the water. Thickets of tall reeds rose over them, concealing the real banks of the lake. Tiny swirls of current circled under the smooth surface, creating gleaming patterns. Further upstream, these currents merged into a standing whirlpool—the Sacrifice Pool. Treacherously calm on the surface, its waters pulled you down to the swaying locks of green slimy weeds on the bottom, which caught you and held you underwater in their net of death. That was the place where the Sacrifice Maiden had to go. Where Alyona would disappear today, as many girls did before her.

I slipped out of my dress and stepped into the water, warm like milk fresh from a cow. Gentle currents caressed my body, pulling me into their flow, letting me float in the cradle of their supporting hands. I watched the smooth spears of the reeds piercing dark amber water, visible all the way to the bottom where the green weeds wavered like long strands of hair.

Once ashore, I submitted to the hands of my servants, who dried my body and hair with a long soft cloth and clad me in my white ritual dress. The only words I could say before I finished gathering the herbs and brewing the Solstice Drink of Love were the words of the sacred chant of the herbs, passed from one Mistress of the Solstice to another.

I enjoyed the quiet evening hour all by myself in the slumbering forest. I walked among the trees, through the glades, along the riverbanks. I was seeking out herbs, collecting them, counting them to the slow rhythm of the incantation. Thick, fresh-smelling catnip stems crowned by their umbrella-like inflorescence of tiny blossoms. Cozy, yellow-and-white chamomiles with their faint, bittersweet smell. Elegant lychnis—its fluffy pink flowers resembling tiny campfires— villagers called it *goritsvet*, fire-flower. Fleshy honeyed balls of red clover, and long and fragile stems of bluebells. In the shade of the forest hedge, I searched for the deep purple flowers of nightshade. Just a pinch.

A glimpse of purple caught my eye. I stuck my free hand into the tall grass and pulled out a flower. As I held it to my eyes, I froze, the pile of freshly collected herbs pouring down from my arms.

Purple leaves on top almost hid the delicate yellow flowers underneath.

Ivan-and-Marya.

I threw the purple-and-yellow flower as far away as I could, and slowly sat down in the grass to collect the pile I dropped, and to regain the concentration I needed to finish my task. I could gather the sacred herbs in my sleep. How could I possibly make such a mistake?

Did this boy, Ivan, put a spell over me?

I forced the thought away and finished my task, taking the heap of heady smelling herbs to the Solstice glade.

The last beams of the setting sun crowned the tops of the trees in the west, leaving the glade deep in shadow. The only light here came from the tall bonfire and a smaller cooking fire behind it. I approached it, my arms full of herbs, my servants in a ring around me. People in the glade hastily parted to make way for us. I walked, the incantation with its slow rhythm pounding in my head.

Herbs of the magic brew, six and six,
Blend at my will into potent mix...

My serving women formed a circle around the kettle boiling over the cooking fire, hiding it from view, producing a lonely spot for me to do my magic. I settled in the grass, chanting, sorting out the herbs, counting their stems to make the exact amount needed for the Drink of Love. Through the air of detachment surrounding me I could hear the voices outside my magic circle—people singing as they danced around the glade. But I paid no heed to them.

Six herbs of darkness, six herbs of light...

My pile of herbs was getting smaller as the brew became

189

thicker, gradually acquiring its rich, sweet smell. I watched it grow dark-blue, swirling as the dark herbs, speck after speck, disappeared in its dark depths. The smell was so dizzying that a carelessly taken breath could easily cloud an unprepared mind.

...*Grant me the power, grant me the sight.*

I threw in the last ingredient and spoke in my head the last line of the incantation. The Drink of Love was ready. I turned to my servants and nodded.

Alyona was beautiful in her ceremonial garb that mirrored mine—a long white dress, a wreath of lilies crowning her long, loose hair. She looked ghostly, almost transparent, as she was led through the glade by a procession of men and women from the palace, each holding a candle in their hands. Her eyes were closed and my father, walking behind, carefully guided her steps.

As the procession stopped before me, I took a mouthful of the rich, bittersweet brew and held out the ladle for Alyona to drink. My father and two serving women had to guide her to me and support her as she took a sip with trembling lips. Then she moved on like a sleepwalker, guided by the women's hands. I served the drink to my father, briefly meeting his gaze. Trying to distance myself from the power of the brew, I continued to hold out the ladle for each and every one of my subjects, until the giant kettle was almost empty, and there were no more people waiting to receive their share.

Everyone by now crowded around the Sacrifice Pool, carrying candles. Tiny dots of light reflected in the still waters of the lake like stars, flickering in the slight movement of the night air. Two women at Alyona's side pulled off her white dress, leaving her naked. I admired her beauty in the wavering candlelight. The aura of the Solstice made her look like an immortal spirit of the river.

Everyone stepped aside as I approached her and laid my hands on her shoulders. "Great God Kupalo. Accept this maiden as our gift to your powers and a token of the coming season. May love stay with your subjects, may our fields be fertile and our cattle be aplenty, may you take what you need and leave us what you will.

"Go," I whispered to her gently, turning her around and pushing her toward the water.

She walked forward on trembling legs, straight into the Sacrifice Pool. The waiting waters reached out to her like welcoming arms. She swayed and disappeared from sight almost instantly, without any struggle. As the water covered the top of her head, her lily wreath came loose, floated a little way and sank.

One by one, the people around us set their wreaths afloat in the glimmering candlelit waters and turned to leave the lakeside.

"A fine Sacrifice, Marya," my father whispered at my side as the last of them walked through the line of bushes into the distant glade.

A crackle echoed through the bushes and a shape emerged into the moonlight.

Ivan.

I was certain I'd never see him again. Entranced, I watched him step forward, holding out a hand.

A faint glow emanated from a small vial in his open palm.

"The Water of Life. I brought it. I did what you asked."

"I don't believe you," my father whispered. "It was a task impossible to fulfill."

A row of silent shadows emerged from the darkness along the edge of the glade.

The Immortals. My breath caught in my throat as I watched my father with sudden fear. Could the rumors about the sacrifice be *true*?

"Impossible for a mortal," Ivan agreed. "But I had help."

My father ran his gaze around the glade. "This is a hoax. Even with the help of the Immortals, you couldn't have done it in three days!"

"It *is* the Water of Life," Ivan said. "If you don't believe me,

Kashchey, I'll show you how it works,"

He tucked away the vial, pulled off his shirt, and jumped straight into the Sacrifice Pool.

"Good," my father said. "He saved us the trouble."

Wings flapped as Raven flew out of the darkness and settled on a branch above our heads.

"The Immortals are gathering," he croaked. "I must join them."

The silent shapes around the edge of the glade nodded their heads. They were all here, I realized. The hag, Baba Yaga, and her cousins Leshy and Vodyanoi, the spirits of the forest, water, and swamps. The ancient and powerful beasts, Wolf, Bear, and Cat. And, my Raven.

"What do you all want?" my father demanded.

The Immortals remained still. After a long moment splashing echoed behind the bushes, followed by rustling of the reeds and a sound of something heavy crushing through the forest undergrowth. A silhouette outlined itself against the moonlit waters of the lake.

A man, carrying a naked woman's body in his arms.

"*Alyona*." Entranced, I watched Ivan come up to us and lay her gently on the ground.

She was quite dead, as far as I could tell. The green weeds covered her arms and legs and tangled in her long wet hair. She was paler than the moon, now shining brightly in the sky, and her half-opened eyes didn't have a single spark of life in them. A grimace of agony twisted her once-pretty face into an ugly snarl.

I sank to the ground, my legs suddenly unable to support my weight. Tears flooded my eyes as I took her cold, stiff hand.

"Don't cry, Marya," Ivan said to me gently. "I brought life to her."

He opened the faintly glowing vial and sprinkled water over Alyona's body.

Her grimace gradually smoothened out into a peaceful expression. Color flowed back into her cheeks. Her eyes closed and then reopened, filled with new life.

"Mistress," she whispered, seeing me bend over her.

I took her into my arms and sobbed until I couldn't cry anymore.

"Here are your clothes," Ivan said to her, reappearing with her white ceremonial dress in his hands.

We helped her back into the dress. She tossed her wet hair behind her back and looked around the glade with fear. My serving women appeared and led her away.

"Give me back the needle," my father demanded.

"Will you uphold your end, Kashchey? Will you give up the Solstice Sacrifice?"

"*Give me back the needle!*"

Ivan reached down into the grass and picked up the rectangular object he had put there earlier.

My Mirror.

"How did you—" I whispered.

Ivan turned to me, his guarded expression melting into a smile. "It's for you, Marya. I brought it here so you could see your past."

"My past? But—"

He reached over and held the Mirror in front of me.

Its surface glimmered, giving way to the familiar gray mist. Then it faded to reveal a forest meadow, with a cozy little house cradled in a curve of a quietly tinkling brook.

A young woman ran into sight. A wreath of wild asters crowned her head and she carried a large bunch of forest bluebells. She sank onto the grass by the brook and dropped the flowers, breathing heavily and looking with expectation in the direction she came from.

She was so beautiful that my breath caught with the longing to watch the perfect movements of her slender fingers rummaging through the flowers, her hands absently smoothing the waves of her long black hair, the elegant line of her neck. Her clear green eyes glowed like two emeralds on her warm, lively face. I shivered as I realized why her face looked so familiar. It was my own face—but warm, happy, so full of

love that it made our incredible likeness almost unrecogniz-
able.

What sort of magic was this?

The girl didn't have to wait long. Another shape emerged
from the bushes at the edge of the glade. A man. Pale, dark-
haired, with dreamy eyes and a beaky nose. He also looked
strangely familiar, but I couldn't place why.

They looked into each other's eyes and laughed. Then she
fell into his arms and, after a lifetime of embraces and kisses,
settled her head in his lap. He looked down at her with such
love that my heart ached for him.

It was so real. I could smell the flowers in her hands, the
fragrance of her skin that resembled a fresh smell of water in
a clear forest spring.

The love in the man's eyes was unbearable to watch.

"I have to go, Elena," he said, his voice low and deep, more
so than I expected from his slight form.

"Will you be long?" she asked, too busy weaving together
two bluebell stems to return the man's look.

Such anguish in his eyes! Such pain at leaving her! Why
was I forced to watch this?

"No, my love," his voice was almost a whisper. "I'll be back
soon."

He gently moved her head from his lap onto a soft patch of
grass and rose to his feet. From her lying position she watched
him like a playful kitten.

The man bent down and in a blink of an eye his form
shrunk into a small black shape. In the place where a man
had stood a moment ago there was now a raven.

Raven?

He spread his wings and flew out of sight.

I drew away from the Mirror, breathing hard.

"What did you see in there?" my father demanded.

For the first time in my life I ignored him. I turned to watch
Raven's still form, perched on a low tree branch.

"You had a human form?" I whispered.

He didn't reply. He merely shut his eyes against my gaze.

"It's not the end of the story," Ivan told me. "Watch."

I looked.

The maiden, Elena, was now alone. She spent some more time with her bluebells and then walked off, forgetting the blue heap in the grass beside the brook. She entered the house and came out again, throwing frequent glances into the sky.

And then she froze as a new figure appeared in the glade beside her.

As I caught sight of the familiar form I felt my heart leap and stand still in my chest.

He walked toward the girl with the confident, springy steps of a born charmer. A conqueror, who had just spotted a prey worth his full attention.

My father, Kashchey the Immortal.

I didn't need to watch further to know what happened next.

It was as I suspected. The maiden fell head over heels for my father's charms. She told Raven that Kashchey was her true love, and the silly bird-man let her go. He even gave her his blessing, instead of beating some sense into her pretty little head.

His grief was hard to watch. He was so heartbroken he gave up his human form for eternity.

But there was still more to see.

I looked into a clearing at the side of the lake, the very same one in which we now stood. I could see the mirror gleam of the Sacrifice Pool with its treacherous currents churning underneath the smooth surface. My father and Elena came out of the trees near the large glade where the Solstice celebrations usually took place and stopped to admire the view.

I could see Elena cradling something in her hands.

"This is a good place to swim," my father said. "The best one in the whole lake."

Don't listen to him! I prayed silently. I didn't care what my father did to his women once he was tired of them, but to watch him kill the one that was Raven's whole life was too much.

I didn't want to see it.

I couldn't look away.

"I'd love to go for a swim," she said, her face glowing with happiness. "But I can't leave my baby. She'll freeze."

"Give her to me," my father said. "I'll keep her warm for you. For us." He gave her an affectionate look that I knew was a lie.

Elena hesitated for a moment. Then she opened her palm and handed the thing she held to my father.

It was an egg. A spotted bird's egg.

"I wish she could grow up to be human," Elena whispered, looking fondly at the egg.

"She will," my father said. "After all, her father had a human form once. After she hatches, I'll teach her to change shape like he used to. Now, go, swim, my love, we'll be waiting for you right here."

Elena was as gullible as I suspected. Without hesitation she pulled off her dress and jumped straight into the Sacrifice Pool. As soon as she did, my father turned and walked back into the forest.

It took her a long time to die. She struggled with a force that I didn't suspect in her slender body. As the air filled with her screams, a black bird flew out of the woods and darted straight to the Sacrifice Pool.

Raven.

He circled low over the water, trying to pull her up with his claws, trying to fetch something big enough for her to hold on to. He got so dangerously close that her gripping hands almost pulled him underwater with her.

He would have given his life for her. But in his bird form he could do nothing to help her. If only he hadn't forsaken his human form!

His eyes were two ponds of despair as he watched her agony, drenched and exhausted, unwilling to give up and yet powerless to do anything for his love except to die with her. In the end, he chose life. Perhaps it was for the sake of the egg, his unborn child, now safely in Kashchey's possession. As her screams finally ceased, as the water closed over her head one last time, he dropped in fatigue on the bank of the lake and lay there for a long time.

I never knew that birds could cry.

Numb, I stumbled away from the Mirror and sank onto the grass.

"What did you do to her?" my father demanded.

"I showed her the true story of her birth," Ivan said. "And, of the first Solstice sacrifice in this kingdom."

"The first sacrifice?" I whispered, trying to make sense of his words.

"Kashchey killed the maiden and devoured her soul," Ivan said. "But her love for him was so great it made him immortal. Or, rather, Undead. This ritual kept him young all these years. But it's time to put a stop to it."

"Who are you?" my father whispered.

Ivan smiled. "A man with nothing to lose. My family left me to die, and the Immortals gave me life back. In return, I promised to carry this through."

Dazed, I turned to Kashchey and met his dark gaze.

"Why?" I whispered. "Why did you kill my mother?"

Raven's eyes opened in a flash. "You killed her, Kashchey?" The air trembled from the force of his shriek. "*You killed her?*" He shot down from the branch like a black arrow and grabbed the needle from Ivan's hand. Rising high in the air, he bit it in half.

The ground shook with thunder. Kashchey twisted in terrifyingly slow motion, losing his normal shape, turning from a dark, handsome man into a misshapen corpse, and then, gradually, to dust. A gust of wind rose from the ground and blew it away, until nothing remained.

As the rustle settled above the tree crowns, the dark shapes of the Immortals turned and disappeared into the forest.

I woke up to the feeling of a hand running down my cheek, arms holding me, supporting my lifeless body. I was blind and unfeeling. I was dead. I was a dove, the daughter of a raven who had given up his human form, and a beautiful maiden betrayed by her love. I had been the Mistress of the Solstice, but everything I did, everything I believed in, turned out to be a lie.

A voice, gentle like the rustle of sunlit wheat and cornflowers on a bright summer afternoon, whispered into my ear. This voice made me aware of my body, limp against the lively form that supported it and kept it from collapsing on the ground. This voice slowly called my senses back to me one by one—the chill of the morning breeze, the soft murmur of the flowing water. But I still couldn't see. My eyes were shut forever, unable to bear the sight of someone I thought to be my father, someone who was my whole world, turning into an evil devourer of souls, blown to dust.

"Marya." A soothing voice, gentle like the hands that caressed me, took away the pain.

I stirred and opened my eyes.

The new day was already dawning. In front of me was the lake, bathed in the soft eastern glow. A low branch was clearly outlined against the mirror-still water, a bird's shape perched upon it, so black that it seemed to absorb the light.

As he saw me looking, he turned and met my gaze.

"Father," I called out softly.

"Be happy, Marya," Raven said gently.

I turned to Ivan, so infinitely close as he held me in his arms that I could never tell the two of us apart anymore. I felt as if I was coming home, as if a part of me that was missing for the longest time found its way back to its rightful place, making me feel, for the first time in my life, complete. Like the yellow flowers of a small forest plant, I found my way into the shelter of the purple leaves, which together made a complete living thing, a single inflorescence.

Ivan-and-Marya.

BUT CAN YOUR LET HIM GO

by

Cindy Lynn Speer

This is me. The caution in your tale, the one with the thousand guises. Right now my disguise is nothingness, as I follow a farmer, leading his donkey down the dusty path into town. The donkey is well fed and the distance left to travel is long, yet the man has made no move to ride it, or the cart it is pulling.

Kindness, then. It is confirmed when he reaches up and scratches the donkey between its long, dark grey ears, and says, "Not far, now. We will rest in a few minutes." He is not thin, but one of those stocky, stable men, and soaked with sweat from the afternoon heat, so I am not sure if he is comforting himself or the animal. He has an air of being decently well off. Not rich, but his belongings are in good condition and unpatched.

So, what is your vice? That is what I ask, always, as I study the people I meet. Are you vain? Are you greedy? Do you let your resentments fester? Do you lust after what is not yours? His was not readily apparent, which made things more complex. After all, if he abused his animal, I could simply switch his and the donkey's souls and call it a day. Or just trade their heads. I'd done it before, though, and was bored with the idea.

He led us off the road, and soon we were under shade, near

water. I watched him avidly, but he watered his animal first, then let him crop the grass. The land was not well grazed, which made me wonder if many people knew about this spot.

I waited for him to settle down, slipping a short distance away. I changed my hair color to a bright gold, but I let it be matted. My face was pretty, delicate, but my body was thin, my clothes old and worn. There was just enough dirt to make me look poor, impoverished, but not disgusting. Pathetic was what I was looking for.

I ran through the trees, and then tripped and fell into the clearing only a few feet away from my quarry.

I made a little, terrified squeak of horror.

He'd jumped up and drawn a knife when I fell into the clearing, but now he looked at me, trying not to laugh. "Tis all right," he said. "I won't hurt you."

I gave him a doubtful look, but then I turned my attention to the feast he had set out on a cloth, as if unable to maintain my suspicion in the face of food. Fresh brown bread, a half a wheel of creamy white cheese, preserved sausage. "Please." I said, and then I swallowed. "Please, sir... can I have... I am so hungry, sir." I looked up at him with huge brown eyes, silently begging. He looked back at me. I saw his tongue touch the corner of his mouth, and I thought, *Aha. How easy and predictable men are.* I was tempted to heave my chest a little, but I didn't want to encourage him further. Men were perfectly capable of falling all on their own. And his eyes did fall, to the torn blouse, that revealed just on the edge of too much, then back up to my face. He winced.

"I certainly have enough to spare," he said, and turned, kneeling. He cut a generous piece of the bread. I did not need to look into the future to know already what it would be. He would give me food, ask me questions, I would tell him the same story I told everyone, and he would ponder what, if anything, he should do for me. The danger, such as it was, had passed.

When he turned, smiling, his hand filled with bread, I was gone.

"Girl?" he called. "Girl? I promised. I won't hurt you..."
He looked around for me, but I was gone.

I remained on that part of the road for several days, half
waiting for him to come back through. The blue birds were
leading me to the next destination on the path of my life, but
I was dawdling on purpose. Many years ago I'd been in a
battle, one so furious that I'd had to retire to the trees and
sleep. The last full moon had seen me rise again at last, but I
still felt odd. The magic that makes up who I am seemed to be
leaking out of some small hole in me, like fine sand through
cloth. Perhaps, I am fading at last, but I can't just yet. Not
until I have done that one thing that I must.

The farmer was in a better mood when I next saw him, and
I knew his business had gone well. Who should I be, this
time? A crone, of course...is there anything else? I made
myself ugly, misshapen, one eye milky, the other seeming to
wander of its own accord. Soon I was making my way up the
road toward him, leaning heavily on my stick. He passed me
without looking at me, and I knew I was disturbing, but a
truly good soul would not care. "Sir," I called in my twisted
voice, "Sir, I am so hungry, do you have bread to spare for an
old woman?"

He sidled closer to the donkey. "I am sorry...I have nothing."

"But you are just back from town. Did you not do well in
the market? Did you not pack something for your journey
home? I do not ask for much, just a crust..."

"I told you, I have nothing!" He quickened his pace.

"But you had plenty when you thought I was young and
beautiful." My voice changed before my body, so he turned
and looked. Confusion becoming revulsion, as I changed before his eyes, warped into a delicate, golden-haired urchin.
"You even thought about bedding me, did you not, for the
price of my supper?"

He stepped back again, hand on the cart wheel. He was
still afraid, and he was wise to be so. "Yes. For one moment I
did, but I wasn't going to. And I mean it. I have nothing..."

"Don't lie to me." I sniffed the air, tilted my head. "You have two...no, three wheels of cheese in the back, a basket of preserved honeyed apples, three barrels of decent ale...on your person, there is ham and bread..." I met his eyes. "Winter provisions? Something to give you warmth and joy during the bleak, hard winter? But there are real people with nothing in this world. What about the old ladies and homeless maids? What about the men who can no longer work or the abandoned mother? What joy or warmth do they get?"

He looked ashamed, I'll give him that.

"I'm not expecting you to lead a crusade, Farmer, for we all hurt the world though our own selfish natures. I just expect you to do good when the opportunity is presented. Now, what shall I do to you?" I squinted at him, pointing a finger, rotating it, considering his fate. "How shall I make an example of you ?"

He did not plead. Usually they do. They beg, they make promises of varying grandeur.

He did not.

He did not try to reason, as often happens. Nor explain why he had done what he had done, or to prove that really, it was a mistake, and in general he was a pretty decent man.

He did not.

He did not try to bribe me. Some do. They try to show me that they are my friend, and that they are willing to give or do something to help me, just make it all go away.

He did not.

What he did was meet my eyes, levelly, with some little bit of resignation, another twist in the road of life, to be accepted and lived through.

We stared at each other a long time. I kept trying to think what to do, but nothing came to me. Nothing I could bear doing to him. "Are you sorry?"

He blinked, and then said, after a moment, "I am, yes. Not because you've told me to be so, but because I think that you have a point." There was a bit of pride in those words, but I let them pass.

I folded my hands, slowly, over my waist. I let go of the spell, and he saw me as I am. As tall as he, slender, darkened from long days in the sun, hair a sun-streaked brown with a little green. "I think I'm changing." I said, and I was frightened.

"I suppose we all must." He said his words carefully, as if talking to a wild horse. "Where are you going? Do you wish a ride?"

I shook my head furiously. I'd lost the heart for it all. I should do something. People didn't leave my presence unscathed.

"Be good." I said, fiercely. "Be good." And between one blink and the next, I was gone.

I tried to forget him as I followed the path through the forest. My blue-feathered companions fluttered impatiently ahead of me, leading me to the bank of a wide river. They did not cross yet, nor did they lead me to a suitable crossing, so I conjured a small boat. A bird settled on the bow, a tiny blue speck of body and long, curled feathers of red.

He and I floated down the winding river, the forest fading into a new kingdom. High on a hill, a castle overlooked the river and city. The city gave way to villages, villages spread out into what looked like rich farm land. It was cupped in a valley formed by mountains. I thought it beautiful but familiar, though after all this time, my destinations always looked familiar.

It called something inside of me, as I stepped out of the boat and up onto the bank. The bird flew three circles around me, and then took off, showing me that I truly was at my destination. The boat disappeared with a word, and I stretched. Truthfully, I had been wandering for so long I scarcely remembered what the place I had started from was like, but as I picked my way down to the main road, I realized it did not much matter. I had my job ahead of me, the familiar, endless task. There were two people to find, to be brought together.

To find her is not hard. You listen for the tales of a girl who is kind. She rarely, if ever, has a mother. Usually the father, if he is still alive, has remarried.

To find the man is even easier. Find the handsomest one. The wealthiest, the highest of the nobility, and you've probably located him. It has even been so, and will be, time and again, until the end of the sun.

Forgive me if I sound bored. I have lived this story so many times, the search, the hope, the sorrow. I know the ending already. It is etched in my bones, and I am not certain how to stop it.

Although the players in this tale are easy to recognize, sometimes it is almost as if they are purposely hiding from me. Stone is no friend of mine, so I cannot feel for her through the cobbles that make up the path toward the town center. My steps were taking me to where the village lapped up against the city, where tall walls surrounded homes. I was tired, but I wanted to find her ere I took my rest.

Listen, I told myself, *breathe and listen.*

> *Your voice, to me,*
> *is the sweetest wine.*
> *I long for to hear it.*
> *It brings me joy. . .*

She had a sweet singing voice, clearer than air, more delicate than a nightingale. It came from the other side of a courtyard wall, so I followed it, hoping the gate was open. It was, and the dark iron, open on each side, framed a young woman hanging laundry, shaking sheets out with a snap, and then pinning them into place. I leaned against a tree, begging for strength. My eyes closed, and I felt for the reassurance of the wood.

A damp, cool hand touched my brow. I looked at her.

Eyes like the sky.

"Are you all right?" She held a cup out to me. "Here, I have drawn you some water. Take it, you will feel restored."

"This is the second time," I wanted to tell her, "That you have offered me water." Instead, I took the cup, and drank.

"You are kind," I said. "Thank you."

She smiled and patted my arm. "I am happy to help. Come, sit in the courtyard. The family is not home, they will not speak against it."

I allowed myself to be led to a bench, and I watched her, feeling myself warmed by her spirit as if by the sun. Through the years, I've grown to love her. There has never been a time—not once—when she has not been kind. I have been in a million forms, and always she has been a friend. It is a bittersweet love, for it stabs me every time I see her, yet I am drawn to it.

"What can I do for you, my child, in return for your kindness?" I fall back into my habits, to save me from thinking too much.

She knelt by a large, wooden bucket. A cauldron was boiling on a fire, and she used a smaller pail to scoop some of the water out and pour it on the laundry. "Tell me a story? As you can see, I have much work, but a story would make it go much faster."

I drank some more, and then said, "I will tell you a very, very old story..."

She smiled, tucked soft, golden hair behind one ear, and resumed her work, listening as I spoke.

This is what I told her, with a little less honesty.

"Once," I said, "There was a woman. She had no real home, for her people lived in the trees of the forest. They slept snug and safe in the very fibers of the wood. And this young woman had a favorite place to go, deep in the heart of the forest..."

In this forest, there is a tree so huge and so great with age that it takes time to walk around it, and a dozen large men joining hands could not circle it. It was large when I first knew it, and my parents, my little sister and I could clasp hands around it, but the last time I saw it, it was practically a fortress.

As I tell her the tale, I long to I sink myself into that tree, allow myself to move into it, my body becoming wood grain, my blood becoming sap. It is a dangerous tree, because it is so very deep that you could get lost in it. The further you go in, the more isolated from the world you become. The deeper you sink, the less likely you are to notice the passing of days, the flight of the birds, the presence of a man sitting at your base, taking his ease.

Would that I had sunk ever so deep into the center of the tree the day he came. Would that we had never seen each other at all.

But no. Back then, I liked to be able to open my eyes, take a peek at the world around me. I was young, and did not need the solace of the very center of the tree, did not need the comfort, the energy of the earth pumped right into my heart. And one time, when I opened my eyes, I saw a young man, a hunter, with strong limbs, and pale eyes, and hair like the sun.

He was sitting against my tree, carving away at a chunk of fallen wood, cutting away the bark, the weathered skin, bringing up pale, clean flesh. He smoothed it gently as he worked, creating subtle, smooth curves. I stepped out of the back of the tree and leaned against it, looking over his shoulder. "What is it?" I asked. "Is it a shoe?"

He jumped quickly, the knife readied to carve into me. I hid my face against the rough bark of the tree, and smiled coyly at him.

"Where did you come from?" he asked, relaxing his stance, but not, I saw, his eyes. He was ready in case I had friends about to attack.

"Not far from here."

I stepped away from the tree, dressed in a long dress of cloth only a little finer than the rough fabric that adorned him.

"I still call my father's hearth home. He lives up there." I pointed with my chin.

It wasn't really a lie. My people gathered there from time to time.

"And you? Where do you come from?" I stepped closer,

and he let me.

I put my hand on his warm skin, and he did nothing but watch me, warily. "So warm," I muttered, and partly closed my eyes, like a lizard on a rock. I wanted to get closer to that sun-blessed skin.

He looked down at me, his eyes studying my face, a bemused look edging his expression as I made myself look beautiful to him, as I subtly changed myself to match what seemed to be found pleasing in his eyes.

Do you know the myth, that one should never eat the food of faery, or be forever trapped? That is true, in its way. To eat or drink of the things of faery is to taste of something so uncommon, so blessed and lovely, that one is forever spoiled. Mortals who taste of us either stay with us forever, or spend their lives wishing for what they'd experienced. They search for the taste, the feeling, the joy, but find them not in human things. Some are fortunate enough to find one of us who will take them into service, but most of them pine away, unable to enjoy what they have for the longing of what they do not.

It is the same with lovemaking between faery and human, which is why we are forbidden to touch their kind. I will not lie to you. I knew that. I looked into his eyes, and into that face that rivaled even my own kind for perfection....and I forgot.

"She doesn't sound like a very nice lady, this faery," she said, scrubbing a muddied hem. I blinked at her, and then drained the cup.

"I don't think she was intentionally cruel," I said. "I rather think...I think she just didn't understand herself. Anyway, it's just a story. What's your name?"

She stopped, and I wasn't certain if it was because she was surprised at the abrupt change in topic, or because she wasn't sure if she wanted to say.

"Eleanor." She stood and shook her skirts, and then took the empty cup from my hands. "I need to fetch aught from the house...may I bring you anything? I should like to hear more."

I shook my head, and watched as she went into the house. I still could not believe I had allowed the farmer to pass and worried about what it meant. I consoled myself that his sin was not so great, but in truth I knew I had failed in my task. Failure was not a new concept, but usually it wasn't something I could help. I was getting weak. Perhaps I was fading, after all, to become nothing but the whisper of wind through the trees... if I was lucky.

She came back out, her arms full of cloth. After a moment of settling in again, she asked, "So, what happened to the man? Did the faery free him?"

"She could not. But one cannot think of the man she had taken as her lover without thinking of another woman that, by doing so, she had wronged..."

My clearest image of her is this: standing by the road, hugely gravid, the wind playing with her pale gold hair and rough spun clothes. Her feet were bare, as an unmarried woman's would be. She looked to the left, and the wind pushed her hair into her eyes. Her hands shook slightly as she pushed the strands back. He comes around the bend, but he is different. Hunger and anguish and longing had brought winter to his summer far too soon. His face is gaunt, and though she steps out onto the road and waves to him, calling his name in a hopeful voice, his eyes look right through her.

The mother of his child watches, her face turning like a flower to the sun, her hair streaming behind her.

I was there, forced to stand and watch by my father, who was furious at me for what I had done. They had sent physicians and magicians alike after him, to break the bond between us, to cure him of me, but it could not be done.

I did not try to speak to my father. I had already discovered that he would not allow it. After she gave up and began to wander down the road, he grabbed my arm and took me into the forest, and I turned one last time, and looked at her. "At least do something for her," I said. "Let me try..."

My words were cut off as I was thrown into the tree. It closed around me, gentle, as if it understood that I was not such a bad person, but firm, for it would not let me out of my punishment.

I was trapped there when he died—of starvation, or exposure, or madness, no one ever told me.

But I was told that he died, and more, for my father leaned against the tree, and spoke to me. He spoke of one night, when the sky was filled with stars, of a pregnant young woman going for a walk. Her eyes fastened on the bright shining lights above.

She looked neither left nor right, but kept walking, her night-dark eyes reflecting the cosmos above. She walked up a hill, a place that chieftains often used as a look out, for it was a tall place, and the view was far.

She walked off the edge of the cliff, there. She did not look down. She did not pause.

We all pay for our sins.

That is what I have become.

I see you in your weakest moments, and I strike, merciless, harsh, and without stay or reprieve. It does not matter who you are, or what you were, what good you have done or plan to do. All that matters is now.

This is what my father condemned me to in his last words to me. It seems to me a cruel punishment, but he was disappointed. He thought I would turn out better than my sister.

Most of you are not as dark a sinner as I. After all, I am responsible for the deaths of two people. What you have done is nothing compared to me. And yet, I judge you. I do so because I must.

"The poor woman was cast out from her family?" Eleanor rinsed the petticoat, inspected it one last time, then wrung it out and hung it on the line. "Poor thing."

"She murdered two innocents through her actions."

"She didn't really. She didn't know what would happen."

I helped her carry the wash tub to a corner of the yard, where we dumped it.

"But she was selfish. If she had been good, and thoughtful, things would not have come to pass as they did."

Eleanor looked unconvinced, but her shoulders moved under her ragged dress, as if to push it aside. "Thank you for the story, it really did pass the time. It is so rare to receive such a treat. I am very grateful."

"Perhaps," I said, "If you like, I can come back."

There was a clattering at the gate, and she looked up, resigned.

She moved forward as the coach came into the yard, and then looked behind her, to say something, perhaps to warn me.

I knew she would be punished if her family saw me, so I became invisible.

She frowned, looked around, but they were calling her name, barking it shrilly, so she hurried away.

There were two sisters, one tall and very pretty, though her face was quite pinched. She would have to wed soon, for when the bloom of her youth was gone in its place one would see a sour, bitter visage.

The second was a bit shorter, homier looking. Weak, I could see. Left with good people she would have blossomed and been quite sweet, but she did not have the inner strength to fight her family.

Lastly, out came the girls' mother. I drifted back, shock running along my being. I knew her. I knew her like my own self, but could not place her. She was beautiful, with a cruel mouth that seemed forever twisted in some secret joke. I was surprised she was not married again already, but then, perhaps her husband was not dead.

"You stupid girl! You've hung the laundry too close to the front gate," she said, though I could tell from the curve of the drive that she had ordered the coachman to steer toward the clothesline.

He looked uncomfortable and ashamed.

Eleanor said nothing, but the look she gave the driver was kind.

It was true that the dust from the carriage coming off the drive and into the dry courtyard had risen like a thick cloud and drifted toward the laundry, but not one speck of dirt had landed on the newly washed sheets and clothes. I had made sure of it, so when the stepmother wandered over to inspect her handiwork she saw nothing to complain about. She frowned and walked into the house, her daughters following.

I did not need to follow, to see the kind of life she lived. I already knew. Instead, I decided to find the other half of the puzzle.

The castle was huge, a long bridge leading across the moat to marble stairs that led up to the entranceway, a huge gate thrown open to the world, but guarded by soldiers who flanked every step.

No one stopped me, not even when I entered the palace proper, because they saw me, and yet did not, so it was easy for me to enter the gilded sunroom where the ladies of the court settled, to bow to the queen, who nodded and waved me aside. No one asked me who I was or what I was doing there. Some of them frowned at me, but ignored the questions in the back of their minds, knowing that I must belong right where I was, and everything was perfectly the way it should be.

"As I was saying," the queen spoke to the woman in gold and green on her left, "I don't know what goes on in his mind. Surely he realizes that he should marry, but he wants to wed for love. Love! Can you countenance such foolishness? Surely I cannot." She took a sip of wine.

The other woman muttered something incoherent, as if afraid of being understood.

"Exactly. I certainly didn't love his father, but I did well enough, did I not?"

I cleared my throat, and inched forward on my knees. "Your majesty, I beg your leave to speak?"

She looked at me, as if trying to place me. She knew I belonged there, but how? Was I a trouble maker? Was I a sycophant?

I smiled shyly, not raising my eyes.

"Well?" she asked.

"May I venture the idea that, perhaps, an illusion of love will do? Hold a ball. Invite the finest and most eligible women, dressed in their most marvelous clothes. Surely, one will catch his eye, and maybe even his heart. If you move quickly, you can have him wed before the shine comes off of her."

I put careful power behind my words. I made the idea feel like her own. I made it feel like the most magnificent idea ever.

"Yes." She leaned back in her chair, her eyes a little dazed.

I might have pushed too hard.

"We will have a ball. And whom he chooses, he shall wed." She smiled a little, and I rose and disappeared from the room and from their memories.

"A ball? Do you think they will really hold one?" We were in Eleanor's kitchen, where she was kneading bread.

"I have heard it would be so from the most reliable of sources. All the eligible maids of the kingdom will be invited. It was the queen's own idea. Apparently they are quite desperate to marry him off."

Her blue eyes went dreamy. "I should like to marry him. You will not believe me, but when I was a child and papa still alive, I met the prince. We played together in the garden while papa and the king talked about things. I never knew what. The prince was the sweetest boy. And a handsome man, now. I wonder if he would recognize me? I have not been a part of genteel society for so long. . . ."

There was a long silence, as she remembered the boy she'd known. I wonder if they'd recognized each other, even as children.

"You are melancholy. Let me tell you another story."

She smiled at me, looking up through her eyelashes. "I should like that above all things." The bell at the front clanged, and she sighed. "Duty first. You will wait, won't you?"

As always, the silence gave me time to think. I sat on a

stool in the sun and looked out at the yard, at the goat, the chickens, the small garden.

I knew the tale I would tell her. When she came back, I told her the following story, more or less.

Once upon a time, I was freed from my prison. I wandered the world, my wooden cloak the only thing to keep me warm, my silver knife my only possession. The rest was imagination. I found myself following the stars, like her, but unlike her I did not fall, I kept my gaze down. I became a fish and swam to new lands, and eventually I ended up in a land made of patches of verdant green and lush riverbanks edged with an endless desert.

The people there lined their eyes with kohl and wore fine linen, their flesh never seeming to know winter. I spelled my cloak away and let the hot sun pour into me. I made my hair dark and carefully cut, my skin bronze, and gave myself a beautiful pleated sheath of linen decorated with gold and jewels. Excitement made my heart pound, but I did not know why. Perhaps it was simply being part of the world again.

I saw a man beating his slave. I turned his staff into a snake, and it bit him. I gave the frightened slave a jar of ointment and told him how to use it to cure his master. I was about to switch the souls of a mistress and her servant, so that the kind, gentle servant could live the live the life that the hard-eyed, calculating mistress took for granted, when I heard someone call.

Many guards; oiled, handsome, strong men surrounded a litter. On it rested a man whose eyes were never still, who despite looking relaxed, seemed to be taking in every detail of his people.

"Do not look directly at Pharaoh, girl! Your eyes will be burnt out, as if by the sun!" the mistress hissed at the servant.

His eyes met mine, and it felt for a moment as if the words proved true, that I was burning. I smiled, coyly, and dropped my eyes, but I could feel the weight of his stare as he passed.

My heart leapt in my breast, for I realized that my lover had been reborn. I walked away as if on air. He was handsome;

kohl outlining eyes that seemed brighter than the gold that decorated the tombs. That had not changed. And his body was still so strong. How to get to him? How to meet with him again?

I had wandered into the slave market unknowing and I found myself looking at a girl with eyes like the sky.

"A foreign slave! Look at this jewel from another world! Hair like gold, eyes like lapis lazuli!"

She looked a little scared, but also brave, as if she would make the best out of the situation.

Of course, if he was born again, so was she. I did not feel great joy at this, but as if a heavy weight had been placed upon my shoulders. A good weight, I tried to tell myself, a chance at redemption.

A man, heavy, but not grossly so, looked at her with quiet longing. Finally, he started bargaining with the seller, another man competing with him. The three haggled until I be-spelled the newcomer, causing him to forget his interest in the girl. He wandered off, and the first man purchased her, gently untying her and taking her hand. He said something earnestly to her, and she nodded.

I followed them home, becoming nothing but shadow. I could do nothing else, for I knew she was my lover's intended bride. If I wanted to appease my angry father, I must find a way to make things right.

Still, my stomach hurt with anger at the thought of her having him while I could not. It did not seem fair.

Her name was Rhodopis. His name was Amasis.

My name? Well, my name is not one that anyone remembers, not even me.

Rhodopis' master loved beauty, even though he was too sick to truly enjoy it. He slept most of the time in a walled garden, while his slaves—one dozen beautiful women—tended the house and lived a gilded life. Rhodopis was his favorite, for her unusual coloring made her glisten like a star in the darkness, and her gentle nature made her a joy to be around. This caused the other women to hate her. They beat her. They tried to starve her, and they spoke to her cruelly. I watched her carefully, this time a bird that sat in the tree overlooking the garden, but she said nothing.

"I knew the great Aesop, and he told me such stories, my lord. Shall I tell them to you, and ease your rest?" she would ask him, and he would smile gratefully and say yes. She tended him lovingly, dutifully, the only one to do so without being asked.

If there were a pitcher emptied, it was filled before the inside could fully dry. Her capable hands washed his brow, her sweet voice rivaled the songs of birds. The others lounged around and bickered when they had no further duties, but he was too kind to say anything against them.

One night when he was particularly upset, she stood up and quietly swept the blue tile floor. I hopped a branch closer, and watched as she brushed her feet off, then leapt forward onto the smooth tile, and spun. She spread her arms, her hands and wrists moving slowly and gracefully, turning into the steps of the dance.

It was eerie, for she made not a sound save for the slightest shuffle of her bare feet on the stone. There was no music, just the silence as all of us, her jealous fellow slaves, her kind master, and I, watched her move with precision and grace, as if one of the temple spirits had come to visit us.

They say, in stories, that birds weep. They cannot, so all I could do was bury my eyes under my wing while my heart bled, and beneath me, soundlessly, her master wept the tears I could not.

She finished by throwing herself to her knees, inches away from the pillows her master rested upon. I looked in time to see him come forward, rest both his hands on the back of her bowed head, and lower his face to kiss her hair. "What can I do for you? Shall I free you? Shall I give you this house when I am gone? Tell me, dear child."

She looked up at him. "I want shoes."

With that, I flew away, and as a woman I wept, and pounded my hands against the dirt, devoured by guilt as ugly as hate. Though her mind did not know why, her soul still longed for the shoes her beloved had been carving for her the day we met.

And oh, what slippers he, her master, gave her. They were made of rose-colored gold, crafted especially for her by one of the best slipper makers in the kingdom. They were patterned with ocean waves. She wore them constantly, both because she loved them, and because, if she did not, one of the other servants would surely steal them.

In the mean time, I often went to see Amasis. I watched him in his rooms, mentally stabbing myself in the heart as he paced alone. The excuse was that I was waiting for a chance to do my duty, for it was not easy to bring together a slave girl and a Pharaoh, but the truth was that I so loved being near him that I could not stay away.

I was there when he called for his scribe. "We will celebrate the consecration of the temple to Ptah at Ineb Hedj." He played with the end of a parchment, rolling it idly. "I want the entire kingdom to be invited, from the most insignificant to the greatest. We will have great sacrifices. I am told that our stores are well filled with grain, so we shall celebrate by feeding all those who attend."

His scribe started discussing gently—for no one argued with Amasis—that giving away so much bread might not be the wisest thing, but my mind was filled with other things. This was the chance for Rhodopis to meet Amasis, at last.

The master was pleased by the news, more than pleased. He hired a litter, so that if he needed to he could lie down, and called together his lovely servants, and gave all of them the finest clothes. They all received shifts of equal worth, but no one had slippers to rival the golden-haired one. I watched over her clothes with care, ready to scratch out the eyes of any who thought to despoil them. The ladies were too clever for that, instead, they took sand and dirt and threw them on the master's bed clothes. The one who had once been the favorite ran, and told the master that Rhodopis had been neglecting her chores.

216

They all stood gathered. Her face becoming pale under her tan as he came over to her, and took her chin in his hand.

"Is this true? Have you been neglecting your work?"

They all knew that if she said no, then all the women would be punished by not being allowed to go, and her life would be unlivable. If she said yes... she swallowed, and said, quietly, "I had not noticed that it was so. I beg you, let me stay and try to make up for it."

He looked sad. He knew what had happened, but he felt too weak to do anything about it, so he nodded and walked away.

"I want to go see the celebration at Ineb Hedj, too." I squawked at her.

She did not understand, but put out a little grain for me before she went to the river to do her washing.

I ignored it, pacing angrily.

But, when was anything in life ever that easy, even for those who could do magic?

When I finally followed her, she was singing as she worked.
> To hear your voice
> is pomegranate wine to me.

I alighted next to her gold shoes, which sat, safe, on a stone.
> I draw life
> from hearing it.

I tilted my head, and looked at the shoes, glittering in the sun. She was not looking, busily scrubbing at some spot, so I became a much larger bird, a falcon. I grabbed a slipper with my beak and flew off, not minding her pleas to come back.

I found Amasis, diving so I could throw the slipper right into the Pharaoh's lap, then I landed on the back of his throne, preening myself meaningfully while people murmured the name of Horus. I raised my wings and flew away to become a woman and wander the celebration.

"Did you hear? Did you? Every woman in the Kingdom is to try on the slipper, and the one that can wear it, the Pharaoh will make his wife! It is the decree of Horus!"

My eyes widened. I hadn't considered that everyone would

get a chance. I quickly went to get in line so I could watch. Thus far no one fit the slipper. I looked at it, willing it to shrink to refuse to take any foot that tried it on. By the time I got to the front of the line my eyes burned from the effort, and my head began to ache.

I looked up at Amasis, and he looked down at me, and smiled.

Somewhere he knew me, I thought. Somewhere he still was hunting for me. It was tempting to place my foot inside that slipper, to feel it cup the curves of my foot lovingly, to take my place at his side.

I offered my bare foot coyly. He wanted it. I wanted it. Who would I hurt? I slipped my toe into the slipper, and I wondered, if his skin would still taste the same, all heat and honey and salt?

"It doesn't fit." The servant in charge of the testing said. He, too, seemed tired.

Amasis was disappointed. "Are you certain?"

It took all my will power to turn my foot, to show the heel hanging a good portion out. "I am sorry, Great One."

"Sire?" It was Rhodopis' master. "I have just now been able to see the slipper, and I know well who it belongs to. . . "

I bowed and left. I did not look back, for I was filled with pain that was like to make my heart break.

It felt less so when I changed again, became a fierce and strong falcon, and took to the skies looking for Rhodopis, as no one could find her.

The bane of my life, that girl, I thought as I searched and found her hiding by the river, her other shoe hidden in some laundry. Ahead I could see Amasis in his barge. "I'm sorry, my lord, they cannot find her." a servant said.

He frowned. "Very well, then. We shall return to the palace."

He was giving up! I could not believe it. I flew up, and called mightily, and he saw. I circled where she was hiding.

"Rhodopis?" he called into the growing night. The barge drew close to land, and he leapt upon the grass and called again.

She came and knelt at his feet, refusing to look at him. She was terrified. I wished to comfort her but I did not dare.

"I am told that this slipper is yours." He held it in his two hands, like an offering for the altar. "Would you please try it?"

She did so, trembling, then drew the other from the laundry and put it on her unshod foot. He laughed with joy and kissed her on the forehead.

"She will be my wife. It has been decreed!"

That should have been the end of the story. The end of all of this. But it was not.

The master threw a great party to celebrate the joyous union decreed by Horus himself. I, disguised as an older version of my earlier Egyptian maiden sat with him while he told me how very happy he was for her. We all, drunk with wine, curled up and slept in the courtyard, oblivious as each of the slaves took a pin and pierced the sleeping Rhodopis with it. She became a dove, and flew above the crowd, mad with confusion and grief.

There are versions of the story where she is found, restored. This is not one of them.

Eleanor knocked on the loaf, testing its hardness. She wrapped it in a cloth and placed it on the table. "Did the fairy go after her?"

"I think she did." I said, after drinking some honey water to soothe my throat. "She wanted to make things right more than anything, but she was not able to." I tilted my head, hearing hooves. "Your family is home."

"You don't have to leave. They never enter the kitchen. It is my own paradise." Her hands were quick, steady, straightening her apron and her bodice, checking her hair.

"I should, though. I have things I need to do ere I rest."

"Rest? You never tell me anything about yourself. Where do you live? What do you do?"

For once, the stepmother served me well. She was calling out for Eleanor, and she could not be refused.

"Another time, dear child," I said, and soon I was away. I

was struck by the thought of those pins. How had the slaves gotten them? Such powerful magic was not easy to find so quickly.

We almost ran into each other, the farmer and I. He grabbed my elbow to keep me from falling, and I clung to him for a second before leaping away.

"Well," he said, as an elderly lady hobbled up to him.

"Young man, I demand you take something for the food you left me."

He blushed like a beet, and he shook his head. "I was told that you have your son's children in your care. You need it more than I..."

I grinned at him. He blushed deeper, if possible, and finally managed to get away, pulling his donkey's lead gently. I fell into step beside him.

"Have you mended your ways, farmer...Gregory?"

"I should have realized you can read minds," he said, looking none too pleased.

"No, I cannot read minds. Your donkey told me."

He scratched Edgar between the ears, looking at me, wondering if he should be worried. "I decided you had a point, and thought I could help some of those I saw when I was last in town," he admitted. "But I am not doing it to please you."

"Such pride," I chastised lightly. He winced.

"Am I in trouble?"

I shook my head. I would be the last to cast stones for that. We walked in silence for a bit.

"I'm hungry," I said, and walked around to the back of the cart. "There isn't much left."

"I bought what I could on the way back," he admitted. "But it wasn't much."

"What about yourself?"

"I am not such a saint. I will put some food by and go home."

I pointed at the cart. I didn't say anything, just envisioned the things that had been stored in it. The wood told me tales of cheeses, vegetables, game, casks of honey and bags of flour, beer and wine, apples, eggs and more. I added other things from memory, longing for the taste of olives, sour and sweet, soft cheeses and lovely almonds. I had been dreaming of oranges and grapes, and I added them too. Then thought of the wagon frame, the sides, everything straight and hard and new.

I reached in, and took an orange, peeling it with my sharp nails. "What?" I asked, and then offered him a section. "Don't worry. It will never run out. But it will never be too heavy, either. Nor will the axles break, or the wheels need repair, or the sides repainted." I gestured as if this were nothing.

He placed a hand on a cart side, reverently. Shocked did not describe the expression on his face. "Will the food spoil?"

"Good point." I pointed at it, and said, "Not for a long time. But eventually, yes. Everything must fade."

When I saw her next, she was on her knees, picking things off the kitchen floor.

"What are you doing?" I asked. "Where is your stepmother?"

Eleanor sat up, placing her hands at the small of her back. "My stepmother threw a bowl of linseeds across the kitchen, and I have to pick each and every one up before they get back, or she will beat me." She said this straight forwardly. There was fear, but she was not wailing and bawling, like so many I know would have been.

"Why would she do such a thing? That is...indescribably cruel!" Ways to avenge Eleanor tumbled through my mind, but I decided to put it aside. Nothing must risk Eleanor's happiness with her prince. Nothing.

"She found me repairing one of my mother's dresses," she said, clearly ashamed. "I know it is out of fashion, but I truly wanted to go to the ball. I know if I saw the prince again..." She sighed, and for a moment, I thought she would weep, but she took another breath and started picking up the seeds again.

"Hold! Don't touch another seed, young lady." I stalked over to the window and whistled. Birds flooded the kitchen, black birds, sparrows, birds with feathers of red and feathers of yellow. She gaped at them, and I took her arm and pulled her back into the hall while they fluttered around, collecting the seeds.

"Well, now. It looks like you have some free time after all."

Her awe became laughter. "Are you going to tell me another story?"

I grinned, and we sat down together in the parlor, Eleanor gingerly, as if waiting for someone to strike her, I with the gratitude of someone who needed comfort for her old bones.

I thought for a moment, and then began, knowing that this was the right story. "Once upon a time, there was a scholar, who lived in a cave with two wives," I began.

She looked at me, an eyebrow arched. "Two wives?"

"This is not Europe, Dear, but the Far East, a province in Zhongguo. Now, shall I tell the story?"

She nodded eagerly, and after another quelling look, I began. It all came rushing back...

The scholar had two wives; the first wife was as beautiful as the sunset, the second wife plainer, sturdier. The first wife was the favorite, an educated lady who would help her husband in his studies, while the second wife would do more of the work, which she resented.

In the fullness of time they both had daughters, Yeh-Shen, a sweet little girl with a laugh like a brook, and Yeh-Guo, who seemed to have absorbed her mother's resentments in the womb. Things were happy enough, at first, though the second wife always felt some envy toward the first, for the first wife was more of a companion than she could ever be.

It was, perhaps, that very closeness between man and first wife that saved the second, for once the two of them went out, into the deepest mountains to search for certain crystals, and the mountain fell out from under them both.

The second wife forbade the first wife's name to ever be spoken again, even beat Yeh-Shen when she called for her mother, and so I will never use hers, so that she may be as forgotten as those she wanted to forget.

It did not take long for Second Wife to become used to the new way of life. Yeh-Shen was a perfect target to bear the brunt of the stepmother's resentment, for she was beautiful like the first wife had been, and intelligent like the first wife had been, and generous and kind, again, just like the first wife. Rather than warming the stepmother's heart, it made her hate the child more, and she assigned the girl every menial task.

Every hardship was to be suffered by Yeh-Shen, who slept in the cave's mouth while Yeh-Guo slept with her mother on a bed made from the first wife's fine robes, embroidered silks in a rainbow of lovely colors. Every morning as the sun crept over the lip of the cave, she would awake and come out to a small lake to draw water. And that is where she met me...

Being a fish was one of the least unpleasant forms I have taken. I liked it, in fact, liked being suspended in the water, the weight of silence. In this form you can sense far more than most think possible, but there was stillness and solitude to the water, a peace that balmed my soul. One day I felt a yearning for water in my heart, so I changed to that shape, and then let the currents lead me. After many miles I found myself tumbling down into a small, pretty lake below the mouth of a cave.

I had lain in the water awhile, exhausted but exhilarated, when I saw a shadow at the edge of the lake. I moved so I could see better, and there, above me, a young woman dipped her bucket into the water.

I let myself go above the edge of the water so I could see her face better, see her eyes. She was not a pretty blonde, this time, but a beautiful Chinese girl, but her eyes were still blue, still kind. She was humming something under her breath.

"Yeh-Shen! Yeh-Shen! Will you hurry up, you lazy girl?" The voice was strident, harsh, like the cawing of crows, and the young girl winced, her shoulders falling a little. She had hoped, I realized, for a few moment's peace. "Yeh-Shen!"

"Coming, Mother!" She grabbed the buckets and ran, the sort of short, choppy steps of someone bearing a heavy burden, up to the cave. I needed to rise from the lake, take another form, and take a look at Yeh-Shen's life, but for a moment I forgot how to be anything else but a fish. I'd been one for ages, it seemed, and now I was having a hard time remembering what it felt like to be anything else.

I forced myself to remember what it felt like to have arms and legs, what a head felt like on a neck, the neck on a torso, the way I breathed and felt and looked and sensed. I crawled out of the lake and went to the nearest tree, crawling inside the foreign-feeling wood, letting it comfort me. I could feel the core of it like a heart, pumping in time with my own, and I let myself fall away.

The next morning I left the tree determined to go up to the cave, when I saw her approach through the woods. I ran toward the lake, changing myself back into a fish as I leapt the last bit and dove into the pond. I peeked above the surface, saw only delight in her expression, and knew she thought that I had leapt from the water.

"Hello, Golden Eyes," she said. "What a beautiful fish, you are, with your scales of copper, silver, and gold." I disappeared beneath the surface, as if afraid. "Please, don't go... I won't hurt you!" She took from her robes a bit of bread, which she broke and held just under the surface of the water.

I took it from her, making sure that I tickled her fingers with my lips, which made her giggle. I let her stroke my fins, then swam away, building up the force to leap above the surface. I somersaulted above the water and landed again, making her giggle with her hand over her mouth, as if trying not to be caught.

"I will be back, Golden Eyes," she said. "I will bring you food this evening."

She dipped her water buckets, and then walked off again quickly, pausing only to wave a little to me, smiling as if I were the best thing that had ever happened to her.

As I rose up, now an invisible mist, I could hear Yeh-Shen

berated by two angry, screeching voices. Feeling lazy, I let the wind push me to the cave where I settled, like smoke, along the ceiling.

It seemed that Master Wu (for that was the name of the maiden's father) had wed a swan and then a toad, for Yeh-Shen was beautiful and delicate, with tiny feet and hands, and skin that glowed like pearl. Yeh-Guo bore a great resemblance to her mother: Short, with coarse, sallow skin and tiny eyes. She looked as if someone had placed their hand on her head and squished her down, making her skin and bones compress.

Yeh-Guo did nothing to help around the house, lounging instead in front of the fire, playing with some colored stones idly, as if she was a fine lady and had nothing better to do. Yeh-Shen was on her knees, scrubbing the floor of the cave, while her stepmother sat, pretending to doze in a patch of sun that came through the smoke hole, but I could see her mean, little eyes move as she watched the younger girl, as if waiting for her to make a mistake. I felt far less pity for her than I had, for I could see into her heart, and saw nothing but foulness and cruelty.

I watched for a while, but when I could bear it no longer, I left to explore the area. I needed to find her future husband and, I realized, I needed to walk about for a bit as a woman, or I would forget myself altogether and be lost to the winds.

The village was simple, a fishing village that boasted of a small harbor. Not so far out to sea there was an island connected to the village by a long bridge. It was a magnificent thing, this bridge, made of pale stone, and guarded by a statue of the lion-like Suanni on the left, the clam-like Jiaoto on the right.

"Do you like it?" a voice asked sweetly behind me.

I turned with a start, and bowed. *Always the king, my dear sweet boy. Always the king.*

He held his hand out to me, and I realized, in my vanity, I had made myself beautiful, for I could not bear to be anything less. I placed my hand in his, and felt the longing awake like a poison in my blood. He felt it too, and I knew, if I wanted to, I could go back to his palace, across the bridge, to the center of the island, far enough away it would seem like another world.

We stood and stared at each other, and I could sense him trying to place me.

"Your majesty, a thousand pardons, but your mother comes..." one of the guards said.

He nodded and leapt back onto his horse, as if anxiously waiting for his mother, in her palanquin, to come to the bridge. He looked for me then, but I made myself a leaf, and whisked myself away.

A fish again, I rested at the bottom of the pond, and contemplated the meaning of beauty.

But she's beautiful, I thought as I heard her singing voice coming closer. *Why can't I be beautiful too?*

I knew if I thought beyond that I would be forced to face my faults—vanity, pride, selfishness—so I put my thoughts aside, and rose to the surface.

"There you are!" She smiled happily. It was getting close to dark, the dusk giving her some room to hide. She took some bread from her pockets. "I have food for you!" She made to toss it into the water.

"Wait!" I said. "No need to get my food wet..." I crawled out onto the bank, and she stared at me in wonder. "You are most kind, Yeh-Shen, to give what little you have to me. It shows that your heart is a gentle one, and I am so pleased to meet someone like you in my travels."

"Your travels? You must tell me!"

And so I did. Every night she would bring me a little of her food and I would tell her stories. Of course, nothing is meant to last, and as the weather turned colder it was harder for her to sneak away.

It was not an exciting way for me to live either, for every night I would wait for her, the other fish closing around me because they thought me interesting or extra warm, pushing me deeper into the mud, and every day I would wander around righting wrongs and being bored.

Maybe that's why I didn't realize it wasn't her, calling my

name. Maybe I'd gotten dull. I had certainly gotten careless, as I leapt from the water, flopping on the bank.

"Hello, Yeh-Shen. Shall we continue..."

"Hello, Golden Eyes," her stepmother cackled. "I am hungry, and you will make a good meal!"

The knife came down, but I managed to roll to avoid it. She grabbed my tail, but I made myself slippery, and slid back into the water just ahead of the hand she plunged in after me.

She grabbed one of my neighbors, and I did the only thing I could think of. I made the other fish look like me. She threw it on the bank and cut it neatly. The others clustered near me, not realizing, of course, what I'd done. I tried not to feel guilty, to make a new plan, instead.

Back at the cave, Yeh-Shen screamed and screamed, her howls mingling with their cruel laughter. The silence that came was so abrupt I knew someone had slapped her.

I rose out of the pond, invisible, as she came running down the path. She threw herself down next to the water. "Golden Eyes? Golden Eyes?" Above her, a softly glowing gold mist formed, became the shape of the fish.

"Yeh-Shen?" I whispered, and she looked up.

"I am so sorry... oh! I!" She started weeping again, and I settled around her for a second, giving her a feeling of comfort and warmth before I rose away.

"You must find my bones, Yeh-Shen, and collect them up and bury them. This way, I will always be with you. When you are in need, visit my bones and ask me what you will. But you must be careful of the gifts, you must be wise with them, and do not lose them, or I shall not be able to come back to help you again."

"Don't go!" she said, as I let myself disappear.

"I must. Do not forget, Yeh-Shen."

The night was dark again, but not so dark that I could not see the tendrils of her dark hair sticking to her tear-wet cheeks. I watched as she went up to the cave, walking as if she were a million years old, and went inside.

"This time it will be all right," I said, though I knew she

could not hear. "This time, I promise, it will work."

It was almost sweet, the way she cared for the bones, carefully reforming the skeleton and then burying them with an offering of rice and bread under a tree. This was the tree I chose to sink myself into. I could not bear to watch any more. Now was the time to wait, and hope.

"Golden Eyes!" I heard someone calling distantly. I didn't understand it, at first, as I woke, but then I realized it was spring. I could feel the sap pumping in my veins, I felt alive and good and bright. I always feel groggy and dull in the winter.

"Golden Eyes?"

Yeh-Shen!

I allowed myself to pour out of the tree in a soft, gold haze. "Yeh-Shen, my dear child. It is spring, and the world is beautiful. How may I help you?"

"You are right to say it is spring, and there is a festival, oh, a wonderful gathering, in the village. I want to go so much, but I have nothing to wear! If I could go, I know I would find a husband. It is the very point of it, you see." She looked at me pleadingly.

"Yeh-Shen, lift the stone you placed upon my grave and look under it."

She did so, and found a package wrapped in heavy cloth. She blinked, unwrapping it with trembling hands.

The dress she took from it was made of the finest silk the color of the brightest late spring sky, and, even more impressive, underneath the dress was a cloak of kingfisher feathers wrapped around jade sticks for her hair and shoes for her feet.

"This. . . this is fit for an empress!" she said, her eyes looking a little more damp than usual as she gently stroked the feathers: celestial blue, azure, ultramarine, every shade of blue that was possible to dream.

She carefully put up her hair, adorning it with ornate sticks of jade carved like flowers. Finally, she took out the shoes, made of gold and patterned to look like scales. "The shoes are the most important part of all," I said, "Do not lose them, or you will never see me again."

She placed them on her feet reverently, and then looked up at me.

I caught my breath, and softly answered her unasked question. "You look like a queen."

She walked swiftly and lightly away in the enchanted shoes that lifted her just slightly off the ground. They would get her to the village quickly, but still I watched over her, an invisible breeze that lifted her gently and pushed her forward, until finally, not a fleck of dirt on her and not one whit tired from her journey, she entered the village.

It is not hard to predict what happened. How could not all eyes fall upon the most beautiful girl in the village? Especially when she is dressed so beautifully, so royally?

Even the king, sitting on a fine throne set at the end of the bridge, visiting not to find a wife, but to watch the ceremonies, was taken utterly. He did not leave his throne, but his eyes did not leave her.

Under the king's eyes, the people had formed a circle, leaving space for those who could dance or play or sing to come and show their talents to the king and their future spouses.

Yeh-Shen took her place in the center, bowing slightly, as befitted a woman wearing a cloak of kingfisher feathers. There was nothing but silence as she posed, her hands outstretched in front of her, as if she were offering water in her cupped hands to the king. We all held our breath, waiting, and finally someone began to pluck a soft, sweet tune from the lute, and she danced.

As she danced, she sang.

> *I have longed for you*
> *since the world was old,*
> *I have waited for you*
> *since before the leaves knew their color,*
> *I long to drink from your lips,*
> *they are sweeter than plums,*
> *sweeter than rice wine,*
> *but will you ever return*

the love of this maid,
this maid?

Her shoes made her seem as if her feet never touched the ground, and in fact, there were indeed several moments when her feet hovered an inch from the stones.

And when she was done, she knelt prettily, her head bowed.

The silence of the moment was broken. I heard someone complain loudly, and all eyes looked.

Yeh-Shen's stepmother pushed her daughter to the front.

They wore the old dresses of the first wife, cleaned and mended by Yeh-Shen's own hand.

Yeh-Shen used the confusion, as the younger woman was pushed out into the court yard, to get away.

I felt badly for Yeh-Guo for a moment, as she stood, trapped, in the center of all our attention. She wasn't terribly bad to look upon, not as ugly as her mother, nor as bitter, but between the extremes of her mother and Yeh-Shen she disappeared. She did not have elegance in the best times, and she did not have enchanted shoes.

She sang a sweet little children's song in a nervous voice, but no one paid attention, least of all her own mother, who had recognized Yeh-Shen and was trying to catch her, pushing through the press of the crowd.

When I found Yeh-Shen she was running through the forest wearing only one shoe. No one followed, for no longer did she wear the cloak of magic blue feathers or the clothes of a princess, but the rags of a servant.

I was pleased. Everything was falling into place.

The king sent his servants to find the girl, but I knew they would not, so I searched for the shoe.

A man picked it up and put it in his sleeve, so I caused him to trip, and he went flying, the shoe falling far from his reach.

A little girl looked at it shyly, so I threw butterflies at her, gold and green and pink, and she followed them.

Finally the man I wanted to find it came, the same guard who had spoken to the prince on that first day, but he was looking for a girl, not a shoe, so I flicked a tiny pebble at his knee. He picked up the shoe and ran off with it, such a tiny thing that it fit easily in one hand; his fingers could close around it.

When they could not find the lady to fit the shoe, the king placed it on a low pillar at the mouth of the bridge, guards all around it.

I knew I must encourage Yeh-Shen to go and fetch it, but I had told her that she could not lose the shoes or she would not see me again. I did not do this to be cruel, but to make sure that if she did lose it, which of course was my intention, her desperation to have it again would outweigh her fear and caution.

So, I had to wait.

I waited while others tried the shoe.

I waited while Yeh-Shen endured the screams of her stepmother.

I waited while Yeh-Shen gathered the courage to go and try to steal the shoe back.

It took many weeks before she finally snuck away from the cave and by this time everyone's guard was down. Her stepmother was unlikely to miss the girl and the guards were drowsy with boredom.

When the sun went down, she crept out of the shadows like a deer, until she crouched by the pillar. I could not believe she had made it that far. Was it possible the guards were blind from standing out in the sun for so many days?

She reached her small hand up and took the shoe, and that was when the guards grabbed her.

She struggled for a second, but then bowed her head and allowed herself to be led across the bridge and to the island, not noticing the leaf that followed her, bumping across the stone at her heels.

He frowned when he saw her. "What did you think to accomplish, child?"

"It is my slipper, your majesty."

Her words made everyone laugh, even the king smiled

slightly.

"I am sure that you wish it were so, but I am afraid we shall have to deal with you as with any other thief." He looked at her, and I thought I saw longing in his eyes. I willed him to recognize her. It would be nice, for once.

"I beg of you, let me try the slipper on."

She was so brave, so earnest, I felt my own cold heart leap, and I crackled impatiently.

He nodded to the guard, who gave her the tiny slipper. He even put a hand out to steady her, but she did not need it as she slipped her dainty foot into it like a rain drop slipping into the sea.

She took the other shoe out of her sleeve, and placed it on. Just as she did, I cast a spell and her rough spun clothes became azure silk and feathers.

He came down from his throne, knelt at her feet, and kissed her hands. I laughed with joy, even though part of me always wished...

But we have what we have. And that was not ever for me, no matter how much I might wish otherwise.

I thought I had finally seen my happy ending, but lo, it was not so.

A year later, Yeh-Shen, sweet, dutiful Yeh-Shen, would visit her stepmother and her sister to give offerings to her father and mother. The evil woman convinced her to climb to the top of the highest Areca tree to fetch betel nuts. It was an old tree, though it looked strong. The stepmother had a sharp axe, so it did not take much to chop it to the point where it would fall, throwing her in the very pond where we used to spend so much time together. Trapped in the branches of the Areca tree, she drowned in the shallow water.

They say she became a bird and watched over her husband. I do not know. I was not there. But I can tell you that her stepmother and sister died not long after. The cave collapsed on itself, the mountain crushing them and swallowing their remains. It is not an easy spell, to make stone become dirt, and it made my bones ache for many moons.

I visited the King's gardens, and I called her name softly. I hoped, desperately, that she was the nightingale that sang so sadly in the king's garden.

"Call as much as you wish. She will not come back."

The king was sitting at the base of a tree, his face tearstained, his hands cupping a tiny, dark form. I touched the tiny bird with my finger, but could not tell if the rumors had been true or not, for there was no life inside of it. I said a word and the bird became a ribbon of blue smoke that faded against the semi dusk.

Like an unwinding ribbon, I saw the possibilities. She was dead. I could not help that, or her, and here he was, at my feet. It would be so easy. I kissed his forehead with great tenderness, and he sighed and relaxed. The pain left him, at least the newness of it, becoming a memory as he fell sideways, asleep. I caught him as he fell and knelt next to him, my hand on his head and tears on my cheeks.

He would marry, yes. He would kiss other women and he would have children. But not with Yeh-Shen, and not with me.

The story filled me with fierce longing that hung upon my heart long after I left Eleanor to her chores. I felt anguish well in my chest like a boil that needed to be lanced. I was becoming weak, weaker than a dust web. I tried to breathe past it. I closed my eyes and let my feet take me where they would.

When I opened my eyes, I was in a church courtyard. Gregory was sitting on the steps, looking tired, his head bowed. I could see it all, that since I'd given him the cart, he'd redoubled his work, his help for the poor. I put my hand on the back of his head. "I'm sorry. I am so sorry."

He looked up. "Why?" he asked, as I sat down beside him.

"You can't tell me that you weren't happier before you met

me. You'd be out in your fields right now... my gift to you was worse than any punishment could have been."

I'd been telling Eleanor the old stories, poring over them in the hope that I would see a way to repair the mistakes of the past, to help her reclaim her rights and give her a well deserved happily ever after, but all I saw was disappointment, pain, and hardship. Over, and over.

"I have all the magic there ever was, and I still can't do anything right."

He was silent for a moment. Then he put an arm, lightly, around my shoulders. "Well, my dear, you're only a fairy, you're not God."

His mouth curved into a half smile, and I started to laugh. When I laughed myself into weeping, he rocked me while I sank against his sturdiness. *He should have been born an oak*, I thought. If he had been, I would have sunk inside him and never have come back out, even for the end of the world.

When I recovered, I made us dinner, of bread, tomatoes, olives and cheese. I made fun of him for ignoring the olives until now, and he laughed and teased me back.

It made me feel I could face my dear Eleanor again the next day and I met her to walk through the market.

I gave her one of Gregory's oranges, and she broke it open, breathing its scent, just standing in the middle of the road, her expression absolute bliss.

I wanted to tell her about Gregory, I wanted to tell her that she knew him, that she had met him at least twice before.

I was trying to puzzle it out, if it was coincidence or if he meant something to my quest, but so far nothing came to mind that made sense.

"I am buying trim," she said. "I've been working on my sister's dresses for the ball. It's tomorrow night." She grinned at me. "She told me I could go! If I have the gown, I can go!"

"I am so glad!" I grinned back, as she told me how she would fix her mother's gown up for the occasion, though I knew her hope was useless.

When we got back to her house, we sat in the kitchen. I

took out a needle of gold that threaded itself, and started sewing new lace around the hem of the youngest sister's dress.

"I have one last story to tell you," I said, for I had realized that this story was the key to all. "Would you like to hear it?"

"I would," she said sincerely, "I just... why do you tell me these stories? Is it to keep from speaking of your life? Is it because you seek to warn me? Only a fool would not see the similarities. All of your stories are the same." She blushed, and then, hastened to add, "In a couple of places. Not really noticeable... I..."

I laughed. "You're right. They are. Like the refrain of a ballad. But someday, the story will change, and the song will be over."

"That's a good thing, right?"

I smiled a little, and nodded. "To answer your question, it is a warning, because stories are always warnings. It is to remind you that there is good and evil in the world, and that things are not always what they seem."

She thought this over, frowning over her stitches. "I think I understand. I would love very much to hear your story now, if you don't mind."

"Never in life, my dear."

And so I began the last and most important tale.

Once, there were three sisters. The eldest was named Fair, for fair she was, in face at least, but not in deed. Then there was Brown, who looked much like her sister, save her colors were brown like Autumn, and finally there was Trembling. Trembling and Fair were summer colored, blue eyed and golden haired. The youngest sister was sweet, but you know that by now, good and pure in her nature.

They were equals, all princesses, all daughters of a widowed, doting father who never remarried for he was a king who liked his battles, and his freedom, and though he had loved his wife very much, he was not interested in getting another. He was, however, interested in getting an heir, and if he could not produce one himself, he would be happy enough to get one by marriage.

And so it was, that the son of the king of Omanya came riding to their lands, to make a marriage with the eldest daughter. Prince Aodhan, whose name means fire.

I was a henwife, then, tall, deeply cloaked and hooded. One eye bore a patch. Sometimes I would switch the patch to see if anyone dared to comment, but oddly, no one ever did. People came to me in fear, and if I could, I helped them. Mostly, though, they were looking for the wrong type of magic. I am ever amazed at how many people are convinced that love is still love, even if it's forced.

By then I had known Trembling for three years and had been waiting for him, I would have known him from a thousand leagues away, and indeed, I had monitored his approach, listening to the winds as they spoke of him, closing my eyes and feeling him come to us, like the dawn bird waiting for the warmth of the sun.

I wondered, sometimes, if it was right of me to take him from one sister to give him to another, if it was not as cruel a sin as the one I had committed at first, but I also knew Fair's nature. At first she would be like summer honey, sweet and just a little wild, the taste of her something you could not get enough of, but nor could you define. It would intoxicate him, enchant him.

Then, when the claws were in deep, she would slowly strangle the life out of him, leaving nothing but a husk. I knew she practiced spells she should not, and created potions that she tested on the servants, and though I could stop much of her mischief, I did not think it morally right to allow them to wed.

Besides, Trembling would love him, and he her. What was wrong with that?

By this time, Trembling lived in the castle kitchens. Her father did not notice, for he was a careless sort who did not seem to rightly know whether it was Fair or Trembling he passed in the corridor, and I long suspected Fair was doing something to help that along.

Brown was the King's favorite. She rode like a man and

hunted like Artemis. She read with such a calm, rolling voice that I often hid myself in corners to listen. Brown knew that Trembling was forced to live in the kitchen because of her sister, but her idea of help was to tell Trembling to stand up for herself.

Trembling nodded, smiled, and stayed in the kitchen. I did not blame her, for it was easy to tell someone to stand up for herself. It was not so easy to do when one's eldest sister had a nasty sense of humor and a cleverness for traps.

Fair kept away from the kitchen. We—the servants, Trembling, and I—always said it was because she felt it beneath her to enter the room, but I knew there was something about me that bothered her. She did not like being in my presence for long.

The day after Aodhan arrived was the Sabbath, and all and sundry were gathered together for church. Trembling was preparing dinner for the family all alone, for the servants had been given the day off.

"Don't you wish to go to the church and see this handsome young prince for yourself?" I asked, stealing a slice of raw potato; eating it as I awaited her answer.

"I would if I could," she said sincerely. "But I have nothing to wear, and besides, if my eldest sister saw me she'd probably have me killed."

"You can't live in fear all your life." I mimicked Brown's voice perfectly, and Trembling threw a peel at me. "But truly, I could give you a dress. Think of a dress that you would like to wear and the type of horse you would like to ride, and I shall give it to you."

She looked at me, half in hope, half in disbelief. "Very well... I... I'll have a dress as white as snow, with green shoes. And a milk white mare, with a golden saddle and bridle."

"I thought that you would give me a wee bit more of a challenge." I took my cloak and pulled it around myself until I disappeared, and went and found myself a horse, and made it the purest white, and fitted it with the finest gold. The horse, a dun mare from the field, seemed to be pleased by this transformation, and cheerfully allowed herself to be led to the kitchen.

I stepped inside, and allowed myself to become visible, pulling a finely embroidered white dress and green shoes from the depths of my cloak. She gaped, then laughed and hugged me.

"Do not go into the church or leave your steed, but wait and listen to the mass. Once it's over, you must leave, and quickly. I will have dinner ready, but you must return before your sisters. Brown might act as if she doesn't care, but both she and Fair greatly fear the power of your beauty."

She smiled at me, admiring the bright green of her toes against the white of her dress hem, only half, if even that, listening. "I will come home soon, thank you, thank you so much!"

She rode away, looking as happy as the spring, and I went inside, and waved, negligently, toward the kitchenware and the food. Knives began to peel and chop, the spit turned over a crackling fire, spoons stirred, and I sat back on my chair, pulled out a small, stringed instrument, and amused myself by making up a ballad featuring the most terrible rhymes imaginable.

She came home bright-eyed and giggling, and I helped her change again, hiding her clothes in the middle of a favorite tree.

When the sisters came in to see how the supper was coming along, I was sitting next to the hearth. "Something's happened," I said wisely. "What has come to pass, that leaves you so excited?" I did not point out that it must indeed be news, for Fair to come into the servants' area.

Fair looked at her sister, then at the supper, then at me. She was thinking hard with that wily little mind of hers, but she couldn't make sense of what she saw. "A woman, a beautiful woman riding a magnificent white mare, her dress of the finest white silk, came to the church today. A stranger to our lands, I think." There was a slight question in her words, and her eyes met with my single one.

Brown spoke, her voice a mixture of dismay and awe. "Every man who was there wanted to know her, and know who she was. There was not one person there who had eyes for anyone but her."

"Interesting," I said.

"I should like to see her. Do you think she will come again?" Trembling's voice was so calm, so offhand, that you would be excused for thinking she had been in the kitchen this whole time.

"Only if she comes down through the chimney," Fair said sweetly then swept out of the room.

We didn't say anything, but I could see Trembling biting her lip, the happiness in her eyes making my heart glad.

The next Sunday, of course, I went to the kitchen just as the others left for church. "Shouldn't you be at church? What will people think?"

Mischievously, she said, "Oh, I would go, but I have no dress to wear, no steed to take me."

"What a pity," I said, standing next to her, playing with a wooden bowl, rolling it on its rim. I was trying not to smile.

She nudged me, "My sisters have done their best to copy the magnificent dress that the mysterious lady wore last week. It would be lovely if I could ask someone for a satin robe as black as night..."

"And red shoes for your feet?"

"Red shoes?" She smiled, and closed her eyes. "Yes. Red shoes. And a horse so black, with a coat so glossy that I can see myself in her body."

When she returned, I knew things had gone well. All she could speak of was him, and all her sisters could speak of was how taken he was with the mystery woman. One more time should do it.

Aodhan knew her, as she knew him.

He would seek her out.

I would go, the next time, for this could finally be it.

Maybe, if nothing went wrong again.

Sunday, I went into the kitchen. "Have you thought of another dress?"

She nodded eagerly. "I want a dress that is as red as a rose from the waist down, but pure white from the waist up. And I'd like shoes that have red toes, white middles, and green heels and backs. I would also like a cloak of green, and a hat of those same three colors." I tried to imagine this, to weave something in my head that would still be attractive. "And your horse?"

"A mare of white, with gold and blue diamonds for markings, with a saddle of gold, and a matching bridle." She grinned at me, breathless with excitement, and I could not refuse her.

I nodded once, and was hugged so fiercely I thought my bones might break.

When I brought her the requested things, she jumped with delight. I found myself smiling, and when she was dressed, I realized she looked really lovely.

I placed a songbird who sang the sweetest songs between the mare's ears. The mare looked at me, and I could feel happiness radiating from her. She was enjoying herself greatly, and I stroked her forehead lovingly as Trembling mounted.

"Off you go, then," I said, though she was already on her way.

"Supper's not going to make itself." I laughed at my own joke, and set the kitchen wares to their task.

I decided to become a cat to follow her. A grey cat with yellow eyes was soon bounding across the land, dogging the heels of the mare playfully.

Trembling stopped at the church. "Oh, Father in Heaven," she whispered. "Please, oh Dear Father..." Neither of us knew that the fame of her had spread so fart that many young princes from all over the world had come to see her, all desiring to win her.

I stayed in the shadows, batting the lower branch of the bush that was my hiding place.

"What do you pray for, dear maiden?"

Aodhan had been hiding in the shadows of the church, waiting for her.

"For love, sir." She seemed captivated by him, frozen in place as he came closer. He placed his hand on her foot. Mass was ending, and her head jerked up. I could hear her sister, her voice polite but fierce as she worked her way through the crowd.

"I must go..."

"Tell me your name."

"I can't. Please..."

Go, I told the mare fiercely, and it started to run. He ran along side of it, as fast as the steed, unbothered, until the shoe slipped from her foot.

When she got home, she was vexed. "I am so sorry! I didn't mean to lose the shoe! Oh, I can't believe it!"

"Do not worry," I said, "Could be that that was the best thing to ever happen to you." She looked at me as if I had finally gone mad, and waited for her sisters to come home.

The shoe became the topic of conversation in every home in Erin. The princes, headed by the Prince of Omanya, searched as a group, leaving no house alone. It was said he rode with the shoe next to his heart, and that the ladies were delighted to see it, for it did not seem like it was too large or too small. It looked... possible. But it was a deceptive shoe, and though there were some that did themselves harm to fit into it, they could not.

"Perhaps my foot is the one to fit it," she ventured, when the sisters visited the kitchen once to give her orders. "They say that anyone can try."

They laughed so hard and long that she did not speak to anyone for days, feeling deeply ashamed, and perhaps a bit disappointed.

Then, one day, the princes came to the castle. Trembling came to the parlor to press her suit to her father, but Fair and Brown stuffed her into a closet and locked the door. She wisely stayed quiet while the sisters tried the slipper in vain, speaking up only when the prince of Spain asked if there were no more women in the house.

"I am here! I am here!" she yelled at the top of her lungs, and I made sure that her voice was loud enough to be heard.

"She is nothing, just an ash-girl." Fair said, shrugging.

Her father frowned. "Is that Trembling? Bring her at once."

Such a command could not be ignored. As they came for her, I put the dresses in her arms, the matching shoe to Aodhan's on top, and she marched into the room, dressed in the dress from the first day, carrying the others proudly.

"It is her," he said, "I recognize her hair of gold, her beautiful eyes."

"You are truly a woman of rare beauty," the King of Lochlin said.

There were loud cheers when the shoe was proved to fit. The cheers swiftly became arguments. They all wanted Trembling for themselves, and they all demanded the chance to win her.

"It was then decreed that they would all try to win her, competing by right of arms. The next day, the king of Lochlin..."

I saw Eleanor staring at me, and I said, "Don't you enjoy big battle scenes?"

She smiled, and cut some trim for the sleeve. "I am afraid not."

"Care to guess who won?"

"Aodhan," she said with certainty. She looked up from her work. "It doesn't last, does it? Something happens to them."

I nodded, then said, "Well, a year after the battle, which if I had time I could tell in long, glorious and exciting detail...?" I looked to see if I'd convinced her, and she shook her head, suppressing a smile. I rolled my eyes dramatically, sighed, and continued.

Trembling was brought to bed with a son. A fine son he was, the very spirit and image of his father. Sadly, she was taken ill, and her father, hearing of this, sent Fair to care for her.

It may well be that Fair sent herself, but whatever happened, she came, and put on a good face, and took excellent care of her sister. I had not left by this time. I was not satisfied that things were as they should be. I felt something was wrong, even as Trembling bloomed under our care.

I went out into the garden one day, to pick flowers. She was doing very well, so I ventured out to gather some posies to cheer her. How innocent our mistakes are, but deadly, still.

When I came home I saw Aodhan return with his retinue, and Fair come out to greet them alone.

"Where is your sister?" he asked, dismounting.

"She has gone home to father, she is no longer needed."

I could see he was greatly upset by this. "It grieves me that my wife should leave."

"Silly, I am here. My sister Fair is the one who has left." And she reached out, and touched his chest.

"I'm sorry," he said, "Of course." But there was still doubt in his voice, so he said, "We shall sleep with my sword between us tonight, if it grows warm, then you are my Trembling, if it stays cold..."

I took a moment only to make sure the sword would do as it should, and then continued my quest for Trembling.

I did not stop looking for her, but so restless was I, that I almost missed a young cow herd. I found him, sleeping in the shadows near the kitchen garden, and I smelled a potion on his sleeping breath.

I followed him when he awoke, taking the form of his own shadow throughout the next day. I knew, by the way he wandered, confused, that his mind was fighting to overcome the spell. I reached into his mind, when I could, and peeled away a corner of the enchantment.

"The ocean," he said, with certainty. "I have to return to the shore."

I stood next to him, as he stared out to sea. He knew, as I did, that if we waited long enough...

A whale rose out of the ocean. I made myself visible as the whale opened its huge maw and tossed Trembling out onto the strand.

She coughed, and stood, shaking. "I knew you'd find me," she said. "Fair pushed me into the sea, and this whale swallowed me. It was as if it were waiting for me."

I was not surprised. I smelled something of my own sister in the leviathan, and knew if what I was beginning to suspect was true, my sister had arranged things with Fair.

"I am sorry I did not prevent this. I should have known. . . I should have. . . " I shook my head. "You are under an enchantment, am I correct? You cannot move from this beach. . . "

"Indeed. I have to wait for the whale to come back and swallow me again. It will return once more, tomorrow night, then we shall leave here, and I will never see my husband again." She tossed her head. "How could my own sister do this to me? Are you not outraged? Are you not angry?"

"The cruelty of sisters ceased to surprise me long ago."

I could not remember the last time I'd seen my sister, but I knew that she had crossed my path many a time before. And I knew how to defeat her. "Fear not. Tomorrow night all shall be mended."

I was gone by the time the whale came to swallow Trembling back up. But the next day Aodhan and I awaited it, a pistol with a silver bullet in his hands.

"When the whale turns on its back, a brown spot will show on its breast. That is the only weak spot it has, otherwise you will never defeat it."

He nodded grimly. "She tried to come to my bed last night, but I have refused her. She will do something desperate soon."

"You need not worry. She will be taken care of"

He slanted me a look, but I was staring, darkly, at the sea. I had taken the form of the cow lad, a thin disguise, but hopefully she would take his presence for granted. When I knew she was coming, I said, "Be prepared, they come," and hid myself beside an overturned boat.

He ran to his wife, holding her, and the whale, unworried, began to make its turn. He pushed Trembling aside and aimed, his shot piercing the brown spot on its breast.

The whale screamed and became a woman, who threw herself out of the waves and onto the beach.

"Danae." I changed forms again, showing my true self for the first time in years. "Jealousy seems a foolish thing for even you to indulge in, sister."

She healed herself, working the area, transforming it. The silver was not meant to damage permanently. In fact, if I'd wanted to kill her I would have used iron. But the silver stopped her long enough for me to intervene.

"Not jealousy, sister." She stood, and I drew my magic to me, preparing. "But a desire to see that you never redeem yourself,—that you fade to nothing."

I grimaced. If I faded before I corrected my errors, I would disappear. I would not rejoin my family or my ancestors. I would have never been.

We fought like clever women fight. With rain and lightning, with changing shapes, cat to snake, hawk to wolf... but in the end, it was not magic that defeated me. She transformed back to herself, scratched and bloodied, and fell to her knees. I had my hand back, to throw a final spell, when she leapt up, and stabbed me with a dagger. The iron grazed ribs, cutting skin and muscle more than anything else, but it was a cruel blow. I fell upon the beach, unable to move, unable to act.

Aodhan fought bravely, as did Trembling. And that is all I will say. What else is left to say, except that I failed again?

"It is why," I told Gregory later, as I made free of his apples, "I am weak. The wound, it never really healed. It does not bleed, or even hurt. But I feel as if something of myself is leaking through the seam in my body."

"That sounds awful," he said. "But if your sister wants you to fail, she must be here somewhere."

"You believe me so easily?"

He gave me a look that suggested he wasn't certain of my sense, and gestured toward the cart of never ending food.

"I found her," I admitted. "It took some time, but I know

exactly where she is."

"And you've taken care of her? Bound her up and tossed her in the sea? Sent her on a one way trip to the moon?"

"None of the above, I fear. It's not that easy, especially considering that she's managed to become Eleanor's stepmother." I was chewing my lip now. "She has weakened me. I have to find a power that's stronger than her. I have to confound her. Love won't do it. Simply getting them wed won't, either. I need more power..." I felt my jaw drop, and I looked at him.

"You've come to the solution." He leaned forward, eagerly. "What is it?"

"My father was the king of our people... which means he was in possession of the ruling wand. It's... well, a magic wand, it makes the holder undefeatable."

"Something like that, you'll need to go on a long quest for." I could see what he was thinking, that the ball was tomorrow night.

"It's mine for the asking. I'm the eldest daughter." I sounded braver and more certain than I felt. The wand had been denied to me as part of my punishment, but if I could convince who or whatever guarded it that I had to have it, that I was worthy...

I lay down on the wood planks that made up the stable floor. "You should find some place more comfortable," I said, wiggling, hoping in vain for a soft spot.

"My newest occupation has not exactly been focused on making a profit."

"You could sell some of the food to the rich. After all, it's a never ending supply."

He considered this, while I tried to make myself calm. "I rather thought that would break the spell..."

And then I was gone. I sent my soul to the tree I'd loved so much, the one that we had all slept in, the tree that I had thought would always be my home.

The forest, to my soul's eye, was the forest I'd grown up

in, with the council stones set in their neat circle, the carefully coaxed and formed trees and plants forming a cathedral around the glen. It was empty, which it had never been in life, and I wondered why. Did no spirits walk this land, just to remember how things once were?

I walked through it, taking my silver knife out to cut away a few chunks of elder bark. I carried them in my bare hands, imprinting my question into them, as I walked to the great cauldron. The cauldron was a circle of rocks near the bottom of a gently running waterfall. The water would splash and fall, rolling toward the basin of rocks, the water would swirl through, and out. It made an odd effect of constantly spinning water.

I walked to the cauldron, my feet steady on the slippery rocks, instantly cold from the water, and knelt, my back to the current so that it kept me pressed to the rocks, kept me pinned in place by the current and the basin.

I sprinkled the bark over the swirling water, and stared into it, concentrating.

This is who I am, I said. *I know myself, my faults, my good points. My vanities and follies outnumber anything that one could call a blessing, but I beg you to see that I try. And that I am fading, now, so close to the end of my quest. Please, father, if you are still close enough to this world to grant me one wish, please, give me your wand.*

The cauldron glowed, and I reached into it, and pulled the wand from the water. I put it against my heart. *Thank you.*

I opened my eyes, and realized my head was on Gregory's lap. I sat up immediately, and he looked at my hands.

"Well?"

I plucked at the skin above my heart, and pushed out with my mind. Slowly I unsheathed the wand from my flesh. He looked a little pale.

"In shock, farmer? Have you never had a splinter?"

"I," he said, "am not amused."

I avoided the house. I was afraid Danae would sense my renewed power, so I decided to bide my time until they left for the ball.

Elenore was kneeling in the garden. She was weeping, leaning against a stone bench. The ruins of her dress lay on the ground, smoldering.

I sat on the bench. "Now, my child, after all I've said, you still don't have any faith in me?"

She looked up, shaking her head.

"I may not have had much luck in getting you your happily ever after... yet... but I am quite talented in the conjuring of clothes department."

She laughed, and then said, "Will you give me a cloak of kingfisher feathers again, then?"

I drew my wand out of my sleeve, tapping it on the back of my hand. "Oh, no, dear, I'm afraid that is a bit out of season."

"Just a bit?"

I winked at her, and she laughed, rubbing her face dry.

"Well, let's see." I stood. "First, you need a coach." I could sense Gregory in the shadows, and I looked at him. He raised his eyebrows and grinned like a fox. Behind him I could see the shadow of Edgar and the cart, for he did not dare leave them alone. I made a show of cracking my knuckles, and rolling back my sleeves. "I need... a pumpkin."

She ran over to the garden. "Here's one!"

"No, no... don't pick it. The vines are rather nice." I raised the wand with a flourish, and the pumpkin grew and grew, the vines becoming the under carriage and wheels. When I was done, I had a peach-and-pale-green carriage.

Eleanor's mouth was open. She swallowed, and said, "What do we need next?"

"Edgar," I said solemnly.

Gregory took him out of his traces, and urged him forward.

I waved the wand again, and he became a man, dressed in grey, though I added peach facings to his fine jacket. His teeth were predictably bucked, his ears a bit large, but he laughed as he ran his hands over his arms. "Edgar, dear, do you think you could drive?"

He tried to speak, frowned, and then merely looked at me

imperiously.

"Don't spoil my donkey," Gregory said, and Edgar gave him a look that promised he would step on Gregory's feet at the first opportunity.

"Now... mice. We need mice." I called them with the wand, promising something wonderful, and they came out of the garden and the attic. As they appeared, I made each one into a dapple grey horse. They walked meekly into the traces, which harnessed the beasts of their own accord.

"And now for a footman!" I pointed the wand at Gregory.

"No."

"But who else can I trust to see her there safe?" I asked, and lifted my wand just as he said, "but no powdered wig!"

"Oops." I said, as he gave me a disgusted look, knowing full well he wore a powdered wig, along with matching livery.

I had to admit, he didn't look bad, not at all. Well, perhaps the powdered wig didn't suit him, but the rest...

"And now," I said softly, "For you."

She looked at me in anticipation.

"Moonbeams and sunshine on water. Diamonds and silk. Rose petals and lavender."

I pointed my wand, and the dress appeared, white as snow, heavily embroidered in pale blue, beads of diamonds and sapphires flashing, adding to the pattern. She wore a pear-shaped diamond necklace, and her hair was studded with diamond pins. And on her feet...

She gently bent down. "They're glass." They rang as she brought her heels together. "Sorry," she said, embarrassed.

"I've always loved the idea of glass slippers," I admitted. They were clear, but still had a sort of sheen to them.

Like the ones that I had given to Yeh-Shen, they were enchanted.

She covered her mouth with one hand.

"If you cry, your face will be all blotchy. Come, dear, get into your coach."

Gregory helped her up, even making sure her skirt was out of the way of the door.

I turned myself into an owl, and we were off to the ball.

I felt a stirring of pride as I flew above them, coasting around the castle spires before settling on a pediment to watch her walk up the stairs and into the ballroom. The place glowed with a thousand candles, causing everyone to sparkle like the stars.

Except for her. She glowed like the sun, and every eye was upon her, especially the prince's, who came out to dance with her before anyone else could. His smile was pure recognition.

"He recognized her. I could swear it is so," I said as I came around the edge of the coach. Gregory jumped, and cast me a glare.

"They did play together as children," he reminded me, as I joined him. We were sitting on the side of the bridge, cool white marble as wide as a bench.

"It was more than that. I think he truly knew her."

Guards approached us from the castle gates, but we ignored them. They weren't looking at us, but straight ahead. As the quartet passed, we rose as one and crossed to the coach. I stroked the lead horse, while Gregory looked up at Edgar.

"How are you doing, old boy?"

He hadn't mastered speech yet, so he simply sat taller in his seat and grinned. I had to resist the urge to offer him an apple.

The four guards were coming back, and four more were coming from the castle. "That's rather elaborate, two patrols of four at all times?" I asked. "Is that normal?"

"No," Gregory said, for they had stopped, and pointed their swords at us.

"That is them," a voice said, "They are the ones who said they would kill the prince!"

"Really, sister, charming the guards? That's not fair." I said to Eleanor's stepmother, who was currently cowering behind one of the guards.

"Search them. They have weapons."

"Run," Gregory said to me, as two of the men grabbed him by his arms. There was no chance for a fight, we had been caught unprepared, and I had been made a fool again.

"Give up the wand, or they'll gut your human plaything from stem to stern," she hissed at me.

I believed her.

I took out the wand, and looked at it. "It must have galled you, to know father would never have wanted you to have his wand." The clock began to chime, the loud noise distracting as I carefully snapped the wand in half and hoped the backlash would be enough.

The backlash undid everything in its path. Mice ran onto the bridge and climbed onto the guards, who didn't understand why they were here, and not at their post. One of them tripped over the pumpkin. Edgar the donkey nearly ran over my sister in his fear over the sudden transformation. My sister was on her knees, her beauty gone, her features twisted by years of evil and dark magic, rotting away what was left of her soul.

Gregory, in his farmer's clothes, grabbed my arm, and pulled me off the bridge. Behind us, I could hear someone calling.

Eleanor was at the top of the stairs, the sparkles of her dress fading one by one. She tripped and fell, then picked herself back up, running across the bridge. She threw herself past the guards, and into the woods. As she passed us, the final chime of midnight tolled, and silk streamed into rags.

Gregory and I joined her, melting into the darkness.

She allowed Gregory to wrap her in his cloak while we hid her from the Prince's men, who were frantically searching for her.

"I lost the shoe," she said softly.

"Good girl," I said, and she gaped at me, and then laughed.

After I put her to bed and made certain Gregory and Edgar were safe, I took a walk.

I hadn't expected her to come at me in such a way. My

sister was usually subtle. She wanted to be the clever one, but this time she'd used brute force to get her way. That was why I wasn't expecting it, and that was what she'd been counting on.

I took the pieces of the wand out of my pocket. They fit perfectly together, not a splinter missing. To heal such a thing would require a great sacrifice. It could be healed, but I was not sure if I wanted to pay the cost.

So close to winning, every time. But I would never be able to assure the safety of my two charges, not until my sister was defeated.

I had seen more than either of us had bargained for. When the backlash took her glamour away, I saw that my sister was dying. She wouldn't forgive that, or die before me without a fight.

I stood between two trees and placed a hand on each, closing my eyes and seeking. When she faded, when I faded, there would be no more of us. No more fairy godmothers. No more changeling children.

The stories men told would be only the shadows of us, that and the breeze through the trees, whispering to those who had the ability to hear. After a time, no one would remember that we had truly been.

I knelt where I stood and the two pieces of wand were back in my hand. Without the wand, without the magic of my forefathers, I would never win. I poured my own magic into it. Every drop I placed inside the wand, bidding it to heal, calling back the magic of my father, my father's father, his mother, and the line of my people since first we breathed and ruled.

There was no magic left within me, but the wand was healed. As long as I held it, I had power. But the power wouldn't last. It had never been broken before, and the cracks where I had snapped it in two showed red and blue and green. It bled gold, and I wrapped it in a ribbon, and held it against my chest.

One chance and one chance alone. If I failed, it would be for eternity, and I would not be one of the voices that whispered in the trees. I would be nothing. But worse still, Eleanor and her prince would dance the same tragic waltz, over and over, until the world died.

I made sure not to be there when my sister entered the kitchen.

"The Prince wishes to find the maiden who dropped her slipper at the ball last night. He is stupidly besotted with her," she said to Eleanor. "He is coming here, first, and will bid every young woman of this house to come and try it on. We both know that you have good reason to be one of those, but this cannot happen." She raised her hand, and when she brought it down, Eleanor was a dove. She fluttered around, terrified, finally settling on a rafter.

"I love it when things come full circle, don't you?"

Gregory had been watching over Eleanor, and he crept into the kitchen and gathered the terrified bird to his chest.

Meanwhile, I was being very, very useful to the prince himself. For the second... or maybe third, but certainly no more than that, time in my life, I was disguised as a man.

"This is the house, my prince, I am certain of it," I said as I held his horse. He held the slipper carefully, but I told the horse to sidestep, and the prince was too tired to catch himself and hold the slipper at the same time. My hand caught the shoe an inch from the ground and the wand slipped down out of my sleeve long enough to tap the glass with the tip of it.

"Here you go, sir, sorry about that sir," I said as he took the slipper from me.

"All will be forgiven if you are right," he said, and we went up to the front door.

Inside the house, we saw what I expected: The stepmother, regal and cruel, the two daughters—one eager, one cowed.

"My slipper! I was so hoping you'd found it!" The eldest leapt up, looking genuinely happy.

"You aren't the woman who was wearing it," the prince said with certainty. He looked at me. "Is everyone assembled?"

"Of course we are all here," their mother replied. All but the ash-girl, our Cinderella. You don't expect an ash-girl would own such a fine slipper?" She smiled. "Besides, you said you would wed the girl who can wear that slipper. Therefore, my daughters are both eligible."

He flinched, as if hit by a spell. I threw a counter spell. It weakened her curse, but it did not undo it. He was still confused. I did not dare do more for fear of alerting her.

"I suppose that is so..." He allowed one of the guards to take the slipper, and the eldest, her own feet enchanted, slipped her foot right in.

But she could not keep it in. Her foot began to burn and itch, and she jerked it out of the shoe.

"It fit!" she said, triumphantly.

"You did not say anything about fitting... you said who could wear. And she cannot wear it." I coaxed the Prince to say for me.

A dove fluttered in, and sat on the mantle. My sister's eyes narrowed on it, and I did not need Gregory's gestures from the shadows of the hallway to tell me who was now in the room.

"I'll get it, your grace," I said, chasing it from the mantle. She flew away, hiding herself behind the curtains.

"Let my youngest try," the stepmother said. "She has a stronger constitution..."

I cast a spell toward the curtain and hoped I hit her.

"Oh! Oh! My foot is on fire!" I heard the youngest sister say.

"Is there no one else here who can try on the slipper?" the Prince said impatiently.

"I can, if you like?" Eleanor peeked from behind the curtain, and he smiled at her.

"There you are. I was getting worried." He came forward and took her hands, and kissed them.

"I haven't even tried on the slipper yet. How do you know it's me?"

"I knew. I knew it when I saw you last night. I think I even knew it when we played together as children."

Perhaps it was because I was in male form, but I felt sick to my stomach. I should change back, I decided. So I did.

My sister looked at me. "It doesn't have to be this way. I do not want to kill you, after all. If I'd wanted that, I've certainly had my chances."

"I know," I said. "But I can't allow you to hurt them any more, not just to show my father how unworthy I am."

"Do you think he sees?"

I drew the wand and pointed it at her Chest. "I think so."

I took a breath, "Undo."

Her breath caught in her chest, and she began to unravel. As she unraveled, she faded, becoming ribbons, and shadow, and then nothing.

The wand, overcome by this most powerful of spells, shattered, and then vanished in a small puff of smoke.

I fell to the floor, the severing of everything ever was a feeling too great, too empty to take in.

"She was going to kill you. She was going to kill us both," Eleanor said. "You saved our lives."

"I will be all right," I murmured to Gregory, who helped me sit up, but I did not believe it.

Saving the prince and his wife's life grants you many things. It grants you a big pouch of gold and jewels. It grants you an invitation to the wedding. I accepted the first, but not the latter.

"I was never meant to be a part of that," I said to her. "I don't dare attend. I should never have been a part of your lives."

She understood, I think.

Before I had gone to the prince to lead him to his intended wife, I had conducted one great spell. I conjured a ring out of platinum to give to my oldest of friends. When given in marriage, it protects the people who are bound together by it. It gives them healthy, strong children, and guarantees that the worst sorrows will pass them by.

In short, anyone who marries with this ring will live happily ever after.

He had left, Gregory and his never ending cart of food, half a day ahead of me, so I granted myself only a few hours of sleep. I was counting on the fact he had a cart to slow him down. I hoped I could catch up. It was odd, and tiring, to be human, to be so hungry and tired all the time.

I cut over a hill, and saw him. I waved tiredly until he noticed, stopped, and waited for me.

I hugged him, again overwhelmed by the desire to sink into him.

I would never sink into a tree again, I realized.

It was another one of those fist-to-the-chest moments, but I breathed through it, and walked alongside of him, Edgar in between us.

"You need shoes," he said, looking at my bare feet. "We have to get you some at the next town."

I had only ever worn shoes as part of a disguise. I had never needed them. My people had always stayed connected to the ground.

"Where I come from," I said, thinking of my gentle Cinderella and her longing, always constant, for slippers, "If a man gave a woman a pair of shoes, she became his wife immediately, the moment she put them on."

He was silent for a long moment, and I let my mind drift. I felt so empty, like a well in the desert, echoingly, devastatingly hollow.

Some men would ask what I planned to do next, but he did not. Some would ask how I felt, now that I was not one bit what I once was, but he did not.

I only half noticed when he pushed Edgar's lead into my hand, I just kept plodding along like Edgar, one foot in front of the other.

After a while he came back and knelt in front of me, holding out his own shoes, filled with moss and sweet grasses to make them fit me. They would look ridiculous, so huge on my small feet.

I smiled down at his earnest face, and slipped one foot, then the other, into his too large shoes.

They could not have fit me better had they been made out of glass.

Credits

"A Necklace of Rubies" by Cindy Lynn Speer: first published by *Drollerie Press*, 2007

"Come Lady Death" by Peter S. Beagle: first published in *Atlantic*, 1963

"Summer Wind" by Nancy Kress: first published in "Ruby Slippers, Golden Tears", editors Ellen Datlow and Terri Windling, *Avon*, 1995

"Stronger than Time" by Patricia C. Wrede: first published in "Black Thorn, White Rose", editors Ellen Datlow and Terri Windling, *William Morrow & Co*, 1994

"Words Like Pale Stones" by Nancy Kress: first published in "Black Thorn, White Rose", editors Ellen Datlow and Terri Windling, *William Morrow & Co*, 1994

"Every Word I Speak" by Cindy Lynn Speer: first published by *Drollerie Press*, 2007

"Remains" by Siobhan Carroll: first published in *AE: The Canadian Science Fiction Review*, 2011

"Frayed Tapestry" by Imogen Howson: first published by *Drollerie Press*, 2008

"The Cold Blackness Between" by Lucy A. Snyder: first published in *Aoife's Kiss*, 2008

"Solstice Maiden" by Anna Kashina: first published in *Sorcerous Signals*, 2009

"But Can You Let Him Go" by Cindy Lynn Speer: first published in "But Can You Let Him Go" story collection, *Drollerie Press*, 2010

ABOUT THE AUTHORS

For **Cindy Lynn Speer**, the pen and the sword are both equally mighty. She has written three novels, Blue Moon, Unbalanced and the book that you are holding right now. She has also written a number of short stories, to be released from Dragonwell Publishing in 2012 and 2013. When she is not writing, she studies historical combat and is an adept rapier fighter. Both things, in their own way, are about telling stories. You can find out more about her at her website, www.apenandfire.com.

Peter S. Beagle was born in 1939 and raised in the Bronx, where he grew up surrounded by the arts and education: both his parents were teachers, three of his uncles were world-renowned gallery painters, and his immigrant grandfather was a respected writer, in Hebrew, of Jewish fiction and folktales. As a child Peter used to sit by himself in the stairwell of apartment building he lived in, staring at the mailboxes across the way and making up stories to entertain himself. Today, thanks to classics like *The Last Unicorn*, *A Fine and Private Place*, and *Two Hearts*, he is a living icon of fantasy fiction. In addition to eight novels and over one hundred pieces of short fiction, Peter has written many teleplays and screenplays (including the animated versions of *The Lord of the Rings* and *The Last Unicorn*); six nonfiction books (among them the classic travel memoir *I See By My Outfit*); the libretto for one opera; and more than seventy published poems and songs. He currently makes his home in Oakland, California.

Nancy Kress is the author of thirty books, including fantasy and SF novels, four collections of short stories, and three books on writing. For sixteen years she was also the "Fiction" columnist for *Writers Digest* magazine. She is perhaps best known for the "Sleepless" trilogy that began with *Beggars in Spain*. Her work has won four Nebulas, two Hugos, a Sturgeon, and the John W. Campbell Award. Most recent books are a collection, *Fountain of Age and Other Stories* (Small Beer Press, 2012), a YA SF novel, *Flash Point* (Viking, fall, 2012); and a short novel of eco-terror, *Before the Fall, During the Fall, After the Fall* (Tachyon, 2012). Kress lives in Seattle with her husband, SF writer Jack Skillingstead, and Cosette, the world's most spoiled toy poodle.

Patricia Collins Wrede was born in Chicago, Illinois and is the eldest of five children. She started writing in seventh grade and began work on her first novel, *Shadow Magic*, just after graduating from college in 1974. In January, 1980, she co-founded the writer's group that later became known as "The Scribblies." In April of 1980 *Shadow Magic*, sold to Ace Books. In 1985, shortly before the publication of her fifth book, she became a full-time writer. She lives in Minnesota with her two cats. In addition to writing books, Patricia enjoys sewing, embroidery, desultory attempts at gardening, chocolate, not mowing the lawn, High Tea, and, of course, reading.

Siobhan Carroll grew up in Canada and (briefly) Saudi Arabia, where she developed a taste for international travel that will no doubt serve her well in her villainous quest for world domination. She is a Clarion workshop graduate and an English professor at the University of Delaware. Her fiction has been published in magazines like *Realms of Fantasy*, *On Spec*, and *Son & Foe* and has earned multiple honorable mentions from the Year's Best anthologies of fantasy, science fiction, and horror.

Imogen Howson's favorite stories are those that ignore biology, reality and the known laws of nature. She writes romantic fantasy and science fiction, and makes liberal use of the substance known as handwavium. She lives near Sherwood Forest in England, with her partner and their two teenage daughters. Imogen has published several novels and short stories. In the virtual world, she can be found at her website www.imogenhowson.com, blog imogenhowson.com/blog, Facebook page https://www.facebook.com/imogenhowsonauthor, and Twitter twitter.com/imogenhowson. She loves to hear from readers and can be contacted at imogenhowson@gmail.com.

Lucy A. Snyder writes poetry, horror, and science fiction. She is a Clarion workshop graduate and a winner of the Bram Stoker Award for Superior Achievement in Poetry for her collection *Chimeric Machines*. Her collection *Sparks and Shadows* won the 2008 Editors' Choice Black Quill Award for Best Dark Genre Collection. She is also the author of a humor collection *Installing Linux on a Dead Badger*. She writes a column for Horror World on science and technology for writers, and regularly contributes to Storytellers Unplugged. To date, she has made over 80 short fiction sales, over 50 poetry sales, and a bunch of nonfiction sales on topics ranging from faeries to medicinal botany to ethernet switches. She lives in Worthington, Ohio with her husband and co-author Gary A. Braunbeck. You can learn more about Lucy by visiting her web site www.lucysnyder.com.

Anna Kashina is the author of *The Princess of Dhagabad* and *The Goddess of Dance*, two stand-alone installments in Arabian-style romantic fantasy series The Spirits of The Ancient Sands. Her novel *Mistress of the Solstice* is upcoming from Dragonwell Publishing in early 2013. A Russian-born author, she published several novels and short stories in Russia, Germany, USA, and Australia, and is combining writing with a successful career in biomedical research. You can learn more about Anna and her books at her web site and blog www.annakashina.com.

Did you enjoy "Solstice Maiden" by Anna Kashina? Read more in her upcoming novel:

MISTRESS OF THE SOLSTICE

by

Anna Kashina

*a dark romantic fantasy based on Russian myth
upcoming from Dragonwell Publishing in early 2013*

I stood beside my father and watched the girl drown. She was a strong one. Her hands continued to reach out long after her face had disappeared from view. The splashing she made could have soaked a flock of wild geese to the bone. She wanted to live, but there was no escape from the waters of the Sacrifice Pool.

I looked at my father's handsome profile. His pale face, awash with moonlight, looked magnificent. The power of the Solstice enfolded him. It made me proud to be at his side, his daughter, his head priestess. He was the one who mattered. The only one.

The girl's struggle ceased. The rippling water of the lake stilled, glittering in the silvery light of the near-full moon. We watched the flicker of the glowing candles set in the flower wreaths as they floated downstream. A few of the wreaths had already sunk—bad luck for their owners, who would most likely die before the next Solstice. Maybe one of them belonged to the next Sacrifice Maiden?

I felt my father stir next to me, as he too peered into the amber depths of the lake.

"A fine sacrifice, Marya," he said to me. "You did well."

"Yes." I closed my eyes to feel the familiar calmness wash over me. I was detached. I didn't care. I didn't even know her name.

My eyes still closed, I sensed my father throw off his cloak and stand naked, his arms open to the cool night breeze.

"Bring her to me, Marya," he whispered.

I stretched my thoughts, seeking out her body tangled in

the weeds on the bottom of the lake, seeking the spark of life that still remained there, trapped, beating in terror against its dead shell like a caged bird. I reached for it, brought it out, and gave it to my father. I sensed the moment the two of them became one, her virginal powers filling him with such force that the air around us crackled with the freshness of a thunderstorm.

He sighed, slowly returning to his senses. I kept my eyes shut until he found his cloak on the damp grass and wrapped it around his shoulders, once again becoming himself. The Tzar. The immortal. The invincible.

The undead.

We could hear people singing in the main glade. The celebration was at its full. Soon they would be jumping over the bonfire. As the night reached its darkest, quietest hour, they would break into couples and wander off into the forest. "Searching for a fern flower" they called it. Fern has no flowers, of course. But searching for it made a good excuse for seeking the solitude of the woods. Besides, blood of virginity spilled on the Solstice night glowed like a rare, exotic blossom of true passion. Those who found their fern flowers tonight were blessed by Kupalo.

I could hear the whisper of every leaf, every tree, and every flower in the forest. This was the night when the powers of Kupalo roamed freely in the world; this was the night when everyone's mind was clouded by Love.

Except mine. Love had no power over me. My mind was free.

Dragonwell Publishing
www.dragonwellpublishing.com

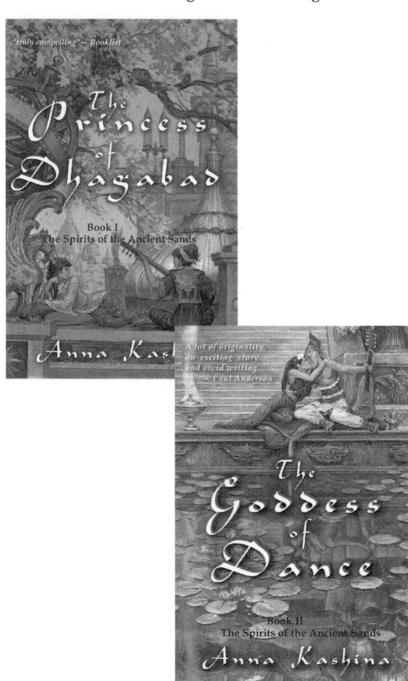

More from **Dragonwell Publishing**:

CPSIA information can be obtained at www.ICGtesting.com
Printed in the USA
BVOW081545241012

303811BV00002B/8/P